The Hijacked Wife

BONNIE K. WINN

*First published in Great Britain 2000
Silhouette Books, Eton House, 18-24 Paradise Road,
Richmond, Surrey TW9 1SR*

© Bonnie K. Winn 1999

ISBN 0 373 07954 0

18-0005

*Printed and bound in Spain
by Litografía Rosés S.A., Barcelona*

'Will you help us?'

Shocked, Summer stared at him, wondering if he could possibly be serious. Deciding he was, she measured her words carefully. 'If I said yes, how could I help?'

'Those guys are looking for a man and a baby, not a couple. I wouldn't ask you if I had another choice—any other choice.' His voice flattened. 'I don't. My back's against the wall. I wouldn't ask for myself. This is for Danny.'

Glancing up sharply, Summer could see he wasn't playing on her emotions. He was completely sincere. She suspected this macho man had great difficulty asking for assistance. 'And you want my help?'

'Only for as long as absolutely necessary.'

She searched his face, once again sensing only honesty and concern. 'I'll do it. I'll be your wife…'

Dear Reader,

You hold in your hand a ticket to a different world—a world full of passion and suspense, a world full of sexy, stubborn and *dangerous* men!

First off the presses is Emilie Richards' *One Moment Past Midnight*, our **Heartbreaker** title, and the hero in this certainly deserves our praise; Quinn McDermott's the kind of man who can find a kidnapped little girl…

Marie Ferrarella's *A Forever Kind of Hero* shows us how a lady private eye and an FBI agent can strike just the right kind of sparks to make fire. This is the second of her **Childfinders, Inc.** books and number three's on the way in July.

In the true tradition of Sensation™ there are two more gorgeous lawmen in *Logan's Bride* and *Cowboy with a Badge* from Elizabeth August and Margaret Watson. And finally, there's a couple on the run with a baby in *The Hijacked Wife*, and a man trying to buy a wife as if he was just going shopping in *Cinderella Bride*. Take a look.

Enjoy them all and come back next month!

The Editors

BONNIE K. WINN

A hopeless romantic, Bonnie K. Winn naturally turned to romance writing. This seasoned author of historical and contemporary romance has won numerous awards, including having been voted one of the Top Ten Romance Authors in America, according to *Affaire de Coeur*. Living in the foothills of the Rockies gives Bonnie plenty of inspiration and a touch of whimsy, as well. She shares her life with her husband, son and a spunky Westie terrier. Bonnie welcomes mail from her readers. You can write to her c/o Silhouette Books, 300 E. 42nd St., New York, NY 10017, USA.

Dedicated to those we have lost too soon:
Caren McCurdy, Max and Eunice Winn, Evelyn Dillard,
Betty Harris Williams, Mark Blacksher, Tommy Hulsey,
Dustin Johnson and Gary Allred.

Chapter 1

Jack Anderson cursed the daylight. It revealed the position of their boat, a bobbing cork amid the offshore waters. They couldn't be more exposed and vulnerable if he'd painted a huge red *X* across the bow.

He bit back an oath as he glanced in frustration at the radio. He couldn't call for help—no doubt the transmissions were being monitored. Irrationally he wished that someone would spot them and provide a hasty tow to shore, while at the same time he prayed they would remain invisible.

Because if rescuers could see them, so could—

Something vital threatened to implode in Jack's midsection. On his own, he could handle whatever anyone cared to dish out. But where his eleven-month-old son, Danny, was concerned, that careless bravado disappeared.

It was up to him to get them to safety. Forget that he should be providing normality. Jack had to think survival.

Hearing the motor of a small boat, Jack felt fear for his son clutch at him. The early-morning sunlight bounced off

the water, but it did nothing to displace the chill sweeping
through him.

His mind raced furiously as he tried to formulate a plan.
This wasn't the time or place he would have chosen to take
a stand, but he would do whatever it took to protect Danny.

Summer Harding pulled down the brim of her baseball
cap and squinted at the reflection against the horizon. It
looked like the listing boat was in trouble. Sighing, she
gave up thoughts of a solitary early-morning run. Another
witless tourist, no doubt. One who didn't think beyond fun
and sun and probably didn't even know how to use the
boat's radio, other than to try to tune in the Top 40.

While Summer appreciated the beauty of the South Carolina coast and especially the small island she lived on, the
popularity of nearby Hilton Head attracted a lot of bone-
headed visitors who thought boats were just like cars, with
the exception of cruising them in water rather than on concrete.

Although tempted to leave the boat to the ministrations
of the coast guard, Summer couldn't disregard an upbring-
ing that insisted she offer help. Increasing her speed, she
reached the disabled craft in no time at all.

"Anyone aboard?" she called out, wondering if the crew
were all asleep below.

A wary yet challenging voice cut through the stillness.
"*I* am."

Startled, Summer glanced up. Taken aback, she blinked.
The man on deck stood with his legs apart, hands planted
on both sides of a trim waist, looking for all the world like
a modern-day pirate. He stared at her grimly, thick black
brows furrowed together, matching the scowl twisting his
lips. A day's growth of dark beard shadowed the man's
face, adding to its harshness. At odds with the darkness
were eyes of the brightest blue, a blue that refused to pale
beside the sea it mocked.

"Who are you?" the man demanded, his gaze taking in her boat, then sweeping the surrounding area.

She found her voice, her eyes still riveted on his confrontational pose. "Summer Harding. You in trouble?"

If possible, his brows drew even closer together. "What do you mean?"

"Engine trouble." She frowned suddenly. "You aren't taking on water, are you?"

"No." He barked out the solitary word as his eyes scrutinized her, apparently missing nothing.

Summer considered leaving the man to find his own way to shore.

Just then she heard a strident wail.

The man whirled suddenly, rushing to pick up something directly behind him, something that squirmed, shifted, then wailed.

It was a baby, Summer realized in amazement. One who looked to be about a year old.

She couldn't refrain from smiling tentatively at the unlikely duo as the man tried to soothe the wriggling child. But he only scowled deeper when he saw her smile. However, she didn't see any actual anger in his dour expression. It was caution, she realized suddenly.

In a protective motion, the man blocked the child from Summer's view. "*Who* are you?" he asked again.

"I just told you. Summer Harding." She glanced at him pointedly. "I didn't get your name."

He hesitated, long enough to make them both aware of his reluctance. "Jack Anderson."

"And *are* you having some trouble?" Belatedly she noticed the screwdriver in Jack's free hand. The rest of his appearance had commanded her attention until that moment. "Maybe you don't need any help."

Conflict raged across his face, and she wondered if he was the sort of man who never wanted to admit he couldn't fix something. Especially to a woman.

"Actually I do," he finally acknowledged. "I'm no engine mechanic."

"Did you radio for help?" she asked, not wanting to haul them in if a tow was on the way.

He shook his head, and Summer withheld her cluck of disapproval. Apparently her initial assessment had been correct. Another tourist with more money than sense.

"I can tow you in."

His brows narrowed again as he stared dubiously at her smaller craft.

"I can tow a boat more than twice the size of my own," she told him. "Think about tugboats and ocean liners— same concept." Still he looked reluctant and she shrugged. "If you'd rather wait for another—"

"No!" He barked out the response, dropping the screwdriver in frustration.

She blinked again. He was a real piece of work.

Apparently struggling to recover his poise, he shoved a hand through his longish hair, adding to its casual disarray. "I mean, I'd appreciate a tow."

"If you'd feel more comfortable about a tow from a larger craft, I could radio—"

"No!" he commanded again.

This time, she simply stared. This guy went way beyond rude. Ballistic came to mind.

"That won't be necessary. I'd rather not have my son stranded out here any longer than necessary."

The reference to his baby hit home as she suspected he'd known it would. On his own, she would be tempted to leave this surly landlubber to find his own way back to shore, but Summer couldn't leave the child out at sea.

With easy competence, she navigated alongside the boat. As Jack watched diligently, she picked up a length of nylon rope, efficiently making up a towline by fashioning a bridle and securing it to the stern cleats of her own boat. Close enough to make a clean throw, she tossed him the length of rope, instructing him where to secure it.

As he caught the rope, she added, "Tie it with a bowline knot." She demonstrated the knot with a piece of rope, guessing he hadn't a clue as to the one she meant.

To his credit, Jack deftly tied the line, listening closely as she talked him through the process of securing the boat.

After several more parting instructions on how to handle the remainder of the tow, she made a wide turn, moving off slowly, bringing the line taut without jerking it. Bound for the shore, Summer maintained a slow, steady pace. Luckily the water was calm, the weather cooperating for the disabled craft.

Glancing back, she saw that the man hadn't lost his glower. Pity. Beneath all that antagonism lurked a devilishly handsome man. *Devilish,* she counseled herself, being the operative word here. Still, it wasn't easy to disregard his looks. He wore his Irish heritage like an ID badge. Wavy black hair and those eyes... And if she cared to dwell on it, a tall, muscular physique—no wonder she'd thought he looked like a pirate.

Shaking her head, she almost wished for a swell of bracing water to clear her thoughts. However, the sea remained disgustingly still. But in a short while, she'd have his boat towed to shore and that would be the last she'd have to see of Mr. Sunshine.

Jack watched Summer secure the ropes on the dock, then gesture toward the shop whose sign declared it to be the Harding Boat Rental and Repair Shop. "My mother runs the place."

As she straightened up, Jack continued to stare at her, his expression tightening with suspicion, his gut filling with it. "Convenient place to tow us."

She threw up her hands. "You're welcome to call for a tow to the mainland. I brought you here because this is our dock *and* the closest place to tow you. Trust me, we don't need the business."

Following the direction of her outstretched arm, he saw

a daunting line of boats apparently lined up for repairs. His stomach sank along with any hope. "How long a wait until my boat can be fixed?"

She shrugged. "A few days if we rush it."

Staring at her in amazed disbelief, he snorted. "You call that a rush?"

"I sure do. Especially since it ought to be more like a week."

"What kind of con are you playing? If I'd known—"

Clearly exasperated, she blew wheat-colored bangs from her forehead and wrenched the baseball cap down more firmly on the remainder of her hair. "If *I'd* known how you were going to act, I'd have left you out there!"

What a strange mix of woman—dressed in mannish, baggy overalls that disguised whatever sort of body she had, her hat doing much the same for her face. At the same time, her behavior indicated that she possessed her fair share of feminine pique.

Another voice cut him off from verbalizing that opinion.

"Summer Harding! Where are your manners?"

Jack watched as his would-be rescuer snapped to attention. "Mom, I was just telling this guy—"

"I heard." The older woman slanted a disapproving glance at her daughter before turning to Jack. "I'm Louise Harding."

Jack glanced at her. The woman was dressed in tailored, practical work clothes, her face deeply tanned by the island sun. He sensed a crusty edge to the woman despite her sharp, intelligent gaze. Next to her stood an alert Australian sheepdog that checked him over with equal thoroughness.

"I would apologize for my daughter's lack of hospitality," Louise continued. "But as you can see, she's an adult and far beyond my control."

For the first time in a very long time, Jack felt the beginnings of a smile. His expression broadened when he saw Summer squirm at her mother's words. "Jack Anderson," he said, then glanced down at the baby tucked securely on his hip. "And my son, Danny."

All the crustiness he'd detected in the older woman melted. "Oh, my." She drew in a deep breath. "Would you look at him. What a beautiful baby." She looked beguilingly at Jack. "Could I hold him?" The dog next to her moved forward. "Stay, Skipper." Obediently the dog retreated, stepping back in place.

Although his gut wrenched painfully, Jack knew it would seem peculiar if he refused, and he didn't need to arouse any undue suspicion. Carefully he placed Danny in the woman's arms.

Louise's face softened as the baby clasped chubby fingers around hers, then reached for a pendant necklace that she wore. "Oh, my. It's been ever so long since I've held a little one." Her misty glance reached out to include her tall daughter. "Been too long since that one was a babe."

That would be hard to determine, Jack thought to himself. Summer could be a cross between Bozo the Clown and Claudia Schiffer for all he knew. There was no telling what her oversize clothes and hat disguised.

Summer cleared her throat and threw her mother an exasperated glance. But Jack saw that her gaze softened a touch when it landed on Danny, who responded by flashing his nearly toothless jack-o'-lantern grin at her.

"Babies are a priceless gift," Louise intoned. "You and your wife are very lucky."

"I'm a widower," Jack responded gruffly, struck as always by the wave of pain that reminder caused.

Summer's eyes widened, and she was the one who spoke first. "I'm sorry. It must be very difficult for you."

Irony and pain were fast companions by now. So much that Jack merely nodded.

"Would you like me to watch him while you have the boat checked out?" Louise asked, tickling Danny's toes and making him giggle.

Jack tried to look as though it were just a normal request,

one that could be granted without concern. The fact was, any time Danny was farther than an arm span away, he worried. Simply having his son out of sight was enough to make him break out into a cold sweat. "It's not necessary."

"You can come up to the house and check things out," Louise offered. "You don't know us, but I assure you we're not going anywhere. 'Course in this day and time, I know a person has to be careful. But you could probably use a little break. Raising a child alone is a lot of work with no one to spell you."

Jack continued to hesitate. Though a quick glance around assured him that it was unlikely the woman could take off with Danny, still he worried. As he had ever since the baby had been born.

Glancing up, he saw the quizzical expression on Summer's face, and realized how odd his reluctance must seem. And it was crucial he remain low-key. Perhaps he could sidetrack the issue by agreeing, and then go to the house to use the telephone.

"How can I refuse such a generous offer?"

Louise smiled as she strolled toward the house, the dog moving in perfect unison with her. Summer continued watching him, and Jack sucked in a deep breath. It could just be a coincidence that she had happened on their boat that morning, and that she just happened to be connected to a boat-repair shop. But coincidences made him nervous. Too nervous to remain on this idyllic-appearing island.

"Did you say there are other repair shops on the mainland?"

Summer bobbed her head in assent.

"And how would I go about finding them?" he asked after a moment, when it became clear she wasn't going to volunteer the information.

Unexpectedly she smiled sweetly, but he didn't trust the taint beneath the sugar. "We have a newfangled invention. It's called the Yellow Pages. And we don't even charge for the service."

Despite her mother's intervention, Summer obviously wasn't any happier about offering hospitality.

Jack met her challenging gaze. "Let me guess. The profit's in the phone call."

"Just let your fingers do the walking and your wallet do the talking," she replied.

So that was her game. His expression tightened even as he thought of his dwindling funds, ones he wasn't certain would support a second tow when combined with the repair cost. "Fine."

"Phone's over there." She pointed. "It's in the shop office, which is connected to the house. Just use the last door on the right."

Relief punctured his worry. So he'd be in close proximity to Danny. "Do you want a deposit?"

She rolled her eyes. "It's not long-distance to the mainland." When he didn't comment, she blew out another exasperated sigh. "So there's no charge. Geez, you take everything so *literally,* don't you? Just don't call the Congo or Bucharest, okay?"

"Thank you," he replied stiffly, glancing toward the shop, wishing Danny were still in sight.

She started to walk away, then turned back. "You don't have to worry about him, you know. My mother's great with kids, and you couldn't have landed in a safer place. Edisto Island makes the set of 'Leave It to Beaver' look wild in comparison."

Startled by her unexpected compassion, he wished for a moment that there could be refuge in this uncomplicated little place called... What had she said? Edisto. But even tucked-away little islands weren't safe.

Summer breezed into the house to grab some iced tea. Hearing the unfamiliar sounds of her mother cooing and speaking nonsensical baby talk, she paused. Quietly she strolled into the living room, watching as her mother played with the baby.

Together, woman and child sat in the ancient rocking chair. Louise was making Danny laugh by twisting her face into some excruciating shapes. It was so out of character for her mother that Summer paused to enjoy the scene.

"You coming in, or you going to stand there all morning gawking?" Louise asked as she blew kisses at the baby.

"Mom, you've got to admit that it's quite a show."

"Don't mock. I waited a long time to have you, and now it's been nearly as long since I've had a baby to play with."

"That's not the only child left on earth," Summer pointed out dryly.

"Well, it's not like you've presented me with any grandchildren," Louise retorted.

Summer rolled her eyes. "Oh, puhlease."

"Don't give me that, young lady. Ever since Tyson left, you've shut yourself off from men. I may be old, but even I know that's not a good sign for having children in your future."

Summer studied her short, practical fingernails. "It's too soon, Mom. It's been less than a year." She purposely left out the fact that her heart was still aching, that the sting of his abandonment wasn't something she planned to dismiss.

"Or not soon enough," Louise answered cryptically. "Tyson was never the man for you, and I hate to see you wasting your life mooning over something that never should have been."

"Mom!"

"It's the truth and I'm not sorry to say so. We've tiptoed around it too long. You won't let yourself even look at another man. And what for? So you can grow old alone?"

Exactly. But she couldn't tell her mother that. "You're being overly dramatic."

Louise's expression mirrored her disbelief. From the untouched gray hair and the plain but handsome face to the practical work shoes, nothing about Louise Harding was dramatic.

Lifting one brow, Louise echoed her daughter's words. "Dramatic?"

"You make it sound as though I'm entering my dotage. It's not that bad, Mom."

"I almost waited too long to have you," Louise countered. A wistful expression settled on her face. "You know I was older when I met your father, then we thought we had more time...." A flicker of old pain crossed her face. "And because I was older, I almost missed knowing you. Don't wait too long, Summer. I don't want you making the same mistake."

"Don't worry," Summer retorted. "I haven't passed the expiration date on my eggs." Still, she leaned forward to pat her mother's shoulder lovingly.

A twinkle returned to Louise's eyes. "That may be, my girl, but don't keep them under refrigeration too long."

Nearly an hour later, Jack had learned there were no repair shops on the mainland that could get to his boat any faster than the Hardings. And most of them offered the unsolicited opinion that he was already in excellent hands. So why did those hands feel as if they were preparing a sneak stranglehold?

He considered ditching the boat, which had enabled their escape from Florida a few days earlier, but then they'd be on foot. He couldn't rent a car or buy plane tickets without using his credit cards, and they would be immediately traced, exposing their exact position. And even though they'd only been on the run for less than a week his hoard of cash was shrinking at a frightening rate.

Opening his wallet, he flipped through the now useless credit cards all embossed with the Jack Anderson moniker. Not a trace of Jack Delancey remained. Everything he had once been was now gone. He walked quietly to the front of the house, searching for his son. Spotting Louise in the living room, he moved closer and watched as she gently rocked the baby. Seeing that Danny was safe, he quietly backed away and retraced his steps to the boat shop.

Before he reached the shop, he spotted Summer. "Any word on my boat?" he asked without preamble.

Summer shrugged, her shapeless overalls shifting with the movement. "I haven't heard yet."

"Summer!"

They both turned at the grizzled voice.

Summer moved first in the direction of a stoop-shouldered man, dressed in coveralls and a battered base-ball cap from which frizzled tufts of gray hair stuck out like slabs of concrete. "Hey, Lloyd," she greeted him. "This is Jack Anderson. What's the verdict on his boat?"

Lloyd wiped his hands on the greasy rag he held and offered one wizened paw. Jack accepted the handshake, appraising the mechanic who looked old enough to be Summer's grandfather.

"It's not bad," Lloyd finally acknowledged. "Mebbe a day to fix it. When I get to it."

"When you get to it?" Jack questioned, trying to hold on to his temper and manners.

"Got boats in front of yours, son. Nearly a week's worth."

Dismay flashed across her face before Summer laid one hand on Lloyd's arm. "But Mr. Anderson is on vacation. He hasn't made arrangements for anywhere to stay."

Lloyd's shrug was eloquent. Clearly the Andersons' lack of accommodations wasn't his concern. "Got boats in front of his," he insisted stubbornly.

Jack opened his mouth to speak, but Summer cut him off, knowing he would only irritate the older man. "Thanks, Lloyd. I'll talk to you about it more in a bit. Right now, I'd better go see if I can help with lunch. We've got fresh fish and hush puppies."

Lloyd snorted. "Can't get enough fish."

Summer's lips twitched. "Not exactly a treat, is it?"

Shaking his head, Lloyd muttered incomprehensibly. A

few words emerged about living next to the ocean and eating fish every day of the world as he ambled away.

Jack stared at the man's slow gait. "He doesn't get in a hurry about much, does he?"

"I'll work on Lloyd," she replied as they walked toward the house. "If I give him a hand in the shop, it'll speed things up."

Jack glanced at her. Clearly she didn't want him on her island any more than he wanted to be there. Then *what* she'd said struck him. "*You* know how to work on boats?"

She gestured at her overalls. "No. This is just a fashion statement."

So she did possess feminine pique, and it had apparently been provoked.

Shifting his glance, he saw Louise leaving the house, alone. He felt a start of alarm and headed toward her. "Is anything wrong, Mrs. Harding?"

"Louise," she insisted. "No, everything's fine. Danny's asleep. I could've rocked him all day." She sighed, then resumed her normal crisp tone. "Don't you worry. I don't have a crib. But I don't hold with putting babies on regular beds, no matter how much stuff you stack next to the child. Danny's on a soft pallet on the floor. Skipper's watching over him. And nothing will get past him to that baby."

Jack glanced toward the house, the constant worry still nagging. "Thank you."

Louise nodded briskly. "We'll be ready to eat in the next hour. You'll be joining us, won't you, Mr. Anderson?"

Jack felt compelled to rush their departure, not join the family hour. "I don't want to impose."

"What imposition? We always have enough fish to feed half the island."

Jack remembered the grizzled mechanic's comment and barely repressed a smile. "I need to be worrying about my boat, not socializing."

"You have to eat, don't you?" Louise insisted.

As Jack glanced up, he saw that even Summer was looking at him strangely. Remember, he told himself, low-key, unobtrusive.

"I know when I'm outnumbered. A home-cooked meal sounds great."

Louise smiled, her face softening. "Did Lloyd look at your boat yet?"

Jack couldn't prevent a grimace. "Afraid so. He says it'll probably take about a day to repair once he gets to it."

Louise nodded. "Lloyd knows his stuff."

"And no one on the mainland can get to it any faster," Summer added.

Jack slanted her a glance. He didn't remember sharing that information with her.

She read the expression on his face. "It's an old story."

"Then you'll need a place to stay," Louise surmised.

"We'll get a hotel," Jack replied.

"Not on Edisto. You won't find one. But no matter, you and Danny can bunk on the sleeping porch."

"We really can't impose."

Louise tilted her head, considering. "Unless you'd rather have the baby stay inside the house—"

"No!" Jack barked.

Louise's brow rose, startled by his emphatic declaration. Still, she seemed to take it in stride. "I always liked having Summer where I could watch out for her, too."

"Mrs. Harding…"

She leveled him a reproving glance.

"Louise," he corrected. "There's no need to feel you have to accommodate us."

Louise fixed him with a steady no-nonsense look. "The porch is there, no one's sleeping on it and there's no reason why you and Danny can't stay with us."

Jack caught the movement of Summer's head as she whipped around. Clearly she wasn't any happier with the invitation than he was. Strangely her reluctance brushed away his. "You say there's no hotel on the island?"

"Only a bed-and-breakfast in one of the converted plantations that's always full. And here you'll be able to keep an eye on your boat.''

Good point. He hoped to bedevil the mechanic into quickly repairing their boat. And then there was the irksome reality of their finances. Hotels cost money. Still, Jack was uneasy. He knew his pursuers weren't that far behind. They had to get moving quickly. ''I want to be honest with you. If I can find a shop on the mainland that'll get to the boat faster, I'll take it there.''

''Fair enough,'' Louise agreed. ''I guess your vacation time's valuable and you don't want to be wasting it.''

''Um, right.'' A shiver coursed unexpectedly down Jack's spine at that reminder. There truly was no time to waste.

''Maybe I can repair your boat tomorrow. I should have the boat I'm working on now finished by then,'' Summer muttered. ''If I start early and it's not too bad, you could be under way by midday.''

Jack's brow lifted. She *really* didn't want him around. All the better for him.

Louise took his elbow as she steered him toward the house. ''Until then, we'll be happy to have you stay with us.''

Jack caught the fleeting expression on Summer's face. Despite her mother's words, she clearly wasn't happy. But he wasn't, either. And wouldn't be until he was off this island, leaving Summer and her contradictions far behind.

Chapter 2

Summer closed the lid of the battered toolbox and pushed at the baseball cap resting on tousled hair hastily pinned up beneath the brim. Her schedule was already crowded between both working as a computer-security programmer and helping at her mother's shop. Despite that, she had hastily finished repairs on the boat she had been fixing to tackle the Andersons' boat. Not because of any newly discovered affection for Jack Anderson—rather, the opposite. Since it appeared that her mother, who had flipped over little Danny, might adopt both Jack and his small son, Summer had decided to hasten their departure.

With a pang she realized her mother really seemed to be missing the grandchildren Summer hadn't provided. And her mother, who'd lost her husband many years ago, had endured more than one human's fair share of pain. It wasn't doing either of them any good for the Andersons to linger. Not that Summer resented the baby—Danny was a charmer. But his father was another matter. Unnerving her with those striking blue eyes that watched her every move.

Summer knew Jack Anderson saw her as a mere annoyance. Not even a female annoyance, simply a sexless, nameless anomaly who stood in the way of his vacation plans. And for some unfathomable reason, that irked her. True, with her baggy overalls she hadn't dressed for the Cinderella ball, but he needn't act as though she were invisible.

Rather than examine why that annoyed her, Summer had considered it wiser to repair his boat and send him on his way. Turning the key in the ignition, she listened to the purr of the engine and grinned. Looked like that plan was working.

"Sounds great."

Whirling around, Summer felt the heat of an unexpected flush warming her cheeks. Jack Anderson's gaze was no less penetrating, and no more interested in anything other than his precious boat.

"Yeah, it's getting there," she agreed.

He frowned, shifting his son who sat comfortably straddled across one lean hip. "Getting there? Sounds ready to go to me."

"Spoken with years of experience as a mechanic?" Summer couldn't hide the sarcasm in her voice even though she pulled the bill of her cap down even farther, shading what little of her face that could be seen.

"No, but it doesn't take an Indy race-car driver to steer a station wagon into a garage, either," he retorted.

She wasn't ready to give an inch. "You try steering this wagon before it's repaired properly and you'll drown your carburetor for good."

"So what are you suggesting?"

"I'll take the boat out later and test the engine. If everything checks out, you'll be cruising again tomorrow."

"What's wrong with now?" Renewed urgency sounded in his voice and showed in his expression.

Briefly she wondered what caused his anxiety. But Summer had already resolved she didn't want to know. Shrugging, she decided just as quickly that she could speed up this process, even if it meant giving in to the overbearing goon.

Danny chose that moment to chortle, flashing his gummy baby grin. For the life of her, she didn't understand how this adorable child could belong to such a domineering man. Her own lips tightened, remembering the domineering man she'd been engaged to, also remembering the pain he'd caused. She paused long enough to chuck the baby under one of his many chins before turning back to the matter at hand.

Summer's voice turned brisk as her gaze challenged Jack's. "All right, I'll test it today. Anything to speed up your...departure."

Her brush-off went unnoticed. "Then let's go." Jack reached into the storage compartment, lifted out Danny's life jacket, strapped it on the toddler, and then put him in a child restraint seat. "We're ready."

Amazed, Summer only stared. "Excuse me. This isn't a group operation. *I* plan to check out the boat."

He wasn't fazed. "Being the owner makes me an automatic member of the group. But you can set the course."

"That's big of you," she muttered. Briefly she considered leaving him to sit on the boat till sundown. But that would only prolong his stay. And the alternative, not testing the engine, wasn't an option, since he was traveling with his small son. She sighed. "This is normally a solo journey."

"Don't you ever stray from the ordinary?" Jack challenged.

Setting her jaw, Summer threw the boat in gear, pleased to see the rocking motion momentarily taking him aback. In moments his long legs were planted firmly on the deck, his lean but muscular body quickly giving in to the natural rolling motion of the sea. Before she could tear her gaze away, Summer had to admit Jack's was a killer body.

Danny chortled his approval at the boat's motion, and

Summer couldn't resist a quick smile. Between them, the two Anderson males were trotting out every emotion she possessed.

Fine spray misted her face, and Summer unconsciously tilted her head toward the source. Love of the ocean and her home had always been such a part of her that she didn't even notice the automatic gesture. She glanced back to see if Danny was uncomfortable. Her heart hitched a bit as she saw Jack tenderly shading the baby's eyes, then his unguarded smile when Danny giggled in glee at the light mist.

Deliberately Summer turned back to the wheel. She didn't need any more tenderhearted feelings for a man. Certainly not this one. Any man would have done the same thing, she told herself. It was probably an instinctive parental gesture that clicked on like autopilot. Still, Summer didn't glance back again as she kept her mind and eyes on the course she had set.

The engine continued to purr as they cruised the gentle coast of Edisto Island. Summer savored the sight of the home she loved. The shore didn't have the sheer boulder cliffs or outer capes that met surf whipped by storms. Like the Carolina life-style, it was softer, quieter. It was still a place where family descendants lived in Colonial-era plantations and passersby waved to one another. Edisto was a place of shady streets, prizewinning camellia bushes, plankboard homes and serenity. It was the serenity Summer valued the most.

Expertly steering the boat through the waters she knew so well, Summer tried to ignore Jack's compelling stare as she listened for anything that signaled a remaining problem. But the even hum of the engine told her she'd diagnosed and repaired the craft properly.

Lulled by the even drone, Summer frowned at the sudden pinging noise. She angled her head toward the engine, wondering what had made it suddenly begin to act up.

"Down!" Jack shouted, rushing forward and grabbing her.

Before she could open her mouth to respond, Jack pushed her to the deck of the boat alongside Danny's carrier.

"What the—?" she protested, raising her head and trying to push herself up on both elbows.

Without a word, he plunked her back into the prone position, one strong arm anchored over her head and shoulders. Twisting to see, she could make out that his other arm was similarly stretched across Danny.

Maybe he was as manic as she'd originally thought. "If you don't—"

"Unless you want to have your head shot off, I suggest you keep it down," he ordered, not giving her a choice as he continued to restrain her.

But her struggles had ceased. "Shot? What are you talking about?"

The pinging sound intensified.

"That's not the engine," he muttered grimly, the blue of his eyes darkening to nearly black.

"It's just missing," Summer replied, hearing her own voice fade as the realization sunk in. Of course it wasn't the engine.

"I wish it was. I'd take a stranded boat anyday."

"Why is someone shooting at us?" She paused. "At you?"

"Is that relevant?"

Summer could only manage a gasp.

"Wouldn't you rather concentrate on staying alive?" Jack asked, crawling forward to slide Danny beneath a storage bin, creating a safe harbor for the toddler.

"I'd like both," she snapped. "To stay alive and to know what's going on."

"I think keeping us alive is going to take all my attention right now," he replied, ignoring her demand. Jack's gaze rested on his son. "Yours isn't the only hide I'm trying to protect."

Exasperation oozed from every pore of her terrified body.

"I wasn't suggesting that it was. But I can help more if I know what's going on."

"Fine," he agreed readily. Too readily, she realized an instant later.

Lunging forward, Jack grabbed the wheel, accelerating madly. The pinging sharpened, screeching along the bow, skittering across the wake their boat left behind in the calm water.

Seeing that Jack's attention was on escape, Summer dared a peek at their pursuers. A sleek racing boat skimmed across the water as though propelled by rockets. Gasping, she realized they were completely outmatched. From Jack's face, it was clear he knew it, too.

"We can't outrun them!" she hollered against the wind.

He spared a glance at her, then at his son. "We have to try."

Summer thought quickly. "We'll have to outmaneuver them." Crawling forward on the deck, she inched closer to him. "Those aren't local boys. I'd recognize the boat. So we can use the home-court advantage."

One of his brows lifted. "Which is?"

"Number one, turning the wheel over to me."

Jack's gaze immediately skipped to Danny.

Watching him, she could see his internal struggle. "You can play macho hero and remain in control, or you can give Danny his best chance at safety."

The struggle showed on his face, and he didn't release the wheel. "And what would step two be?"

"I know these waters, where the shoals and reefs are. I'm betting they don't." Summer fought to sound reasonable, fought not to reach out and rip the wheel from his hands.

Although it clearly was difficult for him, slowly Jack nodded, relinquishing control.

In an instant, Summer captured the wheel. She reversed direction, away from the open sea toward the coast she knew so well. Here, she had learned at her father's knee, navigating the straits, memorizing the underwater ledges that could tear a boat to pieces. And that was where she was headed.

It was tricky maneuvering. One slip and their boat, too, could become driftwood. But confidence born of knowledge and experience took over. She could almost hear her father whispering in her ear, guiding her toward the hidden ledges, the deceptive minefields of nature.

Glancing quickly over her shoulder, she could see the distance between the two boats narrowing. Fear filled her. Meeting Jack's grim gaze, she could see that he fairly itched to regain control, but he kept a check on the desire. Summer knew that she had taken on a huge responsibility. If she failed, she sacrificed an innocent child. For a moment, she hesitated.

But Jack's voice was suddenly in her ear, the litheness of his muscled body surprising her as he moved soundlessly and gracefully. ''You can do it, Summer.''

She gulped, her eyes momentarily locked on his. ''What if—?''

''You can do it. You have to. Danny's counting on you.'' His voice softened almost imperceptibly. ''You won't fail him.''

Her hands tightened on the wheel, and she dared not risk one more glance to see how close their pursuers were. It was blindman's buff with the highest stakes.

Stomach knotted, fingers clenched almost bloodlessly, she tried to disregard the trickle of sweat that beaded between her breasts, the sudden dryness in her throat. Approaching the hidden ledges at a rapid pace, she blocked out everything but the mental map of what lurked beneath the water.

She had to lure the racing boat close, yet she dared not misstep. Spotting her destination, she slowed a bit, enough to bring their pursuers perilously close. A renewed pinging sound reminded her of the barrage of bullets awaiting them.

She nearly froze when one bullet furrowed along the wood beside her, ripping a ferocious path.

Gripping the wheel, Summer whirled around, seeing that they were in position. The racing boat was directly behind them, gaining at full speed. At that moment, she wrenched the wheel, turning their boat in a sudden pivot away from the ledge. But the racing boat, traveling at a high speed, couldn't duplicate the maneuver.

In moments, the sleek boat bottomed out, a huge wrenching noise ricocheting through the air as the fiberglass splintered. Watching the two men on board, Summer gasped in relief as she saw rifles fly through the air and into the water as the men slid wildly across the deck, then careened into the water, grabbing for pieces of wreckage.

But Jack didn't look relieved. She wondered suddenly if he'd hoped the men wouldn't survive the crash. The enormity of that conclusion stunned her. What was he running from? Standing mere inches from him, she wondered suddenly what she'd gotten herself into.

Jack reached over, resuming control of the boat, ignoring the questions in her expression. "You're better off not knowing," he told her, accurately reading her thoughts.

Another shiver of fear skittered up her spine. Then it blossomed into full alarm as she saw him turn the boat away from her home. Licking dry lips, she swallowed the sudden knot in her throat. "You're heading away from Edisto."

His eyes darkened even further, his entire expression grim. "I know."

Jack glanced back at Summer, regretting the alarm he clearly caused. Not that it could be helped, but he hadn't intended to frighten her. He knew he had lingered too long in the seemingly safe harbor. But his choices had been limited. He could hardly remember a time when they hadn't been, when Danny's mother had still been alive, when their future looked bright. Right now, he would settle for simply normal.

But that, too, seemed hopelessly out of reach.

Summer glanced at the coastline they cruised by. "Jack, I think we're getting close to a place where we can dock."

"I can't risk it."

He expected the stunned silence and wasn't disappointed. But she recovered quickly. "What do you mean?"

"I have to put as many miles as possible between me and them."

"But they're not going anywhere on that boat," she protested.

"No, but it won't take long for them to regroup."

Summer stared at him. "And it won't take you that long to dock and let me off."

"I can't afford to take the risk."

Incredulous, Summer continued staring at him. "Surely you don't expect me to ride along until you either run out of fuel or decide it's safe to stop?"

Jack knew she wouldn't like his reply. "I'm afraid so."

"That's ridiculous. I insist that you let me off as soon as possible."

Jack shook back his heavy mane of longish hair. "Can't do it. As soon as I've put some distance between us and them, I'll dock and you can leave. But not before."

He watched her struggle for an appropriately heated response, considering Danny was angled within easy listening distance. Frustration laced her toned-down words that emerged as a hiss. "Don't think I won't add this to your bill!"

If their situation weren't so critical, he would have laughed at the absurdity of her reply. "Let me guess. The labor's gonna kill me."

"No, but I might," she muttered.

Jack turned as the whisper of a smile finally escaped him. He suspected she wanted to throttle him.

"You've thrown them off the trail," she added. "And

I'm guessing by the course you've set that you're changing your spots."

"Not enough." But her words gave him pause. They could change spots, though. He glanced at Summer, his mind turning over the possibilities. New possibilities. Maybe even new hope.

At Summer's urging, Jack agreed that it wasn't wise to navigate the unknown waters in the approaching darkness. When the boat docked, she rose and sighed audibly. "Not that it hasn't been real fun, but I think I'll find the bus station and call it a night."

"Your mother's probably worried," Jack replied, watching her expression. "Don't you want to find a phone first? One that's close?"

Summer stopped abruptly. "Oh. You're right. She's probably called out the coast guard."

Jack scooped up a sleepy Danny. "Let's ask at the pier. They should know of a place close by where I can buy you a cup of coffee and you can use the phone."

She eyed him suspiciously. "Oh?"

"It's the least I can do. Truce?" He shifted Danny. "Your mother was awfully good to this little guy. I don't want to repay her kindness by worrying her."

Summer didn't bother trying to hide her reluctance. "I suppose so. But just a cup of coffee and I'm out of here."

Jack smoothed the soft, ruffled hair over Danny's forehead. "Sure. It's been a pretty big day for Danny, too."

Summer's expression softened as she watched them, then she straightened, stiffening her back. "One cup of coffee."

Jack nodded before she turned away. Coffee was just the appetizer. He thought of the wall he was backed against. Coercion would be the main course.

Summer finished relating an edited version of the day's events to her mother, assured her that she was safe, asked if her mother could use her computer to E-mail the office that she would be away, then returned to the table. "I told my mother I'd call when I knew what time the bus would get to Edisto."

"Uh-huh," Jack replied, coaxing Danny to eat some tapioca pudding while the toddler banged on the tray of the high chair.

"Did you feed him something besides dessert?" Summer questioned, looking at the toddler in concern.

Jack called on his patience. Did she think the child had survived on sugar since his wife died? "He gummed the toast—" he pointed to the empty jar of baby food "—after downing that."

"Oh." Summer glanced at the obviously healthy baby. "I guess you know what he's supposed to eat."

"If I didn't, he'd probably have starved by now," he replied without malice.

"Has it been difficult…raising him alone?"

Jack tried to disregard the shaft of pain. "I suppose parenthood isn't ever easy, but then it probably hasn't been a picnic for Danny, either."

Guiltily Summer regretted the insensitive words. "I didn't mean that. He looks happy and well cared for."

Jack wiped the baby's chin. "Still, he doesn't have a mother. Nothing will make up for that."

At a loss for words, Summer wished she hadn't ventured down this path. "You'll just have to love him twice as much."

Momentarily sidetracked, Jack stroked the child's downy cheek. "That's not so tough."

Strangely moved, Summer reached blindly for her coffee. When not giving orders or kidnapping her, Jack was damnably appealing. "I can see that."

"Then you can also see why I'd do anything for him." When she nodded, Jack met her gaze directly. "Including asking you to help save his life."

Wheezing as hot coffee traveled down the wrong pipes,

Summer tried to imagine what he meant. Jack pulled up her left arm, thumping her soundly on the back. Oddly the thwack eased her choking. She reached for a paper napkin and wiped her mouth. "What do you mean?"

"Danny and I are sitting ducks unless we change our profile. And that's something I can't do alone." He met her eyes, intensity burning in his. "Will you help us? To escape, that is?"

Shocked, Summer stared at him, wondering if he could possibly be serious. Deciding he was, she measured her words carefully. "If I said yes, how could I help?"

"Those guys are looking for a man and a baby boy, not a couple. As far away as they were on their boat—" Jack gestured at her baggy overalls "—and with you dressed like that, they won't even suspect you're a woman."

Summer felt the sting of his words. "Flattery will get you everywhere."

"I wasn't trying to flatter you."

"Good. Because you didn't succeed."

"This is too important to take lightly," he admonished. "I wouldn't ask you if I had another choice—*any* other choice." His voice flattened. "I don't. My back's against the wall. I wouldn't ask for myself. This is for Danny."

Glancing up sharply, Summer could see he wasn't playing on her emotions. He was completely sincere. She suspected this macho man had great difficulty asking for assistance. "And you want my help?"

"Only for as long as absolutely necessary. Then you're back to Edisto—" Jack snapped his fingers "—like that. If I didn't think we needed you for a safe escape, I wouldn't ask."

She searched his face, once again sensing only honesty and concern. "Uh-huh."

"We need a cover," he continued. "They're not looking for a couple."

"This sounds rather well thought out," she noted suspiciously.

"Don't worry. The plan hasn't been hatching for days. Actually you gave me the idea."

Summer blinked. "Me?"

"When you mentioned I was changing spots. I hadn't, but your comment made me realize we could. But I need help—something more than a wig and a fake nose. I need to change the dynamics."

"Enter the convenient boat mechanic," she supplied.

"Exactly. But even better. You're a woman."

"It's too late now to try buttering me up."

Jack twisted his face into a puzzled scowl. "I don't understand."

She sighed. "Clearly. So, you're asking me to be part of your getaway. But there's one hitch."

He eyed her warily. "Which is?"

"I'm not signing on to your Bonnie and Clyde mission until I know what's going on." She stared at him steadily. "Everything."

Jack took a deep breath. It wasn't a story he'd told many people. Relating portions of it, even to his own parents, had been intensely painful. But then, what had happened had been nearly unbearable. At times he wished he hadn't survived to tell the tale. Only his small son had given him the will to live.

In fact, the events leading him to this point had begun when his wife was expecting Danny. "It seemed we had everything," he told Summer. "What you might call a golden life. We were happy, in love, expecting our first child. I had a great job that I loved."

"Which was?" Summer prompted when he lost himself in the memories.

"An architect," he replied, pulling himself back to the present. "We lived in Chicago. I had just designed a sixty-story skyscraper." He paused, bitterness seeping into his voice. "It was the crowning achievement of my career. Based on its success, I was offered a partnership in the firm—unheard of for anyone under forty. I was on top of the world. A successful career, a beautiful wife, a baby on the way—what else could a man want from life?''

Her voice was soft, quietly concerned. ''And then something happened to change that?''

Jack pushed past the pain. He also had to get past the mistrust that dogged him since that fateful time. What if he told everything to Summer and she double-crossed him. Sure, it *seemed* as though she was an unassuming boat owner living on an idyllic island. But what if she was more than that? What if Fisher and Wilcox had somehow gotten to her? ''Isn't it enough for you to know that Danny's life hangs in the balance?''

She showed a sudden stubborn streak. ''No, it's not. You could be stringing me along. How do I know you didn't rob a bank and that's why you're running away?''

Jack realized she was right. He was asking her to risk everything based on little or no information. It was a gamble, telling her everything, but what choice did he have? He met her eyes, willing her to be what she said she was. ''I guess you don't. I'm no criminal. I stumbled onto a high-level crime scheme. Members of a mob syndicate were using the construction of my building to launder money from its drug ring.''

Summer leaned forward. ''What did you do?''

''I did all the right things. I notified the police and they sent DEA agents to investigate. I expected things to be straightened out. Guess I watched too many movies.''

''It doesn't work that way in real life?''

''Not when the 'good' guys are corrupt. Oh, they made a big show of cracking down, vowing to catch everyone involved. If I hadn't continued checking invoices, I'd have never realized the scam was still going on.''

''What did you do then?'' Summer asked in a tight voice.

''I went straight to the agents in charge of the investigation—Wilcox and Fisher. I just didn't realize they were the ones masterminding the cover-up.''

"I suspect that's only part of the story," Summer guessed, her tone questioning.

Reality struck, that fiercely painful reminder of just how wrong things had gone, how the irreversible course of events had changed his life forever. "Tom Matthews, a DEA commander from another unit, was brought in—apparently I wasn't the only one to see that things weren't quite right. He convinced me to participate in a sting operation to take down Fisher and Wilcox." The pain struck, persistent and agonizing. "I discussed it with Linda—told her I thought I should cooperate. She thought it was the right thing to do as well. I had some half-baked idealistic notion that when you're doing the right thing, you're damned near invincible." He laughed bitterly. "For that matter, I guess I was. I'm still alive and kicking."

Glancing at Summer, he could see the realization light in her eyes, as though she suspected what he was going to say next.

"The sting didn't come off as planned. Fisher and Wilcox escaped the initial net. They didn't take it well that I'd been part of it. They came to my house, gunning for me. I wasn't there...but Linda was." His voice tightened, as the memories washed over him. "She never had a chance."

"They killed her?" Summer asked in a horrified voice, her eyes glinting with unshed tears.

"She didn't die...right then. She lived for months in a coma. After the baby was delivered C-section, she died. It was as though she hung on just long enough to give him life...." Jack had to pause, not certain he could trust his voice.

"I...don't know what to say," Summer managed, her tears escaping unchecked. "I'm so sorry."

Jack saw her tears, realized they were genuine. "Not as sorry as I was...as I always will be."

"Are these the men who are after you now?"

Jack shook away the past with a vengeance, knowing he couldn't sink into that abyss right now—Danny's survival depended on it. "Yes. I testified against them, and they were sent to prison."

"Did they get an early release?"

"Not in the way that you mean. They weren't due for parole for years. The only way they could have gotten out was with help from a highly placed insider. Someone inside the agency with enough pull to hide or destroy records and arrange for new records that would allow Fisher and Wilcox to be released."

"Are these the guys we ran onto the sandbar?"

He nodded, remembering how the pair had been flung from the boat, and his disappointment when they had resurfaced. He wasn't bloodthirsty, but he knew that as long as the men lived, he and Danny wouldn't be safe.

"How did you know they got an early release?" Summer asked.

"I'm only guessing about the release—it's not like I saw any paperwork. But I'm pretty certain they didn't bust out of a high-security prison. Also, someone was feeding them information because they knew right where to look for me. And I know they're out because I nearly tripped over them at my house."

"What?"

"I was coming home. I had Danny in his stroller and we were headed toward the back of the house. Just as I turned the corner, I spotted Fisher and Wilcox trying to break in."

Summer gasped, apparently realizing the seriousness of his situation.

"Exactly. If my timing had been a little different, they could have surprised us when we were in the house. We wouldn't have stood much of a chance." He glanced over at Danny, felling the surge of protectiveness that was never far from the surface. "Since the boat was stocked, we rushed there and set off. It's part of why I liked living on the Florida coast. I figured the waterways were the safest escape, especially since Fisher and Wilcox didn't know I owned a boat—at least, not at first. Not until someone filled them in on that as well.''

''And you were making a good escape until you had engine trouble,'' Summer filled in, easily grasping the rest of the story.

''Exactly. I've been trying to reach Tom Matthews, but so far I haven't had any luck.''

Eyes wide with shock and concern, Summer asked, ''And you think he can help?''

''He can find out how my protection was compromised and to what degree. He's the only person I trust.''

She hesitated. ''Are you sure he's not in on what's happening? *Someone* engineered the agents' early release and fed them information. Why not him?''

''Tom was brought in from a completely different unit. He'd never met Fisher and Wilcox before the internal investigation. Because he'd convinced me to participate in the sting operation, Tom felt responsible for Linda's death. He took it hard when she was killed. Afterward, he was a man with a cause—determined to bring Fisher and Wilcox down, which he did.''

Summer tried to assimilate what Jack had told her, but the enormity swamped her. ''But why aren't you in the witness-protection program?''

''I *was*.'' Everything in Jack's demeanor became even grimmer. ''I've been on the run since before Danny was born. I couldn't stay at the hospital and put Linda in danger. So I entered the program immediately. When Danny was born, he was brought to me.'' He paused for a moment. ''Then Linda died, and we couldn't go to the funeral. But we'd said our goodbyes.''

Throat tight, Summer couldn't begin to know how to reply.

Jack looked up at her. ''My cover was blown—from the inside. That's why I ditched my most current disguise—a mustache, glasses and dyed hair.''

''I don't understand. How can your cover be blown from

the *inside?*'' But even as Summer voiced the question, the answer hit her with stunning force. Horrified, she asked, ''How could this happen? Isn't the witness-protection program designed to offer the ultimate protection?''

''Corruption can worm its way into the most unlikely places. I never dreamed that working as an architect would endanger my family, cause my wife's murder.''

Impulsively she laid one hand over his. ''You can't believe that was your fault.''

He ignored her words of comfort. ''I can't even reach Donald Sedgewick. He's been my contact person in the program since the beginning.''

''But you said you were trying to find another man.''

''Tom Matthews. He's the DEA commander, stationed in Washington, D.C. That's where we were headed when the boat's engine gave out.''

''You haven't been able to reach him by phone?''

''The autobots answering the phone keep saying that Tom is away on extended leave.''

''Maybe he is. Maybe he needed a long vacation.''

Jack was shaking his head. ''I don't think so. Tom's always been a workaholic. And why now?''

''Now?'' she echoed.

Jack met her eyes, wondering how she would react to the most damning piece of evidence. ''When I called, they didn't recognize my alias. I was told they can't find my file.''

Puzzled, she angled her head. ''I don't understand.''

''My file, my identity. Everything that was set up to protect Danny and me has vanished from their computer.''

''But if it was in the witness-program files, then how…?'' Summer's voice trailed off as the horror in her expression grew.

''Exactly. Without that protection, we've been thrown to the wolves. And the file could only have disappeared in the agency. Which means everything in the government's arsenal is at their disposal. I also suspect that if my file exists, it has been altered.''

''Altered how?''

''There's no telling. I could be listed as dead, a wanted felon—take your pick.''

''But wouldn't someone notice and get suspicious?''

''They obviously have an important internal contact, one who can deflect suspicions.''

''I could try to research your file on the computer,'' she offered, ''if I could get my hands on some decent equipment.''

Jack shook his head. ''At this point it wouldn't do any good. Besides, they have real experts in their computer department.''

''But—''

''Really, I appreciate your efforts, but you don't know who's behind this.''

''Wilcox and Fisher?'' she questioned weakly.

''I'm not sure how, but I know it's them. Question is, who's their inside man?''

She hesitated. ''Are you sure it couldn't be this Tom Matthews you're trying to find? Do you suppose he's turned? Could that be why he's so difficult to locate?''

The thought had occurred to Jack, but he refused to believe it. He also knew that if he allowed himself to believe that Tom was a traitor, he had literally nowhere to turn. If Tom Matthews had gone against his grain and sold his soul to the highest bidder, Jack knew no place on the globe was safe any longer. It was something he could deal with for himself, but not for his son.

''If I believed that, I'd have to give up, and that's something I don't intend to do.''

Summer had been afraid to learn what he was running from, but this was far worse than anything she might have imagined. And despite his apparent sincerity, she couldn't squelch all her suspicions. What if this was simply a well-concocted story? ''Why don't you go to the FBI for help?''

Jack shook his head. "The long arm of the government has too far a reach. Going to the FBI would sign my death warrant."

She blanched. "But you and Danny..." Her voice trailed off helplessly.

"They'll have to kill me to get my son." The quiet grimness in his voice chilled her; it was far more effective than bravado or swaggering.

Summer realized that he was a powerful man, one who didn't have to brandish that strength. Which made him that much more appealing. It also made her realize that he would only have asked for her help as a last measure. "Surely you don't think they'd harm a baby?" she asked, her gaze settling anxiously on Danny.

"If they had him, they could use him to get me. Beyond that, I don't know what they'd do. They are men without morals."

She gasped. "I guess I never really believed people like that existed outside of the movies and *America's Most Wanted*. I mean, I guess I knew they did—that horrible things happen. But they never happened to anyone I knew before."

"Frankly I felt much the same way until *I* was the someone it was happening to."

"It must be awful," she murmured.

"Sometimes it seems like a bad dream," Jack admitted. "One that I'll wake up from and everything will be normal again. My family is whole, we're leading happy, uncomplicated lives."

"And then reality hits," she guessed softly.

"Yep."

Summer glanced down at their hands. She had not withdrawn hers, nor had Jack pulled away. Heat from his hand warmed her palm, making her aware of the latent strength resting so close. Although she'd offered the touch as a gesture of comfort, she was highly aware of feelings that had nothing to do with comfort.

It was absurd, inappropriate, completely out of place. Yet as they sat in the ordinary little café drinking bad coffee, talking about the magnitude of his dilemma, her pulse quickened at the inexplicable intimacy of their joined hands.

At that moment, his gaze met hers, and the sudden light in his eyes signaled a response. Not sure how to interpret that response, she was flooded with uncertainty.

Danny fussed at that moment, kicking plump little feet.

Not certain whether to be relieved or disappointed at the interruption, Summer turned her attention to the baby.

"He's cutting a tooth," Jack explained.

She reached over, playfully tugging one of Danny's toes. "That's rough."

"And it'll be rougher ahead."

Eyes widening in concern, Summer felt every maternal instinct she possessed kicking into gear. "We have to keep him safe."

"That's the general idea." He paused, his gaze refusing to relinquish hers. "Does that mean you're going to help us?"

Chapter 3

Jack studied Summer's face, waiting for her answer. He had run out of ideas and options. Otherwise he wouldn't have asked. He hated doing it. Since he was accustomed to solving his own problems without help, it rankled to have to ask for her assistance. But she was his last resort. Literally. Summer's cooperation could give them the advantage he'd prayed for.

Her gaze lingered on the drowsy baby. "If I said yes, it could only be for a short while."

Jack released a breath he hadn't realized he'd been holding. "I understand."

"And I'll have to think of *something* to tell my mother."

Pausing, he stared at this unusual woman. Most would have wished him luck and fled. And Summer didn't even like him. "You could tell her I need help with Danny."

"That's why I'm doing this," she reiterated as though afraid he would get the wrong idea. "For Danny."

He nodded.

"And only until you get a good head start."

"I understand." Jack pulled out a plastic-coated menu from a slot behind the napkin holder. "But before we sign a binding contract, let's order some dinner."

"Dinner?" she echoed blankly.

"You know, the third meal of the day, except that by my count we've only had one so far."

"How can you think of food at a time like this?"

"Because we won't get very far running on empty stomachs." He could see by her expression that she hadn't really grasped what running would mean. "Aren't you hungry?"

"I guess so. I just thought we ought to be mapping out strategy." Summer waved her hands in a vague motion. "Or something urgent."

"I map better on a full stomach." Jack managed a smile, hoping to relax her. "And no one feels the urgency more than me. How's this for strategy? We find a hotel and go from there."

Her eyes narrowed. "A hotel?"

"There's not enough room for all of us to bunk on the boat. Besides, it's too high profile. I hate that we spent as much time as we did in the boat. It leaves too recognizable a trail. Wilcox and Fisher will be looking for it, tracing what direction we took. The first thing we do is get alternate transportation."

She nodded slowly.

"Rather, the second thing," he corrected. "Now we eat and then find a hotel."

A hotel.

It was perfectly normal to locate a place to stay. Then why did the idea send her into near panic? Summer wondered.

Because it seemed intimate. One room, usually one bed. No outside distractions. As Danny wriggled to get down, Summer was glad to have him as an inside distraction.

Jack tossed the key on the small bureau top. "It's not the Ritz, but it'll do."

"It's fine," Summer murmured, noting with relief the two double beds.

Jack anchored Danny on his hip. "I'm just going to dunk this little guy for now. He's had a pretty long day. Then the bathroom's all yours."

Nodding, Summer watched him carry Danny into the bathroom. Then she stuck both hands in her pockets, uncertain what else to do with them. She thought of her brief conversation with her mother, the lengthy pause after saying she would be away for a short time helping Jack care for Danny. They were too close for her mother not to suspect she was concealing something.

Despite her independence, family was important to Summer. So important she'd risked her engagement to remain on Edisto and help her mother with the family business. But this arrangement was short-term. It wasn't as though Jack would want her with him on any other basis.

"Summer?"

She whirled around, torn from her wayward thoughts. "Uh, yes?"

"The bathroom's all yours. I'll get Danny dressed out here."

"Right."

As Jack walked out of the bathroom, holding a towel-shrouded Danny, he stopped suddenly. "Idiot."

Summer blinked. "I beg your pardon?"

"I'm an idiot. I totally forgot you don't have anything with you. Not even a toothbrush."

"It's not something I carry in my toolbox," she admitted. "But I'll go to the nearest store in the morning, get a change of clothes—"

"Better get more than one," he advised, expertly toweling off his son, then reaching for a diaper.

"Right."

"And maybe you could get something more…*girlish*," Jack added without glancing up. "Since Fisher and Wilcox saw you in the overalls and probably thought you were a guy.''

Stiffly she nodded and retreated to the bathroom.

Opting for a quick shower, Summer lingered in the bathroom, finally donning the clothes she'd just shed. Self-consciously she reentered the bedroom, expecting to face Jack. She was painfully aware that she still looked *ungirlish,* dressed as before sans the cap.

Glancing across the room, she immediately saw that Jack was sprawled across one bed, Danny close beside him. Hearing a tiny gurgle, she inched closer. Danny stared up at her with his huge, unblinking blue eyes.

''You're not asleep, little one. How'd that happen? I think your daddy thought you were.''

''Da-da,'' he replied, clearly wanting to continue the conversation.

''You'd better go to sleep,'' Summer offered in response.

''Da!'' The baby smiled in appeal.

''Well, as long as we're both awake, I guess it can't hurt.'' Reaching over carefully so that she didn't disturb Jack, Summer picked up the baby. ''So, mister, can't sleep? You did have a pretty big day.''

He reached for a handful of hair in reply.

''Didn't know I had that under my hat, did you? It's only one of my many surprises.'' Wishing for a rocker, Summer settled for the room's only chair instead, rocking her body in a gentle motion.

Danny responded by snuggling close. Feeling a hitch that had nothing to do with the motion and everything to do with the baby she held, Summer traced her fingers over his soft cheek. ''You're really something, you know that?''

But the motion was lulling him.

''It's okay.'' Summer glanced over at Jack, noting the even rise and fall of his chest as he slept. ''I seem to be a master at putting men to sleep.''

Danny's eyelids fluttered, then closed. Cradling the small, trusting body, Summer thought of the threat that lurked far too close by. She couldn't let anything happen to this precious motherless child. And Jack could only do so much. Which was where she came in. With a small smile, she thought of the following day. Maybe she should show Jack a few surprises, as well.

Summer left the last of the two stores she'd shopped in, her purchases nestled in several bags, except for those she was wearing.

Jack had said *girlish*. She was going to give him *girlish*.

And *girlish* meant accessories to go with the clothes, and makeup to accentuate her features. Pale lashes were now darkened, lips glossed. Practical tennis shoes had been replaced with strappy sandals. Her baseball cap was now a distant memory. Instead she clutched a wide-brimmed straw hat that would have done justice to Scarlett O'Hara.

And the shopping bags in her other hand contained more clothes like the ones she now wore. Clothes she had once called impractical, but that were definitely feminine. Summer glanced at her watch, mindful of the danger of wasting time. But she had done all of her shopping and transforming in an hour, rushing like a madwoman. Believing that no one would be tracking *her* movements, she had charged the purchases. But suspecting that the situation might change, she'd also made a trip to the ATM for a hefty advance.

She had arranged to meet Jack and Danny at the coffee shop ten minutes ago. But then, sometimes a late entrance made a statement of its own.

Taking a reinforcing breath, Summer put one hand on the door of the café to push it open, but it was whisked open before she could.

"Allow me," a strange man said with a smile as he held open the door.

"Thank you," she murmured, taken aback by the gesture and the obvious interest and approval in the man's eyes.

"My pleasure," he said with an even bigger smile.

Clearing her throat, Summer looked for Jack and Danny.

Spotting them, she wove through the tables, pausing beside Danny's high chair. "Hi, guys."

Jack lifted his head, lowering his coffee cup. "Hi—" He jumped up. Hot coffee splashed over his khaki pants, and he swore beneath his breath. "You surprised me."

Apparently. Pleased with his reaction, Summer took a chair, watching as he swiped at his coffee-splattered pants. "Does that coffee taste as good as it looks?" Not waiting for a reply, she chucked the baby's chin. "How are you, sunshine? Looks like Daddy's wearing more of his breakfast than you are."

Jack crumpled a handful of soggy napkins. "I wasn't expecting to see you."

"Even though we were supposed to meet ten minutes ago?" she asked sweetly.

"You know...wearing...that."

"That would be—what did you call it?" Summer pretended to try to remember. "*Girlish,* I believe. Yes, definitely, it was *girlish.*"

"Okay. So I wasn't very tactful. I didn't know you were planning to dip into your arsenal."

She felt a thrill of pleased surprise. "Is that what you think I did?"

"You're a woman, aren't you?"

Summer started to reply, but Jack continued speaking. "Good job. Wilcox and Fisher wouldn't recognize you if they were sitting a foot away."

Her smile faded. Of course.

He leaned over and wiped Danny's chin. "Do you mind if we get your order to go? We really need to get on the road."

Summer thought of the danger not far behind. It was a sobering reminder, one that chased away the sting of his words. So she wasn't a femme fatale. That was hardly a surprise. She never had been before.

Summer ordered a sandwich that could be prepared

quickly. Then she looked in puzzlement at Jack. "What are we hitting the road *in?*"

"I traded the boat for a car."

"How'd you manage that—" she glanced at her watch "—so quickly?"

"Danny and I took a walk by the pier. We met an older man fishing. Turns out he owned the car we're using."

"And he traded just like that?"

"The car isn't worth a fraction of the boat," Jack pointed out. "It was a great deal for him."

"Unless the guy gets blown up in it."

"Fisher and Wilcox want me, not him. Besides, part of the agreement is he keeps the boat in his shed for the next two weeks." At her surprised look he continued, "I told him my ex-wife was looking for me and I needed to lay low. He wasn't about to question his good fortune."

"Which means your trail ends here." Summer was surprised at the unreasonable disappointment she felt. She should have been flooded with relief that her part was over.

"I wish it were that easy."

She glanced up sharply. "I don't understand."

"Ditching the boat will throw them for a short while, but it's just a diversion. Remember, they have access to the most comprehensive computer system in the world. One good thing about the trade, it won't cause a paper trail."

"They wouldn't know to track me, would they?" Summer asked hesitantly.

Jack shook his head.

She released a relieved breath. "Good, that's what I figured."

"Why?"

She glanced pointedly at her purchases. "I used my credit cards."

"They don't know who you are—it should be safe."

"But you can't use your credit cards," she realized suddenly. "And your cash can't last forever."

His jaw tightened. "That's not your problem."

She suddenly remembered the expensive boat repair and guessed he must already be running low on money.

"I'll still help you out for a few days."

When Jack's eyes met hers, she felt her pulse doing a little two-step of its own.

"I haven't said it, but Danny and I are grateful—"

Uncomfortable, she waved away his words. "I think you said we had to hurry."

Surprise and puzzlement clouded his eyes. "Right." Then determination replaced both emotions as Jack changed gears. "I've loaded our stuff in the car." He glanced at her packages. "Most of it."

The waitress brought Summer's sandwich in a doggie bag and they left. It didn't take long to reach the car. An older model, black with a light coating of dust, it looked like any one of thousands on the road.

"I can see why you wanted this car," she commented. "It's so ordinary, it's almost invisible."

"Exactly." Jack loaded her shopping bags in the trunk, then hefted Danny into the new car seat strapped in the back.

Summer hung on to one of the bags and the small cooler she'd bought. Flipping it open, she retrieved a small plastic whale. Leaning into the back seat, she offered it to Danny.

"What's that?" Jack asked.

"A teething ring. It's filled with gel. I put it in some ice, so it'll be cool for a while and it should help his sore gums."

Jack lifted his brow in surprise. "Makes sense. I never thought about getting something like that."

She shrugged. "It's just my logical mind, I suppose. I tried to think of what would make me feel better."

"So you're not an old hand with babies?"

Smiling, Summer shook her head. "'Fraid not. I'm an only child, no little nieces and nephews to practice on."

"No baby-sitting as a teenager?"

"I was too busy learning how to take an engine apart and put it back together."

Jack studied her for a moment, watching the sunlight glance off her face, wondering for the dozenth time that day why she had previously chosen to hide it beneath baseball caps. "Which was a good trade to learn. Not everybody's cut out for a lot of schooling."

Summer set her jaw and didn't answer.

"I'm lucky I liked architecture so much myself. Made the studying easier." He laughed, but it was a bitter sound. "Not that it's done me much good. If I want to stay alive, I have to leave that career behind." Jack glanced down at his son, who was happily gumming the cold ring. "But I'm lucky in other ways."

"Uh-huh." She reached into the shopping bag and pulled out a pint-size frilly pink-and-white outfit.

Jack eyed it dubiously. "Isn't that a little small for you?"

Summer unfastened the buttons. "You a fashion critic?"

Shaking his head, Jack watched in horror as she reached over to little Danny and began to dress him in the pink-and-white ruffles. "What the hell do you think you're doing?" he demanded.

"Completing our disguise," she replied calmly.

Feeling the insult to his entire gender, Jack stared at her. "By turning my son into a *girl?*"

"You thought it was perfectly fine to turn me into one," she replied sweetly.

His mouth opened, his jaw worked, but no words emerged.

Summer added a pink bow on an elastic band to Danny's head, the final humiliation. "That ought to do it."

"And then some."

"Don't be ridiculous. You want this disguise to work, don't you? I hardly think Danny's future macho image will be damaged by wearing pink for a few days."

"And ruffles," Jack muttered morosely.

"Lace never killed anybody," she added before glancing pointedly at her watch. "Aren't you in a hurry to get on the road?"

"Right. I want to put as many miles as possible between us and them." He took one last sorrowful look at Danny before starting the car.

The first several miles passed in relative silence. Jack glanced over at Summer, wondering what was brewing in that unusual head of hers. But he found his gaze wandering, noting her completely feminine look, the softness he hadn't known she possessed.

Summer turned just then, her expression questioning.

Jack cleared his throat. "It won't always be safe to travel in the daylight, so I thought we'd only stop when necessary so we can get as far as possible today."

"We'll really have to travel in the dark?"

He frowned, knowing the evil of his pursuers, wishing he hadn't been forced to drag Summer into this. "It'll be safer that way," he answered briefly.

She straightened in the seat, turning to look directly at him. "I've been thinking. Maybe there's another explanation—for why your file's missing."

Jack knew there wasn't, but decided to humor her. "Such as?"

"I'm not sure. The main system could have been in a transfer process and the file just couldn't be accessed when you called."

"I called several times."

"Maybe a disk error or a memory loss," she suggested.

"I see where you're headed."

Summer frowned. "And where would that be?"

"You're trying to think of something other than a conspiracy to explain what's happened. I've already been down that road. It's a dead end." A humorless grin split his features. "Pardon the pun."

Summer shook her head. "Maybe there's something you haven't thought of, a detail you've overlooked."

Jack navigated a sharp curve, then glanced at her, unable to resist the movement. It was something he'd caught himself doing more and more often. How had she managed such a transformation? Sure, the clothes were different, but it was something else. Somehow it was hard to believe she was the same grease monkey who had towed his boat in. "I'd be glad to listen to any suggestions," he finally managed to say, pulling his thoughts back to the conversation. "If I overlooked something that would help us, I'd like to hear about it."

"I didn't say I'd thought of anything, just that *maybe* there's something you've forgotten...or not thought of." She twisted around to look at little Danny, reaching back to straighten his crumpled dress. "Won't we need to stop and let Danny stretch every so often? I wouldn't want to be stuck in that little carrier all day."

"We'll stop." He paused. "If it's too dangerous, we'll stop quickly, then move on."

But Summer's attention was caught as she turned forward in the seat. "What's that in the road ahead?"

Jack swore briefly and vividly beneath his breath. "That's a roadblock." His fingers tightened on the steering wheel. "And we'll have to try and talk our way through."

Summer frowned. "But why would the local police be looking for you?"

He sighed. "They don't call it the *long* arm of the law for the hell of it."

"Oh—oh! Do you think they'll recognize you?"

Jack was already slipping on oversize sunglasses. "I hope not."

She gulped, then glanced back at Danny. "They just *can't,*" she muttered, but with enough volume that the determination echoed through.

Jack dug suddenly in his jacket pocket. Sunlight glinted off the gold ring he retrieved. "Summer..."

"Yes?"

"There's another component to our disguise."

"Oh?" she answered, a slight catch in her voice.

He took her hand with unexpected tenderness, then slid the ring on her finger, pausing before releasing her hand.

"What about you?" she questioned in a husky tone.

Reaching into his pocket again, he produced a matching gold band and started to slide it on his finger.

"Wait!"

Clearly surprised, he watched as she took the ring from him. Gently she slid it on his left hand.

The air in the car seemed suddenly restrictive, the roadblock nearly forgotten until reality intruded once again.

Although there had been a long line of cars in front of them, all too quickly it was their turn at the checkpoint. Jack slid a sideways glance toward Summer, hoping she had the mettle to carry this off.

A patrol car at the head of the road turned on its siren just then, the sound blasting through the windows, waking up Danny, who screamed in protest.

The highway patrolman greeted them with a tipped hat, but quickly replaced it when he heard the baby's cries, raising his voice to be heard. "Something wrong with the little one?"

"The siren," Jack explained. "It startled...the baby."

"Poor little thing," the officer sympathized, now more interested in Danny than in questioning them.

Summer smiled prettily at the policeman, then twisted around to unfasten the car seat. "Babies don't understand the noise."

Jack glanced at Summer. "Do you need some help, honey?"

Honey? She didn't dare voice the thought aloud. Instead she lifted Danny from the car seat. "No, I'm fine."

Jack nodded, trying to look casual as he glanced around for possible escape routes.

"Just the two of you traveling?" the officer asked, his

glance finally moving from the baby back to Jack and Summer.

"Three of us," Summer corrected, stroking Danny's leg in a motherly fashion to soothe him.

The policeman relaxed a trifle when Danny's sobs relaxed into a hiccuping cry. Then he grinned as he spotted the pink bow sitting jauntily across the baby's forehead.

"That's right," Jack agreed. "Just my...daughter and my...wife."

"We're checking—" Just then another siren roared to life and Danny screamed in accompaniment.

"You folks better head on out," the policeman said, clearly uncomfortable with a crying infant.

Jack tried not to look too relieved. "Thanks, Officer. What's going on here anyway?"

"Some coke-head tried to kill two federal agents, then kidnapped a little boy."

"Coke-head?" Jack asked in what he hoped was a normal voice.

"They'd busted him, and he didn't want to go quietly."

Jack's lips thinned into a grim line. "Hope you catch your man."

"No worries about that. Every cop in the bordering states is looking for him. No chance he'll get away." The officer hitched up his gun belt over a burgeoning paunch, then waved them ahead.

"Every state," Summer echoed in a horrified voice as soon as they had passed the roadblock. "We're trapped."

Chapter 4

"Not quite," Jack replied, waiting to release his pent-up breath until they'd eased past the blockade and out onto open highway again.

"How do you plan to get to D.C. without passing through the surrounding states?" Summer questioned, her attention torn between Jack and little Danny. How could she help them now?

"It's time to detour. Fisher and Wilcox must have figured that I'd head for D.C. That's why the roadblocks are set up. So, we'll drive to the east for now and if we have to, we'll double back south. Even though this is a pretty good disguise, I don't want to push my luck with the state cops. If they're looking for a baby, one of them might suspect us despite the ruffles."

She was quiet for a moment, absently rubbing the unfamiliar wedding band. "But eventually you'll have to head north again."

"I'm betting that even Fisher and Wilcox can't keep a multistate roadblock going indefinitely."

"That's quite a gamble," she noted.

Jack glanced at her. "You handled yourself real well back there."

Summer shrugged. "I didn't have much choice."

It was a hell of a position he'd put her in, Jack knew. One many women would have freaked over. He cleared his throat. "I guess it's a good thing you turned Danny into Danielle with the ruffles."

She tilted her head to one side, then acknowledged his comment with a nod. "So where are we headed?"

"To a club I worked in right after I joined the program."

"Doing what?"

"Bartender."

"From architect to bartender... Wasn't that a stretch?"

He thought back over the unbelievable events of the past year. "It was just one of a string of jobs I took while we kept moving. We've changed locations at least half a dozen times in the past year."

"Is that normal?"

Jack's gaze remained on the road, but his hands tightened on the wheel. "Depends. I'm no expert. They don't have a witness support group, so I've never compared notes. I suppose some people stay in one place, but I never really felt safe."

"Did you suspect Wilcox and Fisher then?"

He shook his head. "Not exactly. I didn't know they were out of prison until they came after me. It was just a feeling I had...that something might happen, that we weren't really protected. Maybe it was a premonition. I stashed a hoard of cash, bought the boat and kept it stocked, thinking we might need it. I figured it was easier to disappear on the water. I didn't realize I needed to be a more seasoned boater. A few weekends didn't make me a sailor. I wanted to be ready, just in case."

"Turns out you were right. But why didn't you just get on a plane and fly to D.C. when you stumbled across Fisher and Wilcox? It would have been faster."

"That's the loudest, clearest signal you can send," Jack explained, remembering the terror he'd felt for Danny when he realized his protection had been compromised. "Taking a plane leaves a paper trail with huge banners and signs saying Here We Are. And what if I couldn't find Tom Matthews when I got there? I'd have just delivered myself into their hands."

"Oh," she replied quietly. "Couldn't you contact relatives or friends to find a safe place?"

"When you enter the program, you have to leave those people behind. Contacting them would put them in equal danger."

"You don't mean leave them behind *forever?*"

Jack nodded, remembering the difficulty of those good-byes. His parents, Linda's parents, his brothers. Still hurting from Linda's death, it had been doubly wrenching for him to say those final farewells.

"But surely there's some way...."

His lips thinned. "Afraid not. There's a slow, complicated mail drop, but no phone calls...and certainly no visits."

"You can't ever see your family?" Summer asked in a stricken voice.

"Danny's my family," Jack replied tightly, remembering the tears in his mother's eyes when he had seen her for the last time. "And I'll do whatever I have to in order to protect him."

Summer's glance automatically shifted backward. "So he'll never know his grandparents?"

Jack's jaw clenched momentarily. "No."

"I don't know how you can do it," Summer wondered aloud. "I could never leave my mother, knowing it was for the last time. She's getting older, her health isn't perfect and I can't stand the thought of her being alone with no one to count on. That's why I still live on Edisto."

Jack strove to keep his tone even. "Which is admirable."

"I didn't mean to pour salt on the wound," she apologized instantly. "I was just thinking how difficult that must have been for you. How difficult it still must be."

"It's not the life I'd have chosen. But since it chose me, I deal with it."

"I don't think I could be that strong," she admitted.

"Don't sell yourself short. You've hardly been a shrinking violet the last twenty-four hours."

"I've never considered myself a member of the flower family." Summer smiled unexpectedly, and he noticed the way it changed her face. An unconsciously flirty tug of her lips drew attention to clear, lissome features and tawny-green eyes. Again he wondered why she had downplayed her femininity. It was almost as though she'd run away from being a woman. "And certainly not a violet," she continued. "Shrinking or otherwise."

"Or an orchid?" Jack asked unexpectedly, surprising himself as much as Summer. But he loved the way a sudden touch of pink crept beneath her golden tan.

She made a deliberate show of staring out the window. "So, we're headed to a nightclub?"

"Hardly."

Summer turned her head a fraction. "I thought you just said—"

"A neighborhood watering hole. Clean, but it hardly lives up to the description of nightclub. A bartender and one waitress—nothing fancy."

"I wasn't expecting the Tropicana," she muttered.

"The Tropicana," Jack repeated, running the name over in his memory. "Isn't that the club where Ricky worked on *I Love Lucy?*"

She sniffed. "Your point?"

Remarkably he found himself smiling. "It won't resemble the Tropicana. And I can assure you we won't be running into Ethel or Fred, either."

Jack was right, Summer concluded a little while later. The bar in Damson he took her to in no way resembled the fictional club where Ricky and Lucy had danced and laughed. The Rusty Anchor catered to the working man...and occasional woman. From the way the patrons eyed her, she guessed *very* occasional.

Bart, the owner, greeted Jack in a friendly fashion. "Sure, I can use you. Been tending bar myself the last few weeks. Can't get dependable help anymore. And Rita can watch the kid for you like she did before." His glance shifted to Summer, his gaze roving over her with a little too much interest. "If you're still needing a baby-sitter."

"Bart, this is my wife. We're taking sort of a honeymoon trip."

Summer's gaze jerked around enough to meet his. A *hijacked* wife was more accurate.

Jack's eyes met hers, sending a signal.

But she didn't read the warning.

His lips covered hers, a warm, powerful invasion that she couldn't battle. But it would have been a weak fight. Bart, the dusky club and the danger they were fleeing paled next to the sensations. Ones that rippled from the heat they shared, the heat he ignited.

She was close enough to trace the crinkles near his eyes that suggested he'd laughed often...once. Close enough to see the taut lines of his tanned skin, to memorize the agate-blue of his overpowering eyes.

When Jack pulled away enough that they finally parted, Summer wanted to whimper in protest. Instead she stared soberly at him as Bart chuckled.

"You sure you have time to tend bar?" Bart asked in an exaggerated voice. "While you're honeymooning?"

"I've got time," Jack replied evenly.

"Whatever you say." Bart turned to Summer. "You done any serving, honey?"

Summer stared at the man, instinctively disliking him. "Excuse me?"

"I can use a waitress a few nights a week, too."

"We'll see," Jack replied for her. "The rooms in the back still available?"

"Room," Bart corrected. "Rita turned the rest of it into a studio—whatever the hell that is." He shook his head. "Never did understand that woman."

Jack exchanged a glance with Summer that told her he didn't wonder why. Still, he didn't share that opinion with Bart. "One room will be fine." He shifted Danny and hooked a casual arm around Summer's waist. "Better than fine."

Bart snickered. He led them into the room, which, while small, was neat and clean.

Summer's gaze zeroed in on the solitary bed.

"Thanks, Bart. It looks great. I can see Rita's touch," Jack commented.

"Yeah," Bart agreed. "All she does is paint and clean." He shook his head in bafflement, obviously not understanding his wife. "I'll leave you alone."

"I can tend bar after I bring our things in," Jack offered.

"You want Rita to watch the kid?" Bart asked.

"No!" Summer exclaimed, then calmed her voice. "I'll take care of him."

Bart shrugged. "Whatever, but once Rita sees him, she'll be wanting to watch him, you wait and see."

As soon as the door closed behind him, Summer turned on Jack. "How could you consider letting people like that take care of Danny?"

Jack looked slightly taken aback at her ferocity, but recovered quickly. "Rita's light-years away from Bart. I never quite understood how the two of them got together. She's gentle, kind and loves art almost as much as she does children."

"Are their children more like Rita or Bart?"

"They never had any children, which makes it even more of a mystery why they stay together. But one thing's for sure, she's great with kids."

"I can't understand how you could have worked for someone like Bart."

Jack's expression tightened. "Being in the program doesn't give you a lot of choices. And there's a big advantage to working for Bart. He pays in cash and keeps a low profile himself. I've wondered why—I know it's something in his past, but then I didn't want anyone questioning me either, so it worked out well."

Summer cataloged this information. "I'd still feel better taking care of Danny myself."

"You might not feel that way for long."

Summer set her lips. "Why don't you let me worry about that?"

"I feel bad enough about dragging you into this. I don't intend to turn you into a built-in baby-sitter."

Summer swung back her considerable length of hair, jutting her chin into a posture that for those who knew her, signaled her stubbornness. She held out her hands for the baby. "Why don't you go get Danny's playpen? We'll need it to use for his bed."

"Sure, but—"

She waved him away. "We'll be fine. Just bring in the gear, okay?"

With a shake of his head and an inaudible mutter, Jack retreated.

"So, little man, these are our digs." Danny chortled while she looked around the tiny room, her gaze settling on the bed. With each glance, it seemed narrower, more intimate. She jiggled the baby on her hip as they took the minitour. "I don't suppose you'd like to share your playpen tonight."

"Here's the first load," Jack announced from behind her. Whirling around, she hoped he hadn't heard her words. But he was busy with Danny's paraphernalia.

"It's amazing how much stuff such a little person requires," Summer said nervously, knowing how lame the comment was. But she couldn't stop her chatter.

However, Jack didn't seem to notice anything peculiar. "Yeah. I'll go get the rest."

When he was gone, she paced the compact room. "Okay, Danny, we can do this, right?"

The baby blinked, then reached out to tug at her hair, smiling when he had a fistful.

"We have to find you better toys," she chided gently. "That, or I shouldn't have let you discover my hair."

"I'm glad you did," Jack commented quietly, surprising her again.

Self-consciously she disengaged small, eager hands, then shook back her hair. "It's no big deal. I imagine all babies like discovering things."

Jack's eyes darkened. "Or maybe it's a male trait."

Summer tightened her grip on Danny, needing a firm attachment to something solid. "Maybe."

"Hey! Jack!" Bart's voice echoed down the hall. "You about ready to tend bar?"

Jack glanced at his watch. "Looks like my shift's starting early." He raised his voice. "Sure, Bart. Be right there." He turned back to Summer. "You sure about—?"

"Enough! We'll have a great time, huh, Danny?"

The baby blinked in agreement as he grabbed for Summer's hair.

"If you change your mind, come get me," Jack insisted. "Bart says Rita should be home anytime now."

"Just go," Summer chided. "I'll know where to find you if either of us goes bonkers."

With one last look, Jack reluctantly left.

Summer deposited Danny in his playpen, then shed her sandals, trading her dress for a T-shirt and shorts. "Dresses are okay," she informed the baby. "But between you and me, this is lots better."

Danny waved a stuffed bear in her direction and looked at her in appeal.

Laughing, she stooped to lift him from the playpen.

"You didn't think I was going to leave you in there, did you? We've got lots to do."

After several games of peekaboo, patty-cake and this-little-piggy, Summer sat back on her heels. "Well, you've had your dinner, so I'm guessing we should give you a bath before you're too tired."

Danny didn't protest, content with the neon-green plastic toy frog she handed him as she unpacked his gear and readied his bath.

And, she discovered, Danny loved a bath. Although Summer didn't know much about babies, she guessed that bathtub safety was a big concern. So she cautiously put him in a shallow amount of water, half-expecting him to holler. Instead he laughed, clapping his hands into the water, splashing her in the process.

Joining his laughter, Summer glanced at her drenched clothing. "So much for this shirt, huh?"

Danny answered with another splash, amusing himself with a new spray of water.

Summer let him play until the water cooled, then lifted him out of the tub. "Okay, let's find some jammies."

She put a towel around him, much as she'd seen Jack do, using the top of it as a hood. He peeked at her from beneath the towel, his big blue eyes watching every move.

"With those eyes, you're going to grow into a lady-killer, just like Daddy, aren't you?"

"Da-da?" he questioned.

"Not yet, sweetie." Involuntarily her gaze skipped toward the bed again. "But soon enough."

Summer discovered it was great fun to powder and dress the toddler. "Who'd have thought it?" she asked him, remembering how she'd once shuddered when her friends had begun having babies. From afar, it had seemed like such drudgery. But with Danny's sweet-smelling body nestled close in her arms, she realized how wrong she'd been.

"No wonder people go baby crazy," she told him. "Are all babies as great as you? Or are you just extraspecial?"

He kicked pajama-clad feet.

Summer retrieved the bottle she'd taken out of the cooler earlier. "You about ready for a nightcap?"

His little hands reached up to grip the bottle. Latching on to the nipple, he sucked contentedly, his huge eyes watching her.

"You've got that in common with your dad, you know. All that watching. But I don't mind when you do it." She walked with him toward the window, registering that darkness was recapturing the sky. Stars popped out with astonishing brilliance.

Once again, she wished for a rocker, but this little room didn't even have a chair. Balefully she glared at the bed, then sighed. "Looks like that's the only place in the room to sit down. Shall we pretend it's an oversize maple rocker with a thick cushion? One that's mellow, creaks from age and rocks just so?"

Danny continued sucking his bottle as she settled on the bed. For a moment, she wondered how it would feel if the charade they were playing were real. If she had a beautiful child like this...

If she were married to Jack...

A warmth settled somewhere inside, tugging at her. From the moment Jack had introduced her as his wife, she'd wondered how it would feel and her imagination was only growing.

Summer felt a tug on her sleeve as Danny reached toward her. Did she imagine the connection she felt with him, too? When she stared at his chubby face, all she saw was sweetness and trust. How could that be anything but real? He kicked his feet for attention, and she smiled.

"I'd tell you a story, but I have the feeling your life's been more interesting than any story I could tell you."

Danny didn't blink, as though waiting expectantly.

"Okay. But just one."

Yawning hugely, Danny snuggled closer. Trustingly he drooped his head against her chest as she weaved a tale,

the bottle almost forgotten. Summer felt an unexpected
hitch in her heart. Throat tight, she sat still for a moment,
overcome by the feeling, realizing instantly why Jack was
so fiercely protective of his son.

Summer traced her fingers over the soft cheeks, the
downy hair, and reveled in the wonder. Was this what her
mother had meant? Had cautioned her not to miss?

Seeing Danny's lips slacken, Summer gently removed
the bottle, then stretched out her own legs. She battled a
yawn, thinking it had been a long day for them all. Her lids
drifted downward, but she struggled against sleep. Perhaps...for just a few minutes... But she'd be awake and
off the bed long before Jack returned.

A solitary lamp, turned on low, burned in the corner
when Jack returned to the room. Summer was angled across
the bed, curled around Danny, her arm anchored over him
so that he couldn't roll off the side. Both were soundly
asleep.

It was well past one in the morning, and Jack was equally
tired, but his expression softened as he watched the unlikely
duo. Somehow his mechanic had turned into a woman and
in the process had grown rather protective of his child.

Amazing what could transpire in such a short span of
time. If he'd have had to bet on Summer, he would have
lost his shirt. Based on how she had acted initially, he'd
have sworn she would have bailed at the first possible moment.

Blond hair trailing over her shoulders, she was remarkably appealing. His gaze drifted downward. He sucked in
his breath at the full effect of her long shapely legs. Lord,
she'd hidden quite a bit of punch beneath those overalls.

Right now, that punch was like a fist to his solar plexus.

Deciding that it wasn't wise to continue gaping at her,
Jack walked quietly over to the bed. He hated to disturb
them, but he didn't want to take a chance with Danny rolling off the bed. Carefully, so as not to wake Summer, Jack

lifted her arm from over Danny. Instinctively she rolled to the other side, tucking her knees upward.

Jack picked up his sleeping son. "Come on, tiger, it's been a big day. Let's get you in the playpen."

Danny snuggled against him, not waking. Jack gently laid him down. On his stomach, his diaper-padded rear stuck in the air, Danny released a tiny baby sigh as he settled into the playpen, before Jack turned him over so that he slept on his back.

Jack pulled his shirt from his trousers, then kicked off his shoes. He'd forgotten how exhausting it was to stand for hours behind a bar, making conversation with dull-thinking men. Splashing water on his face, he shook the droplets away as he reached for a towel, then shed his clothes. Clad only in his boxers, he padded back into the bedroom, then paused.

Where was he going to sleep?

There wasn't even a chair to stretch out on, and one look at the wooden floor told him that was definitely a last resort. His mind had been filled with danger, alternate escape plans and worry. He hadn't even thought about sleeping arrangements. While Danny was secure for the night, and Summer was clearly comfortable, Jack wasn't prepared for the inn to be full.

Stepping closer to the bed, Jack noted that Summer's lips were curled in an unconscious pout and he couldn't miss noticing that they were full and moist. Her breath eased out evenly, her chest rising and falling in quiet accompaniment.

He really should have thought out the sleeping arrangements, Jack realized. Summer sighed in her sleep, extending her long legs at the same time. *Really, really* should have thought them out.

Jack glanced again at the floor. There was one blanket folded neatly at the bottom of the bed. It wouldn't make much of a sleeping roll. It would also leave Summer without a blanket.

It was probably upended, backward reasoning, but Jack

decided to go with it. Unfolding the blanket, he covered
Summer, wondering if he was doing it more for her benefit
or his. Staring at the lissome limbs and previously undis-
covered curves might do him in. He clicked off the lamp,
allowing his eyes to adjust to the darkness. Soon only weak
moonlight pushed past the thin curtains.

Carefully, so as not to disturb her, Jack settled onto the
other side of the bed. The mattress sagged slightly under
the additional weight, bringing Summer a trifle closer. For
a moment, Jack held his breath, but she didn't waken.

It was quiet for the first time in more hours than he could
count. Although they'd only left Edisto the previous day,
it seemed as though weeks had gone by. Sheer exhaustion
should have conked him out in seconds. Instead he inhaled
Summer's unique scent. She smelled of sunshine, flowers
and cool breezes. He smiled suddenly in the darkness. Her
scent defined the season she'd been named for. How apt
that she should smell of summer.

She murmured just then, a gentle sigh, an easing of her
lips as they curved unexpectedly. Dreaming, he guessed.
Jack wondered what she dreamed of, this woman of contradictions, this woman who had so effectively hidden her
femininity. Did she dream of long, cloud-swept days, of
beaches rich with the sea's plunder? Or did she dream of
love, of days spent strolling hand in hand with that special
one?

Suddenly Jack wondered if the torture of the unforgiving
floor could be worse than his own thoughts. He had thought
it would be nearly impossible to stay awake long enough
to crawl into bed. Now Jack wondered if he would manage
to sleep at all.

He heard another gentle sigh and watched as the moonlight played over Summer's face. It was going to be a long
night. A very long night.

The sunshine was bright and insistent, forcing Summer
to open reluctant eyelids. Disoriented, she stared at the un-

familiar room. Then she remembered. Jack, Danny... She reached out, feeling only an empty expanse of mattress. Where was the baby?

Terrified for Danny's safety, she bolted upright, then spotted his perky jammies in the playpen. Sagging backward in relief, she realized he was sleeping. A moment later, her eyes flew open. How had Danny gotten into the playpen? The last thing she remembered doing was closing her eyes for a brief moment, intending to waken before Jack returned.

Stomach sinking, Summer slowly turned her head. Broad, tanned shoulders sloped downward to a trim waist, nearly covered by the blanket twisted around his hips and legs. The arm flung over the blanket was equally tan and muscled. Swallowing a sudden gulp, she wondered how he was dressed beneath the blanket.

And how had she managed to sleep in the same bed with him without being aware of his presence? Clearly he wasn't someone easily missed. Taking inventory, she realized he was quite a package. A package that appeared to be completely unwrapped and lying next to her.

She hated to look a gift horse in the mouth. Then again...

At that moment, Danny wailed, a strident cry that couldn't be ignored. Summer pulled back the blanket just as Jack leaped from the bed, stumbling over what she guessed were his shoes. As she raced toward the playpen, he cursed mildly when he thwacked into the bedpost.

They reached Danny at nearly the same moment, and Jack reached down, easily lifting his son into his arms. He turned, his mouth falling open when he finally noticed her. Blearily he eyed her as he comforted his son. "Summer?"

She nodded warily.

"I think we've got a problem."

Her eyes narrowed. "Which is?"

"There's no coffee."

"Excuse me?"

"Why? It's not your fault we don't have coffee." His

gaze traveled down her legs, and she knew her cheeks reddened in awareness. "But it is your fault I need that coffee."

She frowned. "Why's that?"

"Because I gotta know if I'm awake or dreaming." He paused, his gaze meeting hers before lowering to travel down her legs again. "From where I'm standing, I'm having one hell of a dream."

Chapter 5

Coffee was a wonderful thing, Jack decided. Sobering, awakening, stabilizing. And he was practically inhaling his.

Danny was happily ensconced in one of the diner's high chairs, gleefully destroying a paper napkin between bites of oatmeal.

And Summer was still avoiding his gaze, pretending great interest in her fruit and toast. Not that he could blame her after their less than auspicious beginning that morning.

"Summer, I was dead tired this morning." Jack forced still gritty eyes to open wider. "Frankly I still am. For a minute there, I forgot where we were, who you were."

She cleared her throat, picking aimlessly at the berries in her bowl. "It's all right. I told you that."

"I think I embarrassed you," Jack continued, knowing the truth had to be spoken. "And I'm sorry. It won't happen again."

Summer raised her eyes to meet his. Something unexpected simmered in their tawny depths, something he couldn't quite identify. "Fine. No problem."

He wasn't sure, but guessed that somehow he'd said the wrong thing. "I don't know—"

"Jack!" A woman's voice called out his name, and for a moment he froze. Had he mistaken his ability to elude his pursuers? Had his detour been a mistake?

Then Rita rushed to the table. As he stood in relief, the older woman enveloped him in a hug.

"I heard you were back!" she exclaimed in a quiet voice filled with excitement. "And that you'd brought Danny!" She bent down next to the high chair. "Hi, sweetie!" Then she straightened, holding her hand out to Summer. "And that you have a lovely new wife. Hello, I'm Rita. I'm so pleased to meet you."

Jack watched the exchange, knowing how impossible Rita's charm was to resist. When he'd first met Bart and Rita, he hadn't intended to allow anyone to watch Danny, but she'd soon won him over.

"It's nice to meet you, too, Rita," Summer murmured.

"Won't you join us?" Jack offered.

"I don't want to interrupt...." Rita protested.

"You're not," he insisted, grateful for her presence. He pulled over another chair.

Hesitantly she sat down, then turned to Summer. "Are you certain I'm not interrupting?"

"Of course not."

"It's just that I'm crazy about this little one." Rita smiled at Danny, then jiggled his paper napkin so that he grinned back at her.

Summer glanced at the pair. "I can see that."

"If you ever need anyone to baby-sit, I'd love to," Rita told her. "He was such a love to watch before." Longing showed on the woman's face as clearly as the gentle smile on her lips.

Summer couldn't resist the combination. "I think Danny would like that."

Rita all but clapped her hands in delight. "Bart said you might want to do some waitress work to earn some extra cash. If you do, I'd be happy to watch Danny." She reached over and smoothed her hand over Danny's hair. "Very happy."

Helplessly Summer met Jack's gaze. She hadn't wanted to waitress, but it looked as though the decision was being taken out of her hands. Waitressing wasn't completely foreign to her. She'd spent her summers during college working in a restaurant. And from the way things had gone, a little extra cash might not be a bad idea. She suspected Jack's supply was running low and when she'd offered to get a cash advance on her credit card, he had refused. But perhaps he would view this differently.

"If I'm really needed..."

Rita tore her attention from Danny. "Actually Marla, the waitress who was supposed to be on for tonight, has the flu. I know Bart would love for you to work."

It was all happening faster than she'd expected. "I don't have much experience...." Summer began.

But Rita waved away her protest. "It's a casual place—you can see that. You'll be fine." She reached forward to caress Danny's cheek, clearly already enraptured with the child.

Summer managed a smile. "Then I guess I'm waitressing."

Shadows dipped among the boxes in the otherwise empty warehouse. The shrill ring of a cellular phone intruded upon the sterile surroundings.

"Yeah," the man answered. He listened for a few moments, his scowl deepening.

Next to him, a shadow emerged, then took on definition as a second man joined him.

The first man slammed the phone down on a battered desk as he swore violently. "They lost them."

The second man withdrew a thick folder, and in seconds it joined the phone, thrown down on the desk with seemingly careless disdain. But the grim expression on the man's face denied anything casual about the significance of its contents. "Memorize it, dissect it, snort it up your nose. I don't care how, but you comb through these papers until you know how Jack Anderson ticks."

Beads of sweat broke out above the first man's fleshy lips. "What if he's thought of a new angle?"

"Then you'd better find out what it is. I don't want excuses. I want results."

"We could destroy this file," the first man suggested. "Then no one would have to know we can't find Anderson."

"You'll find him or you'll share his fate." The second man let the significance of that statement sink in as he reached for his jacket, flashing his shoulder holster and weapon.

The first man licked his lips, a nervous gesture that emphasized his wide, ugly mouth. He knew the man wasn't making an empty threat. If he didn't find Jack Anderson, he'd wind up sucking wind on the wrong end of a tailpipe. And he didn't have a taste for death just yet. At least not his own.

"We'll find him…if I have to take out everybody in the folder."

"That wouldn't be very wise, now, would it?" the second man intoned, his nearly colorless eyes narrowing.

"No?" A serpentine tongue flicked out again to nervously moisten fleshy lips.

"And wreck our advantage? Right now, we have a road map to Anderson's hideouts. You wipe them out and he runs his own course."

"Yeah, I didn't think of that."

"You didn't think, period." Eerily pale eyes chilled even further. "But you'd better start. You've got as many chances as Anderson, and you've already blown half of them."

The first man tore his gaze away from the other's hypnotic stare. "Don't worry. Anderson won't live long enough to collect the rest of his chances."

Jack watched Summer waitress and knew Rita had been right. She was doing a capable job. She got the orders right, was fast and kept up with him.

But there was a problem. A big problem.

The customers liked her too much. Jack admitted that she looked different now. Hell, he'd felt as if she'd sucker punched him when he'd first seen the change. He just hadn't anticipated her effect on the rest of the male population.

And, he was discovering, it was quite an effect.

As he scowled at her, Summer approached with an empty tray and an engaging smile. His brow lifted of its own accord. Had she ever smiled at him like that before? His gut tightened, and he slammed the glasses on the rack with more force than necessary.

"Four more beers," she announced. "And another whiskey."

"Big surprise," he muttered.

Her smile wavered. "Problem?"

He pulled the beers, then put them on her tray. "Nope. Don't you have a blouse with a higher neckline?"

Summer glanced at the scoop-necked blouse. "Is there something wrong with this one?"

"Yes. No... Look, here's your order. I don't have time to stand here chatting."

Her mouth dropped open. "Chatting?"

"Summer!" Bart hollered. "One more beer over here."

"I heard," Jack muttered, pulling another beer and loading it on her tray.

She turned away as quickly as possible with the loaded tray.

Jack intended to turn away, too. Instead he watched as she walked away. How had those overalls hidden the flare of her hips, the curve of her waist, a derriere that defied description?

Or had he simply been blind?

Although busy with the customers lined up at the bar, Jack was able to see that the patrons weren't afflicted with his handicap. In fact, none of them appeared the least bit blind.

Watching Summer, Jack wasn't sure if he was glad that his own blinders had been removed, or desperately wishing they hadn't.

Summer stalked down the hallway, Jack directly behind her. When she reached the doorway to their room, she hesitated, turning the knob softly.

"You don't have to be quiet," Jack told her. "Rita has Danny. She thought it would be easier to have him sleep in her rooms since it would be late when our shift ended."

"Right." Deflated, Summer found her anger slipping away as she realized she was now going to be alone with Jack in the tiny room.

In the solitary bed.

She had no choice but to move forward. But once inside, Summer regained a fraction of her earlier resentment.

Turning, she faced him. "What was wrong with you tonight?"

"Wrong?" He stalled, fiddling with keys and change.

"Well, I hope something was wrong. Otherwise, you were acting like a jerk for no reason."

"Look, I dragged you into this so I'm responsible for you."

"Responsible? I may not be the best waitress the world's ever seen, but I was doing okay!"

"I'm not talking about your work."

"Then what?" she demanded, her anger reaching a full boil.

"Don't you have something else to wear?"

"Excuse me?"

"Every man in the bar tonight was ogling you."

"Ogling?" Summer repeated, oddly pleased by the false accusation.

"What would you call it?"

"They were just being friendly," she replied, enjoying the look on his face. "So was I."

"Like I said, I got you into this, and I think you're being too friendly. You're not used to men like this—"

"How do you know what kind of men I'm used to?"

Jack stopped, blinked, then stared. "What's that supposed to mean?"

Enjoying the feminine advantage, Summer merely shrugged. "You're right. It has been a long day."

"I don't remember saying that."

She smiled sweetly. "And I don't remember being too friendly."

He stared at her for a moment. "Are you trying to make me crazy?"

"I don't know. Is it working?"

"Am I crazy? Not quite, but don't let that deter you. I'm going to take a shower." He stalked toward the bathroom, halted suddenly, then turned around slowly. "After you."

Something warm settled inside. So, he was a gentleman even under the worst of circumstances. "I'm not in any big hurry."

But he'd already retreated toward the door leading to the hallway. "Look, I'll take a walk or something."

Summer's gaze wandered again toward the bed. "Okay."

Not certain when he would return, Summer showered quickly, changing into the sleep shirt she'd bought along with the clothes Jack seemed to disapprove of so much. She held up the blouse she'd chosen for that day. Examining it critically, she still didn't see anything wrong with the innocent garment.

Avoiding the bed as long as possible, she glanced at the clock. It was late, her feet were screaming from the hours she'd stood on them and there was nothing left in the small room to distract her.

Cautiously Summer turned back the blanket, as though pulling a bandage off a still tender scab. And much like a bandage, the longer she prolonged it, the more painful it was.

"This is ridiculous!" she chided herself aloud. "I'm an adult. He's an adult." It hit her suddenly that her last points weren't an advantage.

Resolutely she climbed in the bed, then reached over to turn the lamp down to low. Folding her hands neatly above the sheet, she lay perfectly still. A few moments later, it occurred to her that she'd adopted the pose of a corpse. Disgusted with herself, she turned on her side, thumped her pillow into a comfortable position and closed her eyes.

A few minutes later, the door opened quietly, yet her eyes flew open. Accustomed to the low light, Summer could easily see Jack move inside, even make out the expression on his face.

She heard the water run in the shower and remembered the tantalizing glimpse she'd had of Jack's shoulders and back. Irrationally she visualized him in the shower, then shook her head to dispel the alluring image. But it remained despite her efforts. As the minutes passed, she could picture the slope of his back, then imagined those long, muscular legs.

At that moment, Jack padded back into the bedroom.

On those long, muscular legs.

Realizing she was holding her breath, Summer tried to settle her accelerating pulse. Then she felt the sudden dip of the mattress as he settled on the bed. Wondering if her body would remember to breathe on its own, she held herself perfectly still.

It occurred to her that there were hours and hours to pass before morning and she couldn't spend that time frozen in place.

Just then, Summer felt the mattress shift and could have

sworn her heart stopped beating. She knew he was scarcely a hand span away, and her hands itched to travel that distance.

Remembering that the next day would be a busy one, she despaired over the inevitable lack of rest, knowing nothing on the planet could induce her to fall asleep.

Jack swore suddenly, and she nearly bolted upright.

Instead she clutched the blanket, wondering which worried her more—that he was going to suddenly rip it away...or that he wouldn't.

But the mattress shifted as he stood up and reached for his clothing.

"Are you going somewhere?" she managed to croak.

"Yeah," he bit out shortly, sounding aggrieved. "For a walk."

"Did I do something?" she asked timidly. "You already went for a walk earlier."

"So I did," he muttered. "By the time we get to D.C., I may have walked to Antarctica and back."

Startled, Summer sat up slowly and watched him leave, wondering what burr had crawled under his saddle. Suddenly his meaning dawned on her. Evidently sharing a bed wasn't any easier on him than on her.

She couldn't fight the smile or the accompanying satisfaction. Thumping her pillow again, Summer realized that she might not get any sleep tonight, but she wouldn't be the only one. And that was more than worth the lost shut-eye.

A waterfall, Summer decided, captured in that state between dreaming and wakefulness. A tropical waterfall that was rushing past jungle vines. Jungle vines that grew on the walls of the bedroom.

Startled, Summer flew upright. Jungle vines on the bedroom walls? She jerked her head toward the bathroom and realized that Jack must be in the shower.

A gentle knock sounded on the bedroom door. Guessing

it had to be Rita, Summer smiled at the thought of seeing Danny.

But Rita's arms were empty. "Morning, Summer. Hope I'm not disturbing you." She thrust a bottle into Summer's hands. "I forgot this when I brought Danny back this morning."

"Thanks," Summer murmured.

Rita waved and Summer shut the door.

Turning, she looked into Danny's playpen, expecting that toothy jack-o'-lantern grin. The playpen was empty. Looking around the tiny room, Summer quickly saw that the baby was nowhere in the bedroom.

Fisher and Wilcox!

Panicked, she ran to the bathroom, jerked open the door and rushed inside. Without thinking, she ripped aside the shower curtain.

"Jack! It's Danny! He's—"

Jack, holding his son in his arms as they showered, stared at her.

Summer's gaze traveled the length of Jack's impressive body. "I thought...I mean when Rita said...and Danny wasn't in his playpen...and you were in here..."

"In the shower," Jack added helpfully.

"Yes, in the shower," she repeated, unable to tear her gaze away.

"With Danny," he added.

"Yes...with Danny...who's okay, so I don't need to be here...so I'll just...that is..."

Unable to form a coherent sentence, Summer turned on her heel and fled to the bedroom.

"Idiot!" she chastised herself. Blindly she grabbed a T-shirt and shorts, dressing as fast as possible, wanting to disappear before Jack emerged from the bathroom. But she wasn't done with her one-sided conversation. "You've done some stupid stuff in your time, my girl, but this was just classic!"

Opening the door, she nearly fell into the corridor. As it was, she ran smack into Rita.

"Hello again," Rita greeted her, linking arms with Summer. "I'm making waffles and I'd love for you to join me."

"Oh, I don't want to intrude," Summer protested, thinking only of escaping. "I'm sure you and Bart would like some time alone."

A shaft of pain crossed the woman's face. "Bart's already left this morning."

Sensing Bart's early departure wasn't uncommon, Summer hated to dismiss the woman, but she desperately needed to be gone when Jack emerged. She glanced back at the bedroom. "I don't know what Jack has planned...."

Rita smiled. "He's a good man, your Jack." Her expression grew wistful. "And you're so lucky to have that beautiful little boy."

Summer's heart melted as it went out to this clearly lonely woman. "Waffles, you say?"

"Belgian. With fresh strawberries and whipped cream. Or maple syrup if you prefer. They're pretty good, if I do say so myself. And lots of fresh coffee, of course."

Summer pressed a hand to her still whirling head, praying that Jack would skip breakfast. "That sounds good. Perhaps I could take the coffee intravenously."

Rita laughed. "And don't worry. Jack knows where our kitchen is."

Summer smiled weakly. "Oh, that's...good."

Rita was right. Her waffles were delicious. And Summer felt slightly reinforced after eating.

Until Jack walked in.

Suddenly the waffles in her stomach started a dance of their own.

But he was remarkably calm. Hoisting Danny easily on one hip, Jack greeted them and reached for a mug of coffee.

"I've already had my coffee," Summer managed to say in a fairly normal voice. "Let me take Danny."

"Sure." He made the transfer easily, then filled his coffee mug.

Jack was so calm and unruffled, it was as though he were accustomed to women walking in on his showers every day. That thought halted Summer. Perhaps he was.

Rita poured more batter in the waffle iron, and the enticing aroma of baking waffles soon filled the air.

Jack sniffed appreciatively. "Rita, you spoil a man."

The older woman blushed, then swatted him toward the table. "Go on with you."

Jack took the chair next to Summer's. "Not having breakfast?"

"Actually I already ate." Avoiding his gaze, she concentrated on Rita. "And the waffles were delicious."

"I like having people to cook for."

Again Summer wondered what kept Rita tied to Bart. She had never met such an unlikely couple. Summer jiggled Danny on her knee. "How would you like some berries?" she asked the baby. "All mashed up with just a touch of whipped cream."

"I imagine that would taste good to him," Rita agreed.

In short time, Summer was spooning the berries into Danny's eager mouth. "You like that, huh?"

"I'd say so," Rita commented, sliding a golden waffle onto Jack's plate.

Danny smeared a glob of strawberries on Summer's T-shirt. She looked at the stain ruefully. "Sharing, huh?"

Jack laid his fork down. "I can take over."

Summer shook her head. "I'll live. Eat your waffle."

Rita sat down across from Summer. "You're awfully good with Danny. I guess it's like he's your own now."

Summer exchanged a startled glance with Jack. "Danny's an easy child to like."

"He sure is," Rita agreed. "In fact, I was thinking I could take him off your hands for a while. I imagine you two would like a little time alone."

This time, Summer felt the scorch as her gaze met Jack's. "That won't—"

"Thanks, Rita," Jack interrupted. "We'd like that."

Summer bit the inside of her cheek rather than voice her protest since Rita was clearly delighted with Jack's agreement.

But once they were heading down the hallway toward the bedroom, she stiffened.

Jack didn't speak until they were inside. Then he turned to her. "You can relax. I don't think your eyeballs have been permanently scarred from seeing me in the shower."

"I'm not acting—"

"Yes, you are. So what? You were worried about Danny. You walked into the bathroom." He shrugged. "No big deal."

Summer wanted to argue that he was wrong, that his naked image still danced in her mind, but she could scarcely admit that when he'd just said it was nothing. "Fine, but I don't think we need a baby-sitter all morning for you to tell me that."

"You're right. I thought you could use a break. I need to check out the town. It's been a while since I lived here, and I need to know if there are any changes that could affect us. Would you like to come along?"

Surprised but pleased, she paused. "Okay, but give me time to change. I got 'berried,' remember?"

Jack grinned suddenly. "Wait until you've been oatmealed. Then we'll talk."

He left, giving her time to regroup. Having spent about two minutes getting ready that morning, she took longer this time, brushing her hair, then applying a light coat of makeup.

Feeling as though she were primping for a date, Summer chose a sundress that she particularly favored and had yet to wear. Realizing she was fussing too much, she finished quickly.

"I want to stay low-key," Jack said as they strolled into

town. "I don't want anything in our behavior to stand out that would make someone remember us later."

"Any suggestions?"

"We act like a loving couple on vacation, something that won't arouse suspicion."

She couldn't help wondering how it would be if they were in fact newlyweds. "I guess that would depend on how loving we are."

Surprised, his brow quirked. "Then again, maybe I'm going about this all wrong. Fisher and Wilcox wouldn't be looking for smitten honeymooners."

Summer cleared her throat. "That's not what I meant," she protested.

"I was afraid of that," he replied ruefully.

She couldn't restrain the smile his words caused. Although their banter was light and Summer enjoyed the ice-cream cones they'd purchased at the corner drugstore, the seriousness of their mission was never far from her mind.

Later, heading back to the Rusty Anchor, she glanced at her watch. "I hope we haven't stayed too long. Rita might have had plans."

"I doubt it," Jack answered briefly. "Besides, she doesn't have enough chances to take care of little kids."

"And clearly she loves them." Summer hesitated. "Why do you suppose she hooked up with Bart?"

"The bartender I replaced was a talker—said Rita was pregnant so they got married."

"What happened to the baby?" Summer questioned.

"Miscarriage apparently. And she never had any more."

For a brief moment, Summer intensely felt the other woman's pain. "But why do they stay together?"

"She doesn't believe in divorce," Jack answered briefly.

"Or happiness apparently."

Jack shrugged. "How do you define another person's happiness? Apparently she's made her peace with the situation."

"I just wish she had more."

"Sometimes that's all you can have," he replied evenly.

Soberly Summer was reminded of Jack's situation. She realized that without some acceptance, his situation would be a constant torment.

Evidently uncomfortable with that train of thought, Jack changed the subject. "Do you think I'm recognizable even though I changed my last disguise?"

Summer frowned. "I don't have a point of reference."

"Would you be willing to see one?"

"Sure. What did you have in mind?"

"A photograph."

She nodded, seeing that they had nearly reached the Rusty Anchor.

Once in their room, Jack dug in his leather flight bag, finally removing a partially crumpled photo. "This was the last Jack Delancey, aka Anderson."

"Delancey? Is that your real name?" She remembered the first time she'd seen him, thinking he looked vividly Irish...and vividly male.

"Yep. So what do you think?"

Summer shifted the picture in her hand, smoothing out the crinkles. "I think I'll have to study it a bit more." Critically she looked at the photo, and then at him.

"Whatever it takes," he replied.

Not thinking of his proximity, she crossed the room, photo in hand. "I have to compare you to the picture."

He angled his head. "I'm hoping I look pretty different."

"The hair's definitely changed enough," she told him, looking at the dyed light brown hair in the picture, which had now been restored to its original black. Idly she reached out to touch the hair that rested on his collar. "Both the color and the length."

"Good. That's why I grew it."

"And the glasses pretty much hide your eyes," she continued, thinking it was a crime to disguise his incredible blue eyes.

"How about when I put on sunglasses?" Jack demonstrated. "Does it look like my old disguise?"

Summer shook her head. "No. Black horn-rimmed glasses are a world away from sleek sunglasses."

He removed the sunglasses. "It's hard for me to know if the disguise is working. I look in the mirror and just see myself, no matter what I change."

"The mustache hid most of your lips," Summer mused, staring at the photo. Then she glanced up to study his clean-shaved face, realizing how close she now stood. She should take a step back she realized, but her feet weren't listening. "And your lips are very full," she murmured, remembering how they'd felt against her own when he'd kissed her for Bart's benefit. But now there was no audience. Somehow that made his closeness that much more exciting. Did she imagine the responding heat in his eyes as her gaze finally slid from his lips?

"And now they look different?" he questioned.

"Different?" Summer repeated unevenly, wondering how her breath had so quickly and efficiently been stolen.

His fingers found their way to the tendrils of hair that had escaped and now curled beside her cheeks. "Like this is different...so soft...so touchable."

Her lips formed an "oh," yet no words emerged.

Jack's thumb eased over her bottom lip. "Or *your* lips, so very ripe..."

Summer's pulse skittered wildly out of control as his fingers journeyed past her chin, gently caressing her neck, then searching and finding the hollow of her throat. Knowing her pulse was signaling an urgent need, she wondered if he could read that code beneath his fingers.

His other hand cupped the back of her neck, drawing her impossibly closer, so that their lips were scarcely a breath apart.

"So very different," he murmured against her lips, his voice a husky drawl.

Eyelids drifting closed, she felt every nuance of longing

when their mouths met. Drinking of each other, they unleashed a beguiling taste, an unstoppable yearning. Summer tried to remember why she should be resisting, why this couldn't be, but her body leaned toward his.

Careening down a path so rapid, so dizzying, Summer caught her breath. "I...we..."

"Shouldn't be doing this..." he finished for her, his voice still ragged with desire. With an effort, he pulled away from her. "It was a lapse."

Her heart quivered.

"That won't happen again," he concluded flatly, walking to the door. "I'm going to check on Danny."

The quiver became a dull ache. Of course, it couldn't happen again. They were supposed to be alert to danger, on a mission to save their lives. And her part in that was strictly temporary.

Yet, as she stared at the closed door, Summer suddenly wished they were what they pretended to be—a young couple in love with all the chances in the world.

Chapter 6

The Rusty Anchor was busy that night, and Jack was grateful for the distraction. Watching Summer all evening had been akin to torture—his own brand. Sweet, slow and unending.

Having lectured himself the remainder of the day on what an idiot he was, still he couldn't keep his eyes off Summer. Especially since the locals seemed particularly taken with her charms that night.

The sudden shrill of the phone caught his attention. He turned to grab the receiver, but Bart had already answered the phone. Frowning, Jack realized that Bart had done that a lot lately. He remembered that in the past Bart had always left the phone to the bartender, not wanting to deal with calls from customers' wives and girlfriends. Strange that now each time it rang, Bart was there in seconds.

Jack shook his head, wondering if he'd grown so paranoid that nothing appeared normal anymore. After all, the Rusty Anchor had been a safe haven before. Jack's gaze lifted, but what he saw only made his frustration rise.

It seemed that every man in the bar had an eye on Summer. True, he had acknowledged that she looked different now, but did every male on the planet have to notice at the same time?

Laughing and joking, Summer moved from table to table. He would have to tell her to watch the flirting, Jack decided. For her own good, of course.

As Jack reached for more glasses, Summer approached. She was readjusting her skirt, and Jack looked at her in question.

"Someone got a little too friendly," she explained.

A sudden, unexpected rage erupted. "Who?" Jack demanded, throwing down the towel he held and reaching for the hinged wood panel that separated the bar from the room.

"No!" Summer's hand caught his. "It's okay. I handled it. He made a grab and basically came up empty—just managed a corner of my hem. He won't try it again."

"He'd better not!"

"Jack, it's okay. I'm a big girl. I can take care of myself. Now, can I get two beers?"

Pulling the beers with a ferocity that sent a waterfall of foam splashing over each, Jack plunked them on her tray. He was responsible for her, he told himself—that was all. Any man would feel the same. But his eyes never left her as Summer walked toward the customers.

Jack continued watching. When one patron slipped an arm around her waist, Jack remained behind the bar with an effort. "Hey, buddy," he hollered, gesturing toward the man's arm.

The man glanced at Summer then at Jack. "You got a problem?"

"Yeah. The waitress is for decoration only. Hands off."

Summer stared at Jack while the man withdrew his arm, then held up both hands in mock surrender.

"I don't want any trouble," the man said, heading toward the pool table.

"Good," Jack responded, turning back to the glass rack.

Summer stalked over to the bar. "Good?" she chided. "I thought we were supposed to be staying low-key. That definitely didn't sound low-key."

"Why don't you let me worry about our cover?"

"I don't think so," she responded evenly. "My neck's on the line, too. And I don't need you chopping it off by suddenly deciding to act like the Terminator."

Jack quirked his brow. "You see the resemblance between Arnold and me?"

Summer rolled her eyes. "All I see is far too much testosterone."

She turned on her heel and marched away. Yet he continued watching. For a while, things seemed calm. Then one of the more boisterous tables grew louder. And Summer seemed to be the center of interest.

Calling on his patience, Jack told himself that Summer was right. She *was* a big girl, capable of handling a few rowdies. And it was perfectly normal that the men were showing an interest.

There was a sudden loud round of hoots. Craning to see, Jack noted that the men's smiles seemed too appreciative. And then he heard a whistle that couldn't be misinterpreted. Flipping up the wooden hinged portion of the bar, Jack stomped over to the table Summer was serving.

"Everybody got something to drink?" he shouted over the noise the customers were making. Jack continued smiling as he got an assortment of nods and grunts of agreement.

"Good. 'Cause I want to propose a toast—to your waitress—"

Glasses and bottles were collectively raised.

"—who just happens to be my wife."

As Summer's jaw dropped, the men exchanged knowing looks.

Jack had just placed a huge hands-off sign on Summer that could be read ten miles away.

"This round's on me," Jack concluded, his gaze firmly locked on Summer.

She all but gaped as he returned to the bar.

"You could have told us the bruiser was your husband," a small, birdlike man complained. "I don't need to have my head bashed in."

"But he wouldn't—"

The other men guffawed, and one replied, "Sweetheart, your man just staked a real loud claim." His eyes roamed over her and he sighed in regret. "Can't say as I blame him."

The phone rang loudly. Jack turned to answer it. Again Bart was already there. When he noticed Jack watching, he turned around so that all Jack could see was his back. And in only moments, he replaced the receiver.

When Bart turned back toward the bar and saw Jack still looking at him, he made a dismissive face. "Wrong number."

"Right," Jack replied. So why the furtive move to cover what he was saying?

Feeling an instinctive frisson of suspicion, Jack paused. Was he reacting to Bart, or to the way Summer had just been treated? Clearly he needed to pay more attention to his surroundings than to her. Still torn, he alternated between watching Summer and Bart. Neither practice pleased him.

One of the patrons warming a bar stool tried to strike up a conversation when Jack put his whiskey in front of him. "So, she's your wife?"

Jack's gaze didn't move toward Summer. It wasn't necessary. He knew exactly whom the man meant. "Yep."

The man cackled. "Now we all know, too."

Jack kept his voice even. "That was the idea."

"If she was my woman, I'd keep her locked up at home."

"Lucky for her she's not."

The man started to laugh, caught Jack's meaning and scowled.

Jack walked away, yet his eyes traveled across the room toward Summer. The way the men fell all over her, a person would have thought a supermodel was among them. Instead it was Summer, the woman pretending to be his wife. The woman who'd shared his kiss, not to mention his escape.

The phone rang just then, jarring his thoughts. Turning quickly, Jack picked up the phone before Bart could. "Rusty Anchor," he barked.

A distinctive click sounded in his ear. It probably wasn't anything, yet Jack cataloged the bit of information, storing it in his mind for future comparison. Slowly he hung up the phone. "Probably a kid," he muttered.

"What?"

Jack hadn't noticed Summer's approach. He shook his head. "Nothing. Just seeing shadows dancing on my grave."

She shuddered. "What a horrible thought!" Concern flashed across her face. "Has something happened?"

"Yeah, I've irked at least half a dozen of Bart's customers, and I just destroyed any chance of getting a tip."

"Very funny," she responded. "You just scared two, three decades off my life."

"Not intentionally. I've just had a touch of paranoia, but hopefully it's not a terminal case."

"If that's supposed to be amusing, you're missing the mark," Summer retorted.

She started to turn away, but Jack captured her hand. "Bad joke. But laughing beats crying in your beer."

Her eyes softened and he read the instant understanding there. How had that happened? he wondered. How had she come to know this side of him so well?

"You told me a certain amount of paranoia is healthy," Summer reminded him.

"Then I should be the American Psychiatric Association's poster kid," he replied, hesitating before releasing her hand. "But let me worry, okay? It shouldn't be your concern. Besides, it's a one-person job."

Jack wondered at the sudden flash in her eyes. If he didn't know better, he would think it was hurt he had seen there.

"Summer!" one of the customers called out.

He tried to ignore the proprietary feeling that came over him. "And the job you've got is keeping you plenty busy."

Momentarily distracted, she glanced back at the patron who'd called her. Then she turned back to Jack, forcing a smile. "That's a lucky break, isn't it? Staying busy will prevent another one of those nasty lapses. I wouldn't want to be worried about something that's clearly not my concern."

Dead tired, Summer counted out the last of the evening's receipts, then dropped them in the register. Jack had already balanced his till. All she wanted was a hot bath, two new feet and a place to hide.

Somehow the tiny room she shared with Jack hardly seemed like a retreat. Delaying the inevitable, Summer lagged behind until she ran out of excuses. Finally she made her way to the room.

Turning the doorknob softly, she hoped that Jack was already asleep. But she saw that he sat in the tiny window seat at the rear of the room.

Although the sound was faint, she could hear him talking quietly. The low light from the lamp allowed her to see that he cradled Danny in his arms.

"And that's the North Star," Jack said softly. "It'll guide you wherever you go. Someday we'll travel by that star. We won't be running away—we'll be going to places you haven't begun dreaming of yet."

Summer's throat closed as she heard his words.

"You don't know it yet, but there'll be lots of dreams for you. And a big world for you to explore. But you're going to have to make that world a better place, so no one has to run anymore.''

She felt the mist gather in her eyes as she closed them. But she couldn't close everything. Her heart thrummed as it absorbed this man.

''Sounds like a pretty big job for such a little guy, but you won't be small for long. Just make sure your heart grows as tall as you do.''

The hitch in her own heart was now painful.

Jack leaned closer to his son. ''You have to know what's right.'' His voice tightened. ''And go after it, no matter what. And you have to believe that whatever the cost of doing the right thing, it's worth it.''

Like the cost he had paid, she acknowledged silently. Giving up everything in his life to follow what was right.

Jack's lulling voice carried to her as clearly as though she were in his arms, rather than little Danny. ''I'm going to be watching out for you as long as I can.'' He paused. ''Unless it means losing you. And whether I'm around or not, you've got to always believe in yourself.''

The chill that went through her had nothing to do with the cool night air. Did Jack really believe that he wouldn't make it? That he would have to give up his life to protect Danny?

She remembered Jack's joking comments about paranoia. Perhaps they hadn't been jokes. She thought of the concern in his expression, his unusual edginess. Did he suspect a new danger that he hadn't told her about? His instincts had cautioned him to keep the boat stocked, which told her they were pretty good instincts. Was that same sixth sense telling him something now?

Again she shivered, not certain which frightened her more—spending another night in the same bed with him…or contemplating that it could be their last.

Summer was too quiet, Jack noted the next day. She had been all evening, just as she had been all afternoon. Something about her had been different since she'd returned to their room last night after work.

At first he thought perhaps she was growing tired of the pretense and possibly Danny, since he, too, was in the room. But she'd spent much of today holding Danny even though Jack had tried to convince her it wasn't necessary. She had even been reluctant to leave the baby in Rita's care when their shift had begun.

It was as though Summer were clinging to something, which didn't fit any part of her character that he was growing to know.

The phone rang and Bart grabbed it again. But this time as soon as he took the call, he disappeared. Jack felt a prickle. Was it instinct or paranoia? He wondered suddenly if there was a bounty on his head. He'd always suspected that Bart had a shady past, but were the man's shortcomings such that he would sell him out? Uneasily, Jack guessed they might be.

A large drink order came in, distracting him. When Jack finished pouring the drinks, he looked around casually while wiping down the bar and restocking the glass rack. He couldn't locate Bart. But he kept Summer in his sights. If something was wrong, he didn't want her to be far away if they had to cut and run.

Summer approached the bar, her mood still hard to discern.

"Pretty good size order," he commented.

She nodded without replying.

He reached over to grab some tonic water and noticed that she was staring at him. When he glanced up, she deliberately looked away.

"Something wrong?" he asked as Summer reached toward the tray.

She jerked her head up at the question, and her hand knocked over one of the glasses. "Sorry."

"It's okay. It's just a drink. I didn't mean to rattle you."

"You didn't," she protested.

"Well, something did."

Summer swabbed at the pooling liquid with a wad of cocktail napkins. "It's just I get the feeling you're having one of those sixth-sense things."

Puzzled, he drew his brows together.

"You know," she continued. "The remarks about your paranoia. It seems like you're feeling things aren't safe."

"Hey. I told you not to worry. Since I joined the program, I seem to see things that aren't there."

But she didn't look comforted. "I want to know if it's more than that."

"Don't worry. You'll be the first to hear."

She searched his face, and he finally saw a trickle of relief in her expression. "I guess I could be seeing things that aren't there, too," Summer admitted. "Maybe I should leave it to you. You know what to look for."

Jack nodded and smiled for her benefit. The hell he did. This wasn't a game with set rules or players. The most obvious thing could be nothing, but if ignored, it could be the most significant. And he was playing blind.

Fisher and Wilcox could have hired an advance scout, someone he wouldn't recognize. Someone he could have just served a drink to.

A few hours passed uneventfully. Jack continued watching Summer. Even though she had seemed reassured, she still looked pensive. And Jack couldn't fight his own premonitions. He had a bad feeling, one he couldn't put his finger on.

Looking up from the drink order he was preparing, Jack saw Bart return to lean casually against the wall near the outer door. When Jack glanced his way, he could have sworn Bart was watching him before he slid his gaze away. Another prickle of sensation darted through him. Jack turned away for a moment and then turned back. And met Bart's watchful scrutiny.

Once again, Bart's eyes slid away.

And this time, Jack knew it wasn't his imagination.

A shiver raced up his spine and settled in his neck. And his body flashed from the freeze of that chill to the instant heat of adrenaline. Adrenaline that had kicked in as soon as Jack scented danger.

Carefully Jack looked around, again checking out exits, quickly taking a mental inventory of what was necessary for their escape. His thoughts clicked in rapid succession as he tried to form the safest plan.

Summer walked up with a drink order. He hoped his Jekyll and Hyde behavior wouldn't frighten her since he'd just assured her they were safe. "Summer…"

"Yes?" she answered absently, digging in her pocket for a pencil.

"Keep acting normal. Don't behave as though we're talking about anything important."

To her credit, she only blanched for a moment, then managed to smile. "Are we?"

"You were right. I have been sensing something. I still don't know if it's anything concrete, but I don't want to stick around and find out."

Her hand shook only slightly as she reached over to put some napkins on the tray. "So what do we do?"

"You get sick."

"Excuse me?"

"Tell Bart you're sick and need to lie down for a little while. Then grab the essentials and stick them in the car."

Although she controlled her expression, Jack could see the panic in her eyes. "What about Danny?"

"In a few minutes, I'll tell Bart I'm going to check on you. I'll wait ten minutes after that. Then we take Danny and go."

"Should I get him now?" she asked, her voice quavering a bit.

He hesitated. "I don't want to tip off Bart. If Rita comes in before I'm out of here, Bart will know you've got Danny and suspect something."

"Okay." Summer firmed her lips. "Do I look like I could be sick?"

She was convincingly pale beneath her tan. Jack nodded. "Be vague and don't overdo it. Tell him you think you'll be better if you can lie down for a little while."

"No malaria?" She tried to joke, but the concern in her voice was evident.

"Right." He laid one hand over hers. "Just keep your head and we'll get out of here."

Deliberately Jack turned away so he couldn't see Summer speak to Bart. He was afraid of revealing more than a poker face himself. But in a few quick minutes, Summer left the bar.

Jack watched the clock tick by with agonizing slowness. When five minutes had passed, he approached Bart, hoping he could sound convincingly casual. "Where'd Summer go?"

"Said she was sick. Went to lie down."

"Sick?" Jack frowned. "What was wrong with her?"

Bart shrugged. "I don't know. Just said she wouldn't be long."

"She thought that fish today tasted a little off. I'd better go check on her in a few minutes. I'll catch up the bar, then can you cover?"

Bart looked annoyed...and something else. Although Jack couldn't put his finger on it, he again sensed something was wrong.

"Yeah, I guess so."

Jack casually glanced at the clock. When ten minutes had passed, he gave Bart the high sign and forced himself not to hurry from the room. Once out of sight, he loped down the hallway. Summer whirled around when he ripped open the door.

"Oh!" She released a whooshing breath. "Thank God it's you! I've got everything else in the car." She held up one small bag. "This is all that's left."

"Okay. Let's go and get Danny."

"What'll we tell Rita?" she asked, hurrying beside him.

"That there's an emergency and we have to leave."

"What kind of emergency?"

"We don't elaborate. We tell her we don't have time to give details. Then Bart might think it's medical, although if I'm right it won't matter." Jack met her gaze. "She won't question it. The important thing is we get Danny and don't waste any time. Our lives could depend on it."

Chapter 7

"We need to get Summer to a doctor." Shooting Rita a disarming smile, Jack tossed the diaper bag in the back seat rather than opening the trunk, which held all of their luggage.

"But wouldn't you rather have me take care of Danny for you?" the older woman asked, longing coloring her voice.

Jack took her hand. "We couldn't ask for anyone to take better care of Danny, but we're not sure how long we'll be."

Rita frowned. "I'm sure Bart loved that."

Jack hesitated.

Rita studied his face. "He doesn't know. That's okay. I'll tell him." She glanced at the three of them. "Later."

Jack hugged her. "You're still the best, Rita."

She waved away his words. "Just take care of yourselves. All of you." She reached out again, hugging him fiercely, her low voice reaching only him. "You've got a good one there with Summer. It's clear you're meant to be together. That doesn't happen too often in this life." Her voice cracked. "You hang on to her."

Startled, Jack glanced at Summer, who was turned toward the back seat, patting Danny's plump leg. *Meant to be?*

But he didn't have time to dwell on the words. He had to get them far away. Perhaps he'd calculated wrong in bringing them here, rather than heading directly to D.C. He just hoped it wasn't a fatal mistake.

"Jack?" Summer prodded, looking up at him from inside the car.

"Right." He turned to Rita. "Thanks again. We couldn't have made it without you."

"You better get your wife to that doctor."

Jack opened the door and slid into the car.

Rita leaned toward the window. "Summer, take care of yourself." Then her gaze found and lingered on Danny. "I'm sure going to miss you."

As soon as she stepped away, Jack drove ahead.

"I know how she feels," Summer murmured.

Jack glanced at her briefly, his eyes scanning the area. "About what?"

"About getting so attached to Danny. He's pretty hard to resist." Summer couldn't prevent another glance to the back seat. Her own heart had been lodged in her throat since the moment Jack had alerted her to this newest danger. She would be lying if she didn't admit being frightened herself, but her thoughts had immediately turned to the baby. Innocent and trusting, he had to depend on them for his protection. What sort of men would hurt a child? Just thinking of their sort sent a new fear skating through her at Olympic speed.

"Yeah. I'm pretty fond of him myself," Jack replied, pulling his focus from the road to glance quickly at his son.

"We didn't tell Rita we were leaving for good," Summer mused. "All of our things are in the trunk, so she couldn't see the bags. How did she know?"

"You picked up on that, too?"

"She was saying goodbye, not see-you-later."

"Despite marrying Bart, Rita's pretty bright. I think she knew something about Danny and me wasn't quite normal the first time around. By now she's probably certain of it."

"Do you think she'll tell Bart?"

"I could be wrong, but I don't think so."

Summer thought again of the sweet woman, then wondered about the man who could even now be calling to turn them in. What price were their lives worth?

Jack turned the steering wheel so sharply, she would have slid to the other side of the car if she hadn't been belted in.

"What—?"

He cursed briefly yet vehemently beneath his breath. "Fisher and Wilcox." Glancing in all directions, he veered into what looked like a dead-end alley.

"What about them?" she asked, trying not to panic as he sped down the narrow passageway.

"They were in the Camaro at the last intersection."

Summer gasped. "Here? We just passed them?"

"Right. And they were headed toward the club." Jack glanced in the rearview mirror.

"Are they following us?" she asked, craning around to see.

"I don't think so. Not yet."

"But when they get to the Rusty Anchor, they'll find out we're gone," she surmised, her eyes darkening with renewed fear.

Jack spared her a quick glance. "Afraid so. We have a five- or ten-minute head start at most. We have to take advantage of it."

Summer couldn't find her voice. Instead she pressed her feet desperately against the carpeted floor, bracing herself since it looked as though they were speeding straight toward a brick wall. At the last possible moment, Jack turned.

The alley opened up onto an unpaved side road. With

no lighting in the dark night, it looked as though the road led into a meadow. Her fingers tightened on the armrest as she held on, wondering if they were about to plummet into a ditch.

Instead the car traveled over a raised culvert.

As she gripped the frame around the window, Summer tried to sound calm. "I guess you know where you're going."

"This is a farm road," he explained briefly.

"Are we going to a farm?"

"No, we're heading out of town, but there's only one main road, which Fisher and Wilcox will be watching."

She glanced out at what seemed to be miles of fields and darkness. "How do you know about this road?"

"I always checked out the alternate routes of escape in any place we lived."

The car hit a particularly large bump. "And you're sure this is still a road?"

"No."

Her head whipped around to stare at him. "No?"

"But I am sure that taking the main road would be like advertising our departure."

Summer swallowed the sudden lump in her throat, leaving the obvious unsaid. If the road didn't play out, they'd be stuck. And although the darkness would conceal them now, the morning's sunshine would be like a spotlight. And like an upended turtle, they would be helplessly trapped.

Glancing in the back seat, she saw that Danny remained soundly asleep, despite the lurching of the car. Taking a deep breath, Summer called on her own store of calm. "Where are we headed?"

Jack didn't pull his concentration from the road. "I'm not sure."

With those words her calm shattered. "But your plan—"

"Is only half-formed. We've got a couple of options. I'm not sure which one to take."

Summer tried not to panic. "Any idea where we're going to spend the night and how long it'll take to get there?"

"That's easy. You're there."

She blinked. "Here?"

"Yep."

"We're in a car in the middle of nowhere."

He spared her a brief glance. "And that's where we're staying."

By sunrise, they had driven the prolonged, unknown route from town. They'd had to slow down to a virtual crawl through some particularly dark and rough patches. And they did get stuck once, bogged in mud. Jack had pushed while she steered, finally dislodging the car although they both wound up wearing a fair share of mud.

While they had left the town, it wasn't so certain they'd evaded Fisher and Wilcox. Once on the main highway, Jack watched the rearview mirror constantly. "We have to stop for gas."

Summer wiggled her cramped feet. "No complaints here. I feel like a permanent pretzel. And Danny can probably use another change and a bottle."

A few minutes later, Jack spotted a small gas station and pulled in. Summer took the opportunity to check the limited selection in the station's minimart. She stocked up on baby food, diapers, juice, bottled water and sandwiches. Spotting paper towels, she took a good supply along with some soap, hoping she'd be able to get rid of the mud soon.

The bored-looking clerk didn't comment on the unusual selection when she piled it on the counter.

"I need to pay for gas, too," Summer told him as she pointed to the pump where Jack stood.

The clerk glanced up casually. Then his gaze sharpened when he noticed the car. "That one?"

"Yes." Uneasily, she followed his gaze as it lingered on Jack.

When the clerk finally turned back to her, she glanced

upward. It took all of Summer's control not to gasp aloud. A Most Wanted poster bearing Jack's face jumped out from the other notices tacked on the wall.

The clerk fumbled nervously as he rang up the items. It took three attempts to get a total, which he told her in a quivering voice. His Adam's apple bobbing, he moved his hands in a nervous fashion, fiddling with his baseball cap, then repeatedly thrumming his fingers on the counter.

Instinctively Summer replaced the credit card she'd taken from her wallet and handed him cash instead from the tips she'd earned.

It took the clerk several more tries to hand her the correct change. "I think that's it," he said finally, his eyes huge in his thin face as he stared at her.

Summer tried to smile normally, then glanced at her purchases, which were still splayed across the counter. "Would you mind putting my things in sacks?"

The clerk stumbled at first, unsuccessfully trying to open grocery sacks, then finally shoved almost everything into one severely overpacked bag.

Summer took the bag without complaint, then tried not to be obvious as she rushed to rejoin Jack. Still, she jerked open her door, scooting across the seat quickly.

"I'll pay for the gas," Jack began to insist, reaching for his wallet.

"Fine, as soon as we're on the road." She shot him a pointed look. "Let's go *now!*"

Taking her cue, he hastily opened the door and slid inside.

"Something wrong?" Jack asked as he started the car and quickly got back on the road.

She craned her head backward, and her stomach sank as she watched the clerk run outside to stare after them. "I was afraid of that."

"What?"

"That clerk noticed something. He was okay until he saw the car and then you."

"Bart must've given away the car," Jack muttered. He stared at the wide-open spaces around them, spaces that offered nothing in the way of a hideout.

"I'm not sure about that. I only know that the clerk acted differently when he saw the car. And just now he ran out to watch us leave."

She gulped. "He had a Wanted poster of you tacked up in the store. I'm pretty sure he recognized you."

The sudden sound of a siren screeching behind them shattered what was left of their hope.

"Take a bow. You're absolutely right." Jack accelerated, and the car flew over the blacktopped highway.

"I'd have been real okay about being wrong," Summer tried to joke, flinching as Jack cornered at a speed so high she didn't dare look at the speedometer.

When the sound of a second siren signaled another car joining the chase, Summer instinctively closed her eyes for a moment. "Jack, we can't outrun a pack of police cars."

"Two isn't a pack," he countered.

"This is no time to quibble." Her voice rose, but remembering Danny, she stopped short of shouting.

A third siren joined the chorus behind them, and unbelievably Jack accelerated even more.

"Jack, we can't outrun every police car in the state! Why don't we stop? We can ask them for help—tell them what has happened."

"You saw the poster. I've been listed as a wanted criminal." He spared her a brief, grim look. "You think they're going to want to chat?"

"Why not take a chance?" she reasoned. "The police aren't the enemy. Their job is to protect us. We should be able to trust them."

"Yeah, and in a perfect world no one should have been able to mess with my file. Someone inside the agency wants to find me. The local police would hand me over so fast your head wouldn't have time to spin."

"But you don't know that!"

"If we take the chance and you're wrong, it's a death sentence."

Summer flinched. "I know the stakes are high, but how can you be sure the police won't listen?"

"Whoever's behind this is smart. I can protest my innocence until I'm hoarse, but the police will still turn me over to the feds. No law officer is going to believe the word of a wanted felon over that of a DEA agent."

Summer sucked in a deep breath. "So, what do we do now?"

His fingers tightened on the steering wheel. "We don't let them catch us."

She thumped her forehead. "Why didn't I think of that?" Summer glanced back at the throng of cars following them. With lights flashing and sirens shrilling, it looked as though there were a hundred cars gaining on them.

Jack spared her another brief glance. "I'm not playing superhero, Summer. I'm flying by the seat of my pants. All I can promise is that I'll do my best to get us out of this."

Hesitating for a moment, Summer reached over, placing one hand on his forearm in a gesture of support. Surprisingly encouraged despite the cars pursuing them, Jack ran a mental scan of the surrounding area. He knew it well.

When he had moved here the first time, still crazed by his wife's murder and the subsequent death of his own lifestyle, he'd had little to do in his free time. So, he had spent it cruising the surrounding area. Instinct told him even then that he might need the knowledge.

Jack had never guessed it might mean his life.

Now he watched carefully as an idea bloomed. Choosing what he hoped was precisely the right moment, he flipped a quick U-turn, heading in the opposite direction. He pressed the accelerator to the floor, knowing the burst of speed was essential to his plan.

Summer's voice was high and reedy. "Are you hoping to get up enough speed to fly?"

"Close to it. You'd better hang on."

"I don't like the sound of that," she trilled as Jack turned abruptly, pulling off the road at the nearest turnaround, sending the car into a fishtail.

But he didn't reverse direction again as she expected.

Jack spotted the washed-out bridge he remembered. Because the new highway ran beside it, the old bridge had never been repaired. Now it was a deserted, overgrown pile of vine-covered timbers and crumbling concrete.

Quickly driving beneath the remains of the bridge, Jack drove as close as possible to the pillars that were nearly obscured by overgrown greenery. Just as quickly, he turned the key, shutting down the engine.

The sudden silence was as startling as the shrill of the sirens had been.

But it didn't last long.

Soon the chorus of sirens approached, sounding for all the world as though a horde of banshees pursued them. Unconsciously both Jack and Summer held their breath, afraid that even that small sound would somehow betray them.

Danny whimpered. Jack pulled off his seat belt and whipped around, reaching for his son. Comforting him, he postponed the wail that Danny was puckering up to deliver.

Thinking quickly, Summer grabbed some fruit juice, poured it into a bottle and thrust it toward the baby's waiting mouth. He wavered between the satisfaction of cool juice or an earsplitting wail. The juice won out and he sucked at the bottle, letting out an intermittent hiccup.

But those tiny sounds were obliterated by the sirens that were now almost directly overhead. The three of them huddled close together.

Unconsciously Summer placed her hands over the baby's ears as though to shield him from the sound. As she did, her eyes met Jack's and she saw the message of gratitude and encouragement he was telegraphing.

The sirens blasted over them now, coupling with the sound of the engines of police cars revving as they drove at high speed. Summer closed her eyes to the sound, as though somehow that could shut out the danger.

A warm, strong hand covered hers at that instant, making her feel incredibly comforted despite the terror of the pursuing sirens.

Jack kept his hand over hers as the cars passed by them, the sirens finally fading into the distance.

Once again, the silence seemed wholly unnatural, almost eerie as the sounds of birds and the gentle rush of the water replaced the sirens. They watched the clock on the dashboard as the minutes ticked away. Nearly an hour later, no police cars had returned.

"Do you think it's safe?" Summer whispered as she rubbed the baby's legs in a comforting gesture.

"You don't have to whisper," Jack replied in a normal tone. His voice was almost as startling an intrusion as the sirens had been.

Summer cleared her throat as she drew back to her own part of the front seat. "So," she began again, "did we outwit them?"

"We'll have to wait and see."

She frowned. "Shouldn't we get back on the road heading the other way?"

"Police cars can come from both directions," he pointed out. "And I'm sure there's an APB out on us by now."

"Then how are we going to get away?"

Jack's mouth thinned. "Now that they've made the car, it's like driving a Times Square marquee. It's guaranteed to draw a lot of attention from a lot of people."

"Then we'll have to get another one," she surmised logically.

"Yeah. I'll just ask my fairy godmother for one."

Summer frowned. "I can get enough cash with my credit cards."

But Jack was shaking his head. "No way. I'm already indebted to you. I never should have put you in this much danger. I'm not draining all of your cash, too."

"And you're going to do what? Strap Danny on your back and walk to D.C.? Or maybe thumb a ride? Fisher and Wilcox should be along soon. I'm sure they'd be glad to pick you up."

"Summer, point's taken. I appreciate the offer, but I can't take your money."

"It's a loan. And when you get everything straightened out, you'll be able to tap into your own money."

"*If* everything gets straightened out," he reminded her. "I could be following a long shot to either a dead end or an ambush."

Summer leaned over to smooth the hair on Danny's forehead. "Nope. You've done the right stuff so far."

Jack reached over to tip up her chin. He would have expected any woman to be screeching her head off by now. Seeing the tender concern in her eyes, he felt the guarded walls around his heart crack a bit. That in itself was dangerous, he knew. Yet he inclined his head toward hers. Remembering the softness of her lips, he longed for one more taste.

Danny squirmed, pushing away the now empty bottle.

With a resigned sigh, Jack leaned back. "I think we can get out now."

Summer reached for Danny, holding him closely. "Are you sure it's safe?"

"No, but I think it is. We won't know if we've escaped detection until we're back on the road."

"Looking for another car to buy," she insisted.

Jack's eyes narrowed. "I was going to say after it's dark."

Summer nodded. "We can look for another car after dark."

"Did anyone ever tell you that you're awfully stubborn?"

"Did anyone ever tell you that you're a control freak?" she countered.

Jack sighed. "It's going to be a long time until dark. I

suggest we find out some other way to pass the day besides verbal badminton. My head's spinning from watching the birdy flopping from side to side.''

''Just so long as you know it's my serve,'' she answered sweetly.

''And your net and rackets, I presume?''

She shrugged. ''I'm willing to share. Just like I'm willing to share my cash.''

''Are you part mule?''

''Back to your flattering ways, I see.''

He grinned unexpectedly, his lips quirking upward. ''Seems like it works as well as anything else.''

Summer tossed back her hair. ''Considering I'm covered in mud, I'm finding it difficult to argue the point.''

Jack pointed toward the water. ''There's an easy solution to that.''

She frowned. ''A creek bath?''

''I don't think we'll be checking into a hotel anytime soon,'' he replied.

''Good point.'' She turned Danny around so that he was standing on her lap, looking at her. ''Well, my fine friend, how 'bout a bath?''

He gurgled, his little mouth crinkling into a baby grin.

''I'll take that as a yes.''

''You don't have to watch him,'' Jack protested, reaching toward his son.

''I know that. I *want* to take care of him.'' Her words surprised them both, and for a moment the car echoed again with silence.

Then Jack abruptly pushed open his door, coming around to open hers. ''I'll get what we need from the trunk.'' He glanced toward the road. ''But only a few things. If they double back, we'll have to leave in a hurry.''

Summer nodded in agreement as she carried Danny toward the grassy slope of the embankment. The water flowed peacefully along the winding path of the creek.

Jack took a few things from the trunk and then watched

Summer and Danny. She laughed with the baby as she dangled his plump legs in the refreshing water. Stripping off his clothes and diaper, she gently bathed him in the clear water, making him chortle with delight as she made it a game.

Leaning against the car, Jack found it hard to believe they were running for their lives. He loved the sound of Summer's infectious laughter and the reaction she drew from Danny. It was as though she'd pushed reality into a fading background. At that moment, they could be any normal family.

Drawn to them, Jack brought a towel to Summer as an excuse to come closer.

"Look what Daddy's got!" Summer made Danny giggle as she playfully covered him with the towel.

Jack noticed how gentle her touch was as she dried the baby and then reached toward the diaper bag Jack had put beside her.

"It's time to get all wonderful smelling, tiger." While powdering and dressing him, Summer blew kisses on his tummy, making him laugh and kick his plump legs.

"Danny, you're going to be spoiled rotten," Jack observed dryly. Yet his eyes warmed as he watched the affection she showered on Danny.

"Daddy's just jealous because you're getting all the attention." She pulled a small sock on over Danny's wriggling toes.

"You could be right," Jack countered.

Summer's eyes flew up to meet his. For once, she seemed at a loss for words.

Jack reached down to pick up Danny. "How 'bout something to eat and a nap, big guy?"

Awkwardly Summer gathered up the towel and bath things.

"I'll put Danny down," Jack told her as he walked toward the car. The portable crib would be easy to grab if they had to leave in a hurry.

Danny eagerly accepted the bottle, his eyelids soon drooping. Jack watched him as Summer rolled up her pants legs and ventured into the creek, staying close to the bank. Soon Danny was asleep, and Jack removed the bottle.

Knowing Danny was safe, Jack headed toward the creek. He didn't speak until he was directly behind Summer, who still stood in water only a foot deep. "I thought you were going to have a creek bath."

She spun around in surprise, then gestured toward the surrounding water. "I am."

He advanced. "You have to get wet to take a bath."

Summer stepped back. "I'm wet enough."

"You were raised by the water. You know this isn't wet."

She brought her hands together, letting the water trickle through her fingers. "It's okay."

"I don't think so." He advanced.

Seeing his intent, Summer spun to escape, but he was quicker.

In moments, she was dunked. Seeing the glint in her eyes, Jack stepped back. But she was fast. In an instant, he tumbled into the water beside her.

"Oh, fine," she sputtered, unable to quell her laughter. "Now we're both drenched."

Jack laughed with her, but then the amusement died away as he looked at her. The white cotton shirt she wore was soaked. And the scrap of lace she wore beneath the blouse did little to camouflage her breasts.

From the sudden flame in her cheeks, it was apparent she realized that at the same moment. She spun around, wading quickly to a point farther downstream.

Jack considered giving her time to regroup. Then she hesitated and turned back around. And consideration vanished.

He advanced.

She retreated. Opening her mouth to speak, Summer looked equally surprised that no words emerged.

Another long stride forward and he was beside her. The
water ebbed gently around them as their gazes met. He
reached out to tuck a strand of hair behind her ear. His
fingers lingered, grazing the slope of her cheek, then skimming toward her lips.

A whispered sigh escaped as he cupped her chin.

Neither invitation nor protest was issued. But then he
wasn't sure he would have listened to either.

Her eyes weren't simply green, he realized as her face
tilted upward to give him an unencumbered view. Flecks
of cinnamon and molten gold warmed the green into a
tawny-jade. Combined with her thick, wild, sun-kissed
blond hair, she resembled a lioness. And from the fire he'd
seen in those eyes, she would be the unchallenged leader
of the pride.

But now there was a different quality simmering in her
eyes. Questioning, a touch of uncertainty, and something
else. And that something stirred him.

Stirred him so that he reached out and closed his other
hand around the back of her neck, pulling her even closer.
There was a trace of quivering in her lips. But that made
them even more desirable. Vulnerability coupled with courage was an alluring combination. One Jack was finding
impossible to resist.

Fleetingly he thought of all the reasons he should be
walking away, leaving Summer and her contradictions behind…leaving her untouched.

Just as quickly, he decided there was little to recommend
in resistance. Angling his head toward hers, he sought the
center of her lips. A jolt of pleasure shot through him as
they parted beneath the pressure, offering him a taste. Sam-
pling both sweetness and mystery, he wanted to savor each.

Initially Summer accepted the kiss, then leaned into his
embrace. Her hands snaked up to grip his shoulders, then
advanced to twine in his hair…to pull him even closer.

The sudden shrill burst of a siren shattered the air…and
all other thoughts fled.

Chapter 8

Summer and Jack froze for the briefest of seconds. Then, moving as quickly as the water would allow, they pushed out of the creek, and ran toward the car.

Scrambling to reach Danny and escape detection, Jack dived beneath the overhanging greenery, pulling Summer with him. For a seeming eternity, the siren ricocheted around them. Finally it began to fade.

Hearts in their throats, they listened. Eventually the noise of the siren died away to nothing.

Panting with exertion and fear, Summer clutched at Jack as he threw open the car door. "Do you think they know we're here?"

Jack shook his head. "No. If they did, that police car wouldn't have passed us by."

"So we're okay?"

"For now. But they're still searching. Let's pack everything and stay inside the car."

"And...?"

"Wait until it's dark."

Summer caught his gaze. A torrent of unspoken emotion, fright and need swirled between them. But she nodded, swallowing her questions, knowing it would seem like forever until darkness reclaimed the sky.

Jack continued to scan the rearview mirror, even though they'd traveled miles since dusk. And he had been thinking furiously the entire time. They had to have another car, and he still hadn't come up with a plan.

"This looks like a good-size town," Summer commented, interrupting his thoughts. "They should have a car lot."

"Yeah, and maybe they'll take a handful of beans in trade."

Summer bit down on her bottom lip. "I know you don't want to take my money, but all of our lives are on the line. This isn't the time to put on your macho gear." Her voice softened. "There's nothing wrong with admitting you need someone—I mean, that you can't do everything on your own."

His gaze shot across to catch hers. He wasn't ready to admit needing anyone, but the reality was he had to have money—and she had some to offer. Still, he didn't like being backed against a wall. It went against everything he was.

Jack tightened his jaw. "I promised you I'd get you out as soon as possible, not pull you in deeper."

"It's my choice," she insisted. "I could have left when we first docked, when we got to Bart's, even today at the gas station." Although Summer omitted mention of their brief respite at the creek, it flashed between them. She turned and stared out the window. "I'll watch for a car lot."

Jack couldn't prevent a snort of exasperation. "You sure you're not part mule?"

Summer sniffed, then turned to check on Danny. "I thought we'd already covered this."

"So did I.''

Summer wrinkled her forehead. "If it'll make you feel better, you can pay me interest on the loan. Just pretend I'm a mobile branch of the bank.''

He glanced over at her. "So you're a *bankmobile?*''

She smiled finally. "And unlike the bookmobile, you won't need your library card.''

But Jack couldn't return the smile. He hadn't intended to pull her this far into his problem and he sure didn't want to make it worse. Uncomfortably he remembered their kiss, realizing that so far he'd gone about everything in the wrong way. But there was one point he couldn't argue. She had cash and he needed it.

An hour later, they were pulling out of Fast Eddie's Cars for Miles. The salesman grinned and waved as they drove off in a battered pickup truck. While probably the ugliest vehicle on the lot, it was one of the few Jack thought to be mechanically sound.

He knew the salesman thought he'd made the deal of the century between the car they'd traded in and the accompanying cash. But Jack was hoping the truck differed enough from the car, yet was still sufficiently scruffy that it wouldn't attract attention.

To take advantage of the seat belt for Danny's car seat, Summer was wedged next to Jack in the middle of the seat. Knowing she must be exhausted, he looked at her in regret. "I hate to tell you this, but we'll need to drive while it's dark...all night.''

She nodded. "I guessed as much.''

"Even though it didn't work before, I'm going to try reversing direction. I'm guessing Fisher and Wilcox will think I won't try it again and that we'll be heading straight for D.C.''

Summer swallowed her fear, glancing down at Danny. "What if this doesn't work?''

Jack's voice was grim. "It has to. We don't have any other choice."

Eyes of ice impaled the thick-lipped man. "Who was running the roadblocks? The Keystone Kops?"

Full lips pulled back over protruding teeth, the man reached toward his graying hair, shoving it off his forehead. "It's like they disappeared. They must have a safe house we didn't know about."

"Or you didn't do what I told you. I expect you to know Anderson so well that his sweat oozes out of your pores."

Fleshy lips twitched. "Most of the background we've got about Anderson is about his wife, and how he got involved in the sting operation. That doesn't do us any good with the wife dead."

The first man pivoted slowly. "It doesn't?"

"I don't know what you mean."

"Anderson went berserk because his wife was killed. Think he wants to go through that again?"

Full lips eased into a smirk. "Yeah."

"Do it right this time…unless you want to be bunking in twin coffins with him."

The smirk dissolved into a quiver of fear.

Pale eyes remained eerily cold as a bark of laughter echoed off the walls.

For one moment the graying man pitied Jack Anderson. Then a fear pierced him so intensely he nearly lost his water. And he knew he had to save all his pity for himself.

The motel wasn't one either Jack or Summer would have purposely chosen, but it had one great advantage. The parking lot couldn't be seen from the highway. They didn't know yet if the police had traced their new purchase, and they knew it was wise to keep the truck out of sight.

"Hideaway Lodge?" Summer questioned. "Do you suppose it can live up to its name?" Weak rays of morning sunshine valiantly struggled to push past the thick foliage of trees that camouflaged the motel. But even in the dim light, Summer could see the fatigue on Jack's face.

"Just be glad it's not the Bates Motel," he replied, keeping a grip on his weariness through sheer determination alone.

Danny continued sleeping as Jack unbuckled the car seat, lifting out the entire carrier. Summer tried to look appropriately motherly as they trooped into the small office.

The overweight, unkempt clerk looked nearly as bleary as they felt. "Can I help you folks?"

"We need a room," Jack replied, placing Danny's car seat on the low, wide counter.

"How long you planning to stay?" The clerk's gaze sharpened, and he looked them over as though memorizing faces for a future lineup at the local police station.

Uncomfortably, Summer tried to fade into the unbecoming background of the run-down office. Yet she couldn't help studying the clerk, thinking what an unappealing sort he was. Despite plump cheeks, his face looked pinched, almost mean. Tiny eyes set above a sharpish nose nearly receded into the numerous folds of skin that served as a disguise for any sort of cheekbones.

"How long we stay will depend on how we like the area," Jack replied noncommittally.

"I see." The clerk's gaze continued assessing them as he tapped plump, sausagelike fingers on the counter. Grimy, ragged fingertips said that he was a nail biter. "What credit card will you be using?"

"I won't." Jack reached for his wallet. "I'll pay cash…in advance."

"What'd you say brought you this way?" the clerk asked suspiciously. "We're not on the main highway."

Jack leaned forward on the counter in a confidential manner. "My wife and I like out-of-the-way places." He laid one hand over hers. "This is sort of the honeymoon trip we never had."

The clerk grinned slyly. "Don't say."

Jack turned to Summer.

This time, she expected the kiss, but still it overwhelmed her. She had shared kisses before. What was it about this man's that knocked her flat?

The clerk chuckled. "Looks like I'd better let you two get on with that honeymoon." He thrust a well-worn key on the counter. "It's the room on the end. No joined walls on the north side—it's our most *private* unit." Shuffling to the back, he returned with a handful of towels.

Taking them, Jack thanked the man, collected Danny and, with Summer in tow, they escaped.

"Could this have been any seedier?" she asked with a shudder as soon as they were out of hearing distance.

"Sorry about that. I just didn't want him dreaming of any other scenarios that might involve reward money."

Summer stopped short. "I never thought of that."

"That's what I'm guessing motivated Bart. He probably picked up on how I was acting. And I'm sure he hasn't forgotten the first time I worked there. I blew in fast, left just as quickly. Drifters don't often return to the places where they've worked. He was bound to be suspicious."

"What about Rita?" Summer hesitated. "Do you think she knew what Bart was doing?"

Jack shook his head. "I doubt it. And he sure won't tell her."

They arrived at the room the clerk had assigned them. Uneasily Summer looked around, wondering if, even now, they were being watched.

But Jack was opening the door. "'Be it ever so humble—'"

"Don't even joke." Dubiously she eyed the worn interior before gingerly entering.

In contrast, Jack moved briskly, quickly carrying in a few of their things. They had agreed to bring in only what they absolutely needed, leaving everything else in the truck for a fast getaway if necessary. "I'll be back."

Surprised, she glanced up at him from her crouched position beside Danny. "I thought you were tired."

"I'm half-dead," Jack admitted. "But I've got a few more things to do—locate a pay phone and try to reach Tom Matthews, then find some mud and cover up the license plate."

Knowing he had backed the truck into the parking stall so they could pull forward quickly, she felt a chill of danger. "Do you think they're that close?"

"I'm hoping they're not, but it doesn't pay to get careless. If we're asleep all day, we can't watch the truck. We wouldn't know if someone came nosing around."

Throat suddenly dry, Summer couldn't form a response. It was something that had always made her nervous—the thought of someone breaking in when she was asleep and defenseless. The fear had probably been born of too many late-night fright movies, but it was the subject of her infrequent but recurring nightmares. And no matter how often she'd chided herself that they were simply dreams, each had shaken her deeply.

"I won't be long," Jack continued. "If you want to take a shower, go ahead. Just put Danny in the playpen. And don't be surprised if I'm already sacked out when you're through."

Still distracted, she managed to nod, watching Jack leave.

Automatically Summer unbuckled Danny's car seat as he thrashed to get free. Reaching for a blanket they'd brought along, she stretched it over the worn carpet, not certain how clean the floor covering was.

A quick inspection of the room made it clear they were completely vulnerable. A weak lock, easily opened windows and no rear exit all spelled disaster. It was the setting from her nightmare come to life.

Beads of perspiration popped out, dampening the V between her breasts and running a similar moist line down her back. "Oh, Danny, what are we going to do?"

But the baby was more interested in the phone cord than

a response. Quickly retrieving the phone before it fell on his head, she searched for and found his favorite toy—a ball that jingled merrily when he rolled it.

"As soon as you finish crawling around the room, it's bath time," she told Danny, guessing his little legs might not be too clean after he finished exploring.

Having been fed along the way, the toddler was content to roam for a while. As he did, Summer thought of the danger they were fleeing, what she'd left behind...and what Jack had sacrificed to do the right thing. How must it feel to know he could never pick up the phone and call his parents? She couldn't begin to imagine how bereft that made him feel.

The door opened suddenly, and Summer was relieved to see Jack.

"I thought you two would be dead to the world by now," he said by way of greeting.

"Actually I was just going to give Danny a bath." Since she could see that Jack was practically asleep on his feet, she took pity on him. "But we could play for a while if you'd like to shower first."

"Actually I think I'll just sit down for a few minutes."

"Why don't you stretch out?" she suggested. "Danny and I don't mind a bit."

Jack reached down to pat Danny's diaper-padded bottom. "Maybe just for a minute." He couldn't prevent a longing glance toward the bed, and Summer smothered a grin.

Scooping up Danny, she headed with him toward the bathroom, guessing Jack would be out in moments. But after driving nonstop for hours on end, she thought it was a wonder he'd hung together so long, staying in control. "Okay, little man, it's bath time."

Danny squealed when she produced a bright orange-and-green rubber dinosaur. Although she was tired, Summer let Danny splash in the bathwater she'd drawn until it began to cool. Wrapping him in a big towel, she held his wriggling body and made a game of the powdering, diapering and dressing process before carrying him back into the bedroom.

As she had suspected, Jack had fallen asleep. The even rise and fall of his chest told her it was a deep sleep. Quietly she cuddled Danny after positioning a chair near the window. If someone spotted them, she didn't intend to be caught completely unaware.

From her vantage point, she could see the truck as well as the corridor to the office. Just glancing in that direction made her picture the clerk's weaselly face. Repressing a shudder, she didn't doubt for a microsecond that the man would relish turning them in, reward money or not. She suspected he was the sort who would enjoy torturing small animals.

Drawing her knees up a bit, she gently rocked Danny, amusing him with a distracted game of this-little-piggy. Within a short time, Summer gave him a bottle and although Danny fought it, sleep overcame him.

Despite the gritty fatigue that made her reddened eyes scratchy and her limbs ache, Summer forced her eyelids to remain open. For a long time, she held Danny as she kept watch, her gaze drifting down to study his sweet baby face. Long, dark eyelashes feathered over his cheeks, shuttering blue eyes that keenly resembled his father's. Small pink lips eased open as his sleep deepened. He was so vulnerable, so trusting. Tracing the curve of his plump cheek, Summer felt a fierce surge of maternal protectiveness. Nothing could happen to this precious child.

What was it about these tiny people that could so completely and overwhelmingly capture a person's heart? How could she have known the completeness, the rightness of bonding with a child? Had there always been a place in her heart reserved for a little one?

Summer's hands sifted through his dark, silky hair, and she felt her eyes moisten at the flood of feeling. Suddenly she understood what her mother meant, what other women had always tried to convey. But it was something a person had to experience, Summer now knew.

When she realized Danny would be more comfortable in his portable crib, regretfully she laid him down. He sighed, then settled back into baby dreams.

Summer resumed her vigil, leaving her post only to check occasionally on Danny. As the day wore on, she didn't spot anything suspicious, but she refused to give up her watch. She didn't intend to let anything happen to her little one. Although that thought ricocheted through her brain, shocking her with its truth, Summer didn't try to convince herself it wasn't true. In her mind, she now had a vested interest in the child.

Her eyes drifted toward Jack, and unconsciously she rubbed her lips, remembering the kiss they'd exchanged for the clerk's benefit. Yes, her interests were now entwined with this child. Even though his father didn't have an interest in her.

Dusk was sneaking across the sky, displacing the day. It was a pleasant dream, one in which he was warm, comfortable and rested. But the conscious nudged aside the subconscious, and Jack's eyes popped open. Heart pounding, he twisted to leap from the bed.

Spotting Summer in a chair by the window, he halted just as suddenly. One rapid glance across the room assured him that Danny was safe.

"Summer?" he questioned quietly.

She twisted around. "You're awake."

He pushed one hand through disheveled hair. "How long have you been sitting there?"

She shrugged. "Do you feel rested?"

Although Jack was still waking up, his gaze sharpened, focusing on her. "You did sleep, didn't you?"

"I'm not the one who drove all night."

Shocked, he stared at her. "But didn't you sleep? I know it's difficult to sleep during the day, but we don't have any choice. Or if you're uncomfortable about the bed, you could have wakened me, or simply pushed me off. I can sleep anywhere.''

''It's not that.''

Summer's face was closed, and he found it difficult to read what she was hiding. ''Then what?''

But she only shrugged.

Rising from the bed, he crossed the room to stand by the chair. Stooping over, he followed her line of vision as she looked out the window. Suddenly it struck him. ''Were you doing sentry duty?''

''Something like that.''

Astonished, he turned to face her. ''Then why didn't you wake me? You didn't intend to stand guard all night, did you?''

She glanced up at him. ''If necessary.''

Jack squatted, bringing his face to her level. ''Summer, you're astounding. But you didn't need to do this. I'm a light sleeper. I've kept one eye open while I've slept ever since I got into the program.'' He paused, studying her face. ''What if I'd slept all night, as well?''

''Then I'd have kept watching,'' she replied simply.

Jack reached out to touch her cheek. ''You truly are amazing.'' Meeting her sober yet elusive eyes, he wondered again about this woman. Eyes an intriguing mix of green and gold, hair tawny and untamed, she again reminded him of a lioness—proud, fierce and beautiful.

''You would do the same,'' she replied.

''But this is my battle.''

''I guess somewhere along the way, I forgot that.'' Summer's gaze wandered over to settle on Danny. ''I didn't intend to let someone sneak up on us while he slept.''

He reached out to take Summer's hands, searching her face, seeing the deep shadows beneath her eyes, the worry etched across her features. While she was fiercely protective, at the same time he could see her vulnerability, the concern that had extended to embrace his son. It occurred to him that she needed someone to protect her...perhaps even cherish her.

The thought sent a shiver of fear through him that was far worse than the threat of Fisher and Wilcox. Abruptly he stood and moved away. "I think it's time to figure out how to get you home."

She stared at him. "I agreed to help you get Danny to safety. I'm not going back on that promise."

Frustrated, he passed a hand over his forehead. "Summer, this isn't what I meant when I asked for your help. I only hoped you could help us establish a new identity. I think we've done that."

Stung, Summer stuttered, then glared. "If you think I'm deserting that child, you're crazy!"

Jack steeled his voice, purposely ignoring the spurt of gratitude her words caused. "That's not your choice."

"You're forgetting something, aren't you?" Her eyes narrowed.

Jack didn't like the look. "What's that?"

"Money. The fact that I can get my hands on more and you can't."

For a moment, he cursed the situation that had turned the tables on him. His ego dented, then sprang back to shape. "I didn't ask for your money."

"But you need it. Without it, you and Danny won't make it to D.C."

"That's not your concern." Jack turned away, wishing she hadn't brought up such a valid argument.

"I'm just supposed to hit the road and forget about the fact that two thugs are after you?"

Frustration was a lethal acid in his gut. "I think you should just forget about Danny and me, period."

He could see her throat working, the hurt that flashed across her face, the unexpected betrayal that sprang to her eyes, darkening them so that the gold disappeared into their emerald depths.

"I'm not made of stone," she finally uttered, nearly

choking on the words. "Do you think I could walk away, knowing the danger that you bo—that Danny is in?"

Jack felt guilt and the need to wipe away the hurt he'd inflicted. Both obliterated his initial fright that she'd grown too important. That was his handicap. It wasn't right to hurt Summer because of it. "I haven't thanked you."

Cautiously Summer raised her head. "For what?"

"Keeping watch over us."

Her eyes met his, searching, as the trembling of her lips eased. "You're welcome."

Jack started to reach out to her, but his hand fell to one side. Restraint was a recalcitrant companion, difficult to control—even harder to understand. Glancing down into her eyes, Jack could see her confusion...and knew it didn't even begin to match his.

Chapter 9

Despite the relative seclusion of the Hideaway Lodge, Jack wasn't comfortable staying any longer. Both he and Summer were uneasy about the clerk's prying questions and suspicious looks. As soon as darkness completely settled over the highway, they loaded their belongings in the truck and left.

Again the night was their friend, providing camouflage and security against predators. Jack pushed hard, risking attention by speeding as fast as the old truck would go. Uncomfortably he realized that wasn't very fast, certainly not fast enough to elude pursuers in a high-speed chase.

"I'll feel better when we've put that place far behind us," he commented.

Summer nodded in agreement, then realized he couldn't see the motion in the darkness. "Me, too."

He glanced across at her. "Why don't you sack out? You must be dead tired."

"I'm okay," she insisted.

Jack didn't argue the point, but in a few minutes he could

see her head wobble as she tried to remain upright. Despite his better judgment, he reached out and pulled Summer close, nestling her head against his shoulder.

Summer stiffened for the briefest of moments, then relaxed against him, her warm body a welcome distraction. A short time later, he heard her whispery sigh. As the minutes passed, he sensed her sleep deepening.

She tried so hard to be independent, strong, self-sufficient. It was rare that Summer allowed any unguarded moments. Like now.

Taking advantage of the respite, he inhaled her unique scent—that distinctive aroma of sunshine and roses. She moved her head, sending a shaft of silky hair across his arm.

The headlights from an oncoming car illuminated the cab of the truck. In the dim light, he could see the soft curves of her face, the open vulnerability she so rarely displayed.

As the truck ate up the miles, Jack's thoughts drifted...and his heart ached a bit. For the tomorrows that wouldn't be...for the future he wasn't certain he would have.

Suddenly, bright lights loomed in the rearview mirror. His fingers gripped the steering wheel. The car behind him approached, drawing closer...and closer. Adrenaline flowed, and he cast a protective glance over Summer and Danny.

The headlights of the pursuing vehicle seemed to flood the interior of the cab as the car closed the distance between them. With every warrior instinct engaged, Jack's control remained steady. Just as he prepared to accelerate and shoot ahead, the other car pulled out and into the lane beside him.

Deciding an offensive move would be suicide at that point, Jack switched to defensive mode. But even as he was changing tactics, the car sped up, continued past him, then swung into his lane ahead of him.

As the car sped ahead and out of sight, Jack slowly unclenched his death grip on the steering wheel, realizing that if the car had been driven by Fisher and Wilcox, they would be riding into a death trap. One without escape.

Summer came awake slowly, aware that her neck was kinked and that her body felt incredibly warm. Pale, early-morning sun highlighted the dewy grass along the roadside. The sky was still that gray-blue shade of first light.

"Morning," Jack greeted her.

Slowly she straightened up, belatedly realizing what that wonderful source of warmth was. Some of that heat traveled into her cheeks. "Hi."

But Jack didn't seem at all fazed. "I'm about ready for some coffee. How about you?"

"Sure." Summer pushed at her hair, wondering what it must look like after a night sleeping in the truck. She wished she hadn't been asleep. She would have enjoyed knowingly experiencing so many hours nestled at Jack's side. "Where are we?"

"Not far from where I was headed."

She blinked. "D.C.?"

Jack laughed. "Afraid not. We just crossed the state line to West Virginia. We're headed to a safe place—a job I had in the program."

"One like Bart's?" she questioned dubiously. Any more safe havens like that and they would be toast.

"No. Different sort of place, different sort of people. I didn't know Bart very well...should have picked up on how he was acting. But we won't have that problem to deal with here."

Summer digested this, wishing she had the coffee he'd mentioned to swallow it with. "You're the expert."

"Let's hope you keep thinking that way." Jack pulled off the highway and onto a farm road. After a few miles, they approached a large, gated road.

Summer spotted a sign proclaiming it to be the Appleton Horse Ranch. "Horses?"

He nodded. "This is the safe house."

Struck by mixed feelings, Summer looked around as they neared the ranch house. The isolation could prove just what they needed...or a ticket straight into Wilcox's and Fisher's hands. If they were caught in such a secluded area, she and Jack could be easily eliminated without witnesses. Nervously she glanced around, but everything appeared normal.

Pulling into the circular driveway at the house, Jack climbed out of the truck, then held open the door for Summer when a voice rang out.

"Jack Anderson! As I live and breathe, I can't believe it's you!" A dark-haired woman ran out the front door and down the three wide steps to the truck and flung herself at Jack.

Summer, heart in her throat, moved to slide out of the truck to help him. But he'd picked up the tall, leggy brunette, and was twirling her around.

Jack beamed down at the woman, the sort of easy, open smile Summer had never seen on him. Unexpectedly a fist of envy punched her squarely. Especially when she realized the woman was gorgeous. Not just Barbie-doll pretty, but out-and-out stunning, drop-dead gorgeous.

Summer wondered suddenly if this woman was the reason Jack had tried to talk her out of continuing on with him. A wave of hurt and embarrassment assailed her. Had Jack reluctantly allowed her to tag along simply because he couldn't find a way to shake her?

Jack returned to hold open the driver's-side door so that Summer could slide out without crawling over Danny. "Cyndi, I'd like you to meet Summer."

Staring directly into the other woman's model-perfect face, Summer wanted to take her mussed hair, wrinkled clothes and crumpled self and sink out of sight.

But Cyndi was already holding out her hand expectantly.

Gamely Summer stepped out of the truck. "Hello."

"I'm so pleased to meet you," Cyndi told her with an-

other wide smile. "Let's go inside and have some coffee.
Have you two eaten breakfast? Probably not, it's so early."

"That sounds great," Summer managed to say.

Jack unbuckled Danny's car seat and lifted the still
sleepy child. "Cyndi, look at how my boy has grown."

Cyndi's eyes widened, and a look of pure delight trans-
fused her beautiful face. "He's adorable. You're right, he
has grown. He was so tiny when you were here before.
Now he's more like a real person." Long, slender fingers
with manicured nails reached out to gently caress the
baby's plump leg.

Summer swallowed, looking between Jack and Cyndi.
Danny could easily have been the product of these two
beautiful people. Is that what Jack saw, as well?

Cyndi looked up just then. "Aren't you lucky." Then
she laughed again. "I'm sorry. Here I'm carrying on and
I'm sure you're hungry. Let's go inside and have that
breakfast."

Feeling like the rumpled end of the parade, Summer followed them into the house. As they reached the stairwell,
Cyndi turned to Summer with a smile. "I don't know about
you, but car trips get to me. Would you like to go upstairs
and freshen up? There's a ladies' guest bath at the end of
the hall. I keep it stocked with all the necessities."

Geez, she was nice, too. It would be easier to hate her
if she weren't. But Summer thanked her and headed upstairs. From below, she could hear Cyndi's and Jack's
voices blending, and the occasional laughter before it
drifted out of range.

Summer took in the home's tasteful decorating as she
gingerly made her way down the hall. At the entrance of
the bathroom was a full-size mirror. She took one look and
groaned. Her hair was worse than she'd expected, and her
makeup was horrendous. If it were possible, she would simply hide. Knowing she couldn't, Summer entered the bathroom.

Once inside, she blinked as she saw the fully stocked

counter. Everything necessary to repair her makeup and hair was there. Short of a fresh change of clothes, she could transform herself. Clearly their hostess knew how to take care of guests—even unexpected ones. Summer didn't know whether to be grateful or resentful toward the gracious woman who had provided for them.

If Jack was interested in Cyndi, Summer could make arrangements to return to Edisto. Her heart syncopated in a dull beat of pain. It shouldn't bother her so much, she realized. She had known from the start that she was only along for the ride until Jack and Danny reached safety. But her heart wasn't hearing any logic. Still, Summer reached for the cosmetics. If this was her exit, she planned to look her best.

Sometime later, hair and makeup restored, she wandered downstairs. Following the aroma of freshly brewed coffee, Summer found the kitchen. From there, it wasn't a big leap to locate the breakfast room. Danny had awakened and Cyndi was holding him.

Jack sat across the table, clearly at ease. He glanced up as Summer entered. "Hey!"

Cyndi noticed her at almost the same moment. "Summer, come sit down and have some coffee. Breakfast is kind of casual, I'm afraid. Muffins, fruit, an omelet if you'd like."

The thought of food made Summer's stomach revolt. Jack picked up the coffeepot, filling her mug. He had slipped into the role of host, she noticed. "Thank you."

Jack smiled. "Sure."

"Smells good." Summer forced the words past the lump in her throat.

"I was just telling Jack that if he wanted to work here for a while, I can use the help," Cyndi said, tweaking Danny's toe. "You're welcome here forever, as far as that goes. But certainly as long as it suits your plans."

Summer looked at both Jack and Cyndi and wondered if their plans were changing. "You breed horses?" Summer managed to ask, calling on the manners her mother had ingrained in her.

"Yes. It's been a family business for several generations," Cyndi replied. "Hard but rewarding work. Jack can tell you that I was in over my head for a while. In fact, I don't know what I would have done without him."

Somehow Summer managed to smile and nod. "I see."

"This little guy must be a handful," Cyndi commented.

Belatedly realizing that Cyndi was addressing her, Summer glanced at Danny, her emotions fracturing again. "That he is."

Seeing Summer's gaze on him, Danny began wriggling in earnest.

"Looks like he wants you," Cyndi said with regret, then handed him over to Summer.

"Hey, big guy," Summer said softly. "You finally woke up, huh?"

Plump fists promptly reached for Summer's hair. Accustomed to his fascination with her hair, Summer smiled as she gently untangled tiny fingers.

"I guess motherhood teaches you how to deal with that," Cyndi said, watching them. "Jack is lucky to have found you. No one would know Danny's not your own."

Not certain what Jack had told Cyndi and uncomfortable with the line of conversation, Summer concentrated on Danny, offering him a bite of banana as she stalled. "You don't have children?" Summer finally asked.

A look of unexpected pain crossed Cyndi's face. "I'm afraid not." Then she smiled again. "Jack, you remember where your old room is, don't you? Do you think it will be large enough? It does have the small sitting room."

"It will be fine," Jack assured her.

His old room? Summer thought. Somehow that sounded a tad too intimate.

But later she had to admit it was a lovely room. Just as everything in the house was. Just as Cyndi was. Why wouldn't a man like Jack be attracted to her? She was beautiful, gracious and warm.

"So you told Cyndi I was Danny's stepmother?" Summer asked when they were alone.

He shrugged. "She assumed so."

So that was how it was. "I see."

"Are you all right for now? I thought I'd go check out the situation, see what needs to be done."

Nodding, she watched him leave. Once he was out of the room, she crossed to the window and pulled back the curtain. Within a few moments, she saw Jack walk toward the stables, then pause when Cyndi joined him. Together they headed away.

Slowly Summer allowed the curtain to fall back into place. So this was the safe house Jack wanted to reach. Unfortunately she could see why.

"They couldn't have just disappeared," the pale-eyed man replied grimly.

The graying man shrugged nervously. "It's as though they fell off the planet."

"Since we both know that's not possible, you'd better come up with a better scenario."

"I'm running everything in Anderson's file through another computer scan. Got somebody working on it—a profiler type. Should be able to tell us where Anderson will run."

"The last *expert* told us he'd head straight to his relatives, then to the police."

Thick lips twitched in agitation. "This profiler's supposed to be more accurate."

Pale eyes chilled. "You'd better hope so."

The horse-breeding business was a demanding one, Summer soon learned. Long hours, hard work—it wasn't as glamorous as she had assumed after seeing the well-appointed home. But Jack thrived on it.

Taking to the fresh air, the arduous work, he was more at ease than she'd ever seen him. And all of that couldn't be credited to Cyndi.

Summer realized that Jack was a man of action. He would never be content to sit on the sidelines. He wanted—needed—to make things happen. She wondered how he dealt with the frustration of not being able to do that because of the restraints he'd been placed under.

Summer guessed she was only just beginning to realize how many changes and sacrifices Jack had made in order to live his ideals. Having done the right thing, now he was living with the consequences. How many men had she known who were willing to live their principles despite the cost? Briefly she thought of Tyson, her ex-fiancé. He hadn't even been willing to commit to a woman who couldn't further his career. And that was after she had put her life on hold for four years waiting until Tyson felt the time was right.

And ultimately the time had never been right.

Unwillingly her mind raced to compare Tyson to Jack. Quickly she realized there was no comparison. Jack was unlike any man she'd ever known. Commitment, morality, strength—it was quite a combination. And she could see why that combination would appeal to an exquisite woman like Cyndi.

Closing her eyes in pain against that thought, Summer brushed her hair for the second time, wishing she could reinvent herself as a stunning brunette. Sighing, she stopped procrastinating and made her way downstairs.

Cyndi had wanted an opportunity to play with the baby, and Summer had painfully acknowledged it was probably a good idea. If the woman was going to be a permanent fixture in Jack's and Danny's lives, she should become accustomed to the baby.

Taking a deep breath, Summer forced herself to smile as

she stepped into the dining room. Danny, normally cheerful and content, was fussing.

Cyndi smiled at Summer in relief. "I'm not sure what's wrong with Danny. He doesn't seem too happy, and Jack's outside looking at Black Star. I'm worried about a tendon strain, and that horse is my prime player. Since Jack's dad is a veterinarian and he grew up with horses, he's practically an expert. While Jack was here before, he cut the vet calls in half.

"Really," Summer murmured. "I had no idea."

"Yes. I'm pretty good myself with horses, but I haven't a clue about babies."

"Hey, big guy," Summer greeted Danny. "What's wrong?"

He held out his hands toward Summer, and Cyndi lifted him into Summer's arms. "Looks like he wants you."

Automatically Summer felt his forehead and cheeks. They were a touch warm, but nothing to be alarmed about.

"Is he okay?" Cyndi questioned anxiously. "Like I said, I'm a total incompetent with babies."

"I'm sure you're fine," Summer said, allowing Danny to cuddle against her. "Maybe he's just been in too many strange places in too short a time."

"Trips will do that," Cyndi agreed, looking relieved. "So you think he's not sick?"

"I'm no doctor, but I think he's okay."

"You're a mother and that's just as good," Cyndi protested. "My mother always knew just what was wrong when I didn't feel well."

Summer's throat ached with unspoken words. Knowing they had to remain unsaid, she concentrated on the immediate. "Could I have an ice cube?"

"Oh, of course." Cyndi disappeared into the kitchen and returned quickly with a glass of ice cubes. "I don't know how many you want."

Summer found one small cube and showed it to Danny before easing it into his mouth and then sitting with him in the rocker. "Is it your gums, sweetie? Is there a new tooth trying to come in?"

"Is that what it is?" Cyndi asked in relief. "I was afraid something more serious was wrong with him."

Jack walked in just then, his gaze jetting between the two women and finally resting on Danny. "Is something wrong with Danny?"

"Like an idiot, I panicked because he's teething," Cyndi explained. "Luckily Summer recognized it and she's already dealt with the problem."

Jack crossed the room to squat beside Summer's chair. He reached out to pat Danny's tummy, then checked his forehead.

"I don't think he's warm enough to worry," Summer murmured. She had learned that teething could cause babies to run a mild temperature.

"Right," Jack agreed. Then his eyes met hers, and she read the silent gratitude.

"He's sure a love," Cyndi sighed. "Teething or not. Such a handsome boy." Her brilliant smile rested on Jack. "Just like Dad."

Summer bent her head toward the baby, shading her expression. Yes, just like Dad. And like Jack, Cyndi was one of the beautiful people. People who belonged together.

Feeling like a mutt intruding on the Westminster Kennel Club show, Summer wished she could simply fade into the background. She tried for the second-best solution. "Since Danny's not feeling that great, I think I'll take him upstairs for his supper. I suspect he'll be fussy. I'm not that hungry myself, and we could call it an evening."

"Do you have to?" Cyndi questioned with what sounded like genuine distress.

"I don't have to but—"

"I'd rather you stayed," Jack inserted quietly, still squatting close by.

"Cyndi's lovely dinner won't go as smoothly," Summer protested.

"It will be wonderful having the interruptions," Cyndi declared. "I have far too many quiet, undisturbed dinners. A baby is an immensely appealing distraction."

Jack would have to be comatose to miss that hint, Summer decided. So, Cyndi's dinners were solitary ones. Apparently there was a vacancy in her life she wanted to fill.

Reluctantly Summer joined them at the table a few moments later. It was especially comforting to have Danny acting so clingy. She cuddled his warm body close. Despite the envy she couldn't squelch, Summer knew that she would experience lasting pain when she separated from both father and son. However, seeing Cyndi's concerned glance resting on her, Summer shored up a smile.

"I'm sorry. I don't have a high chair," Cyndi apologized. "I don't have many guests Danny's age. But I could hold him for you," she offered. "Then you can eat, too. And if I can't handle things, you're right here."

Jack smiled fondly at Cyndi. Summer watched his easy, relaxed grin as she tried valiantly to ignore the shaft of pain it caused. Because even though the smile wasn't directed at her, she realized she cared enough about Jack to want to see him smile like that. He deserved happiness. He'd made sacrifices most people couldn't begin to fathom. Could she begrudge him happiness now? Despite the cost to her?

"Summer," Cyndi repeated, trying to gain her attention. "Would that be okay—for me to hold Danny while you eat?"

"Sorry. Of course, if you're certain you want to."

Cyndi all but clapped her hands together. "I'm afraid I'm a total boob when it comes to babies. But when I'm sure I'm not doing anything to hurt them, I just love being able to take care of one."

Disguising her reluctance, Summer tried to hand Danny to Cyndi. But Danny chose to be obstinate.

Bless his little heart.

Fists waving, cheeks purpling with agitation, he put up a terrific howl when Cyndi tried to take him.

To her credit, Cyndi was graceful about the rebuff. "I don't blame him. I suspect I'd feel the same way. I wouldn't want a stranger taking care of me if I were sick."

Summer strove for an equal share of graciousness, especially when she saw the yearning in the other woman's eyes. "I'm sure that by morning Danny would love to be given a second chance."

Cyndi smiled softly, her voice quiet. "Thank you. I'll take you up on that when I get back from town tomorrow." She glanced at Jack, raising her voice a fraction. "What a lovely family you have, Jack."

Jack met Summer's eyes across the table. "Yes, I'm a lucky man."

Startled, she couldn't force her gaze to leave his.

Cyndi's warm chuckle broke the intense stare.

Embarrassed, Summer glanced away.

"Young love, how magnificent," Cyndi said with a trace of longing.

Summer's eyes seemed to travel back toward Jack with a will of their own. She wished suddenly for a stargazer's crystal ball so that she could discern the truth behind all the longing in the room. And discover how *she* fit into the cosmic puzzle.

Stark fingers of dread snaked over her, entrapping Summer in their relentless grasp. Dark, nameless terror attacked. Her head whipped from side to side as she tried to elude her pursuers.

But only a deepening black void greeted her. Summer struggled, trying to force her leaden limbs to move, to run, to escape. But despite her most valiant efforts, she was frozen in place.

Overpowered and outnumbered, she searched for strength and found paralysis instead. A cold sweat drenched her.

Finally her frozen vocal cords responded to the overwhelming terror and she screamed, the sound bouncing off the walls, echoing through the room.

Strong hands clamped over her shoulders, shaking her gently, then with more force. "Summer, wake up, you're having a nightmare."

Heart pounding so hard that it was painful, she slowly came awake. As always when emerging from a nightmare, it was hard for her to separate reality from the frightening dream that had her in its grasp. "Jack?"

He smoothed her hair back from her forehead. "Shh, it's okay. You just had a bad dream."

Remembering, she shuddered.

Jack drew her close. "It's not real. It can't hurt you."

"But it *seemed* so real. They always do."

"I won't let anything hurt you," he promised, continuing to run his hand through her hair.

Briefly Summer remembered being in the clutches of her captors, then felt remarkably soothed as Jack held her. "I'm sorry. I didn't mean to wake you. Is Danny—?"

"Sound asleep. Guess it was a big day for him. Don't worry about waking me up. You let me sleep the other night. It's my turn to pay you back."

"Could you just stay here with me for a few minutes?" she asked, hating that she still felt so weak and afraid.

He stretched out beside her. "I'm not going anywhere. Why don't you tell me your dream?"

Embarrassment waged with the desire to be comforted. "You'll think it's silly."

Again he stroked her hair, his thumb skimming over her cheek. "Nothing that frightens you is silly. Come on, tell me."

She hesitated, then the words spilled out in a rush. "Someone was chasing me...and they caught me."

He pulled her even closer. "That's understandable. We're fleeing—it spilled over into your dreams."

Summer's eyes were troubled as she raised them. "But

you don't understand. I've always been plagued by night-mares—it's as though I never feel truly safe."

"But your family is so solid."

"I know." She hesitated again. "The nightmares began when my father died. I guess I felt abandoned—that I had no protector. Then when my fiancé left... The dreams grew worse." Appalled at her revelation, she tried to pull away.

Jack drew her closer. "Any man who walked away from you is a fool."

Startled, Summer searched his eyes, wondering what was hidden in their dark-blue depths.

"I'll protect you, Summer. You can count on it."

Briefly Summer thought of the bedroom sofa that he'd chosen to sleep on and she was inordinately glad that he was willing to abandon it. She thought of the sexual tension that had stretched between them as inescapably as the danger pursuing them. But now it wasn't passion she craved; rather it was the strength and comfort he offered.

Relationships had as many facets as people themselves, she realized. And right now, she wanted pure companionship. Jack was providing that and more. And for the moment, she pretended it could last.

Jack was restless. Summer wasn't certain why, but she could see it in every move of his body.

She tried to concentrate on feeding Danny his cereal, but she couldn't shake the feeling that something was wrong. Jack had joined her for a midmorning break, having gotten up in the wee hours of the morning to begin working. She wondered if even now he was thinking of Cyndi. Was that what weighed on his mind?

Danny smacked his cereal bowl, sending a glob of creamed wheat flying.

"Danny," Jack gently chided him. "Save your ammo for when you need it." He grabbed a sponge, then wiped up the damage.

Summer sent him a baleful glance. "Now, that's great advice."

Jack ruffled Danny's hair. "He likes to test out cause and effect." He walked quickly to the window, then stared outside.

Summer managed to feed Danny another few spoonfuls. "Watching for something in particular?" Or someone? Like Cyndi, she wanted to ask, but didn't dare.

He shook his head. "Just keeping an eye out."

An unexpected chill skittered up her spine. Was he experiencing his sixth sense again?

Just then the back door banged open. Cyndi rushed in, her pretty cheeks flushed, her hands filled with packages. "Good, everyone's here. I was hoping to have coffee and play with that adorable baby."

Summer managed to smile. So, he wasn't watching for anything in particular? Convenient that Cyndi had strolled in at just that moment.

Jack took Cyndi's packages, and Summer looked away, unable to watch.

"How's Danny feeling this morning?" Cyndi asked.

"Better," Summer replied, feeling the spokes of being a fifth wheel poking at her.

"Well enough that he's hurling cereal," Jack added.

"I've felt that way often enough myself," Cyndi confided to Danny.

Surprised, Summer looked at the other woman. What would ruffle this seemingly perfect woman?

Cyndi poured a mug of coffee. "I heard something unusual this morning in town."

Interest piqued, Jack abandoned the packages on the counter. "Oh?"

"One of my neighbors, Alice Freeman—you remember her, don't you, Jack?"

He nodded and Cyndi continued. "She said she'd overheard someone at the drugstore asking about you."

Jack's gaze collided with Summer's.

"Alice thought I'd want to know since she knew you'd once worked for me. Actually she asked if I'd seen you lately, but it struck me as odd that someone was asking after you. I told her I had a migraine coming on and that I had to head home before it got worse." Cyndi glanced at Jack and then Summer. "Don't you think it's odd that someone's asking about you now? So soon after you arrived?"

"Yes," Jack replied, his tone clipped.

Fear robbed Summer's words as she stared at him.

"Cyndi, we're going to have to leave now," Jack continued.

Soberly Cyndi glanced at Jack and then Summer. "It has to do with this person asking about you, doesn't it?"

He nodded, not offering an explanation.

"I thought so." She hesitated for a moment. "Do you need money?"

Jack shook his head, his stubborn male pride still firmly in place. "No, just the pay I have coming."

"Surely I can do something else—"

"We have to leave quickly."

"Do I have time to finish feeding Danny?" Summer asked, holding a spoon in midair.

"If you hurry."

Cyndi glanced at Summer and the baby. "I'll help you."

Distracted, Summer looked at the other woman. "Thanks."

Jack hurried out of the room, and Summer knew he would have them packed before she finished.

Cyndi glanced after him briefly, a worried look on her face. "I'm sorry you have to leave so soon. As I've told you, I don't know what I'd have done without Jack when he worked here the first time."

Summer tried valiantly to repress the pang of jealousy stabbing her, hoping her face didn't betray her feelings.

Cyndi reached over to pat Danny's cheek. "My husband was dying, you know."

Summer's gaze shot up to meet hers. "No... I didn't."

Cyndi searched Summer's face. "I hope you haven't taken what I've said about Jack the wrong way. Without him to lean on when Bill was so ill, I'm not sure I would have made it." A shadow passed over her face, and her gaze intensified. "It wasn't anything more than friendship. Not that I wanted it to be, but in any case Jack isn't that sort of man. He would never take advantage of a situation...or break a trust. He's truly an exceptional person." She laughed suddenly. "I don't know why I'm going on like this. Of course you know that—you married him. I just didn't want you to mistake our familiarity. I wasn't fortunate enough to have any brothers of my own, but if I could have handpicked one, it would have been Jack."

Summer felt suddenly small for her unnecessary envy. "It's rare that we get to choose our relatives. I think you've both made an excellent choice."

Cyndi smiled. "Why don't I wipe down this little guy while you collect your things? I suspect Jack will be pacing in a minute."

Feeling the urgency herself, Summer stood, started to walk away, pivoted, then hugged Cyndi. "Thanks...for everything."

Cyndi nodded and Summer rushed upstairs.

Jack had nearly everything packed. But his face fell into lines of relief when he saw Summer. "If you'll finish packing, I'll carry the gear to the truck."

"Right."

He quickly grabbed the playpen and portable crib.

"Jack?"

He paused at the doorway, clearly impatient to be gone.

"Do you think it's Fisher and Wilcox?"

"It's not the tooth fairy," he replied curtly, then paused again, swearing lowly. "Sorry. I was just hoping for a respite. By now, you'd think I'd realize there aren't any respites. I shouldn't have bitten your head off for asking."

Realizing the cause of his stress, it was easy to forgive him. "It's okay."

Within minutes, they had everything packed into the truck. Jack buckled Danny into his car seat.

After feeding Danny, Cyndi had filled a sack with a substantial stash of food. "Bread, lunch meat, chips, fruit—stuff like that," she explained.

Jack took her hands, but this time Summer didn't quiver with envy. "Thanks, Cyn. Someday hopefully I'll be able to explain."

Cyndi smiled, but Summer could see a mist of tears in the other woman's eyes and the way her throat worked as she tried to look brave. "No explanation needed. Just take care of yourselves. I want our next visit to be longer. Summer and I hardly had a chance to get to know each other."

"You got it."

Cyndi hugged him fiercely. Then she turned to Summer, giving her an equally hearty hug as she whispered, "Take care of him, Summer, and yourself. You'll be okay. Just believe in what you have."

Unable to speak over the lump in her throat, Summer hugged her back before they quickly jumped into the truck.

She twisted around, watching Cyndi wave to them as they sped away. When Summer finally turned back around, she glanced at the seemingly safe-looking countryside. "Where to?"

Jack clenched the steering wheel, the tightness in his grip matching that in his voice. "I wish I knew."

Chapter 10

Daylight was the enemy, but with no other choice, Jack made himself concentrate on the road. He had driven hard and fast for over an hour, but he knew that he couldn't keep up the pace without attracting the unwanted attention of the highway patrol.

"Are there any hiding places you know about from when you lived here before?" Summer asked.

"Unlike Bart's, I didn't have much free time. Just keeping up with the ranch took all my time."

"Do you think we have much of a head start?" she asked, twisting around to look at the road behind them.

"Your guess is as good as mine. I'm hoping Fisher and Wilcox just arrived in town since Cyndi's neighbor heard them asking around, but we can't be sure of that."

"They certainly seem to be tracking us pretty well."

Jack glanced over at her. "I noticed that, too. It's as though they're reading my mind, figuring out where I'll head."

"Do you think—no, that's stupid."

"What?"

Summer hesitated. "Do you think they hired some sort of psychologist to study you—predict what you'll do next?"

Surprised at the concept, but impressed with her insight, Jack thumped the steering wheel with the palm of his hand. "You're probably right." He paused. "So, what now? I think like somebody else? Or just deny my natural inclinations?"

Summer shook her head. "Your instincts have kept us alive so far. Unless I'm missing my guess, you were having a premonition this morning."

Startled, he turned to look at her. "How did you know that?"

"I guess I've gotten used to the way you act, your body language...."

"Right," Jack replied, his voice huskier than he intended.

Summer twisted her hands, unable to contain the thoughts that had been plaguing her since they'd left the ranch. "You didn't tell me about Cyndi's husband."

"It's still hard to talk about. Bill started out as my employer and quickly became my friend. I didn't know when I met him that he already knew how sick he was. Then, losing him... I'd already given up my own family. It was hard doing that again, seeing someone so young and vital dying for no reason."

"Like Linda?"

Summer's instant understanding was like a balm to that wound. "Yeah. I always thought those platitudes about the good dying young were just that, but when it happens... You know it's true."

"Sometimes I've wished I could just start over again, do things right this time," Summer confided. "Be a better person, a *good* person. I guess I'd go back to when I was about eighteen. Any further back would be too painful. I was such a geek."

His gaze lingered on her. "I find that hard to believe."

"Where were you when I went to my prom with the king of the geeks?"

"Busy being a *good* person, I guess."

"Don't scoff. I would like to be more pure of heart, be a better person."

"How many people do you know who would give up their own ambitions to stay near an aging parent? You could have opted to put your mother in a retirement center instead."

Summer barked out a caustic laugh. "Can you imagine that? She'd have killed me."

"But you never considered it. And that's strictly pure of heart, Summer."

She reached over, her hand encircling his arm. "I haven't felt very pure of heart lately. Thanks."

Jack wondered what had been bothering her, but just then he spotted a highway-patrol car. "Hell."

"What is it?" Summer's eyes followed his, and she saw the police car. "Do you think they're looking for us?"

"Hopefully they don't know what vehicle we're in. But we're going to have to get off this main road."

Summer stiffened as she watched the patrol car. "Everyone and everything can't have conspired against us."

"Back to that issue of *good?*"

She nodded. "We can't outrun the entire world."

"I used to think that. But I learned that if I had to, I could." Jack looked at his son, who represented all the good that had otherwise become tainted.

Summer followed his gaze and stroked Danny's plump leg. "I can understand why."

The roads Jack chose took them through lush, thriving countryside. But Summer couldn't enjoy the green meadows or the late-season wildflowers. Worry ate at her. It seemed no matter which direction they had taken, Fisher and Wilcox nipped at their heels. What would happen to them if they couldn't outrun or outwit their pursuers?

Now twilight was approaching. Summer didn't know whether to be grateful for the cover of darkness or worried because they had no destination as they drove into the night.

Jack turned off the road suddenly onto a narrower one.

"Why are we turning here?"

"I want to get off the main road before it's completely dark. We need to find a place to camp. We can't chance staying at a hotel on the main highway."

Intrigued, Summer watched closely as they drove forward.

When Jack stopped the truck at the end of the road, it was hard to say who was more surprised.

"An amusement park?" Summer questioned, her eyes roving over the tall chain-link fence.

"A *closed* amusement park," Jack corrected, seeing that the Fun Time Amusement Park sign over the gate was faded, hanging crookedly in neglect. "I didn't expect that."

"But you wanted to come here?" she asked cautiously, wondering if the strain had pushed him over the edge.

"I tried to think of some place the normal Jack Anderson wouldn't choose, some place their profiler wouldn't pinpoint before we got there. I guessed we could camp somewhere close by."

"I've never seen an abandoned amusement park," Summer said in wonder.

"Abandoned..." Jack mused.

"What are you thinking?"

"How adventurous are you feeling?"

"Considering we're probably only a few steps ahead of men who want to kill us, I guess all in all, pretty adventurous." Any more adventurous and they'd be hanging upside down out of airplanes. But she kept the thought to herself.

"Good. Let's figure out how to break in."

She blinked. "Why would we want to do that?"

Jack unfastened Danny's car seat, then reached for the toddler backpack carrier. "Can you think of a better place to hide?"

Summer climbed out of the truck. Since she couldn't think of any place to hide, she shook her head even though she was doubting the soundness of this plan.

Jack strapped the carrier on his back. Automatically Summer reached for Danny, lifting him from the car seat and placing him in the backpack carrier.

"Let's see if there's an alarm system."

Summer gulped. "Alarm system?" She hurried behind him. "What if there is one? What do we do?"

"Disengage it," he replied calmly.

"You know how to do that?"

He flashed that devilish grin. "One of the advantages of having so many jobs. Not to mention my training to become an architect. Helps to know how wiring works."

Of course. She should have thought of that, but then she wasn't sure what a person should be thinking about when breaking and entering.

It didn't take Jack long to disengage the simple alarm system. And from the easily broken locks, it appeared the owners didn't anticipate many intruders. But the park, located away from any towns, wouldn't attract vandals or fun-seeking teenagers. Summer wondered if the park's remote location had contributed to its demise.

"We need to bring the truck inside," Jack told her. "Parked out here, it's like a flag."

"I doubt many people come down this road."

"It would only take one," Jack replied grimly.

Sobered, she nodded.

"If you'll drive the truck through, I'll close the gates behind you," Jack instructed.

As she climbed inside the truck, it occurred to Summer how bizarre her actions had become. But then Jack was motioning her forward. Automatically she accelerated. The gates clanged shut behind her, an ominous sound. She tried not to think about it as she parked in the work shed that housed what remained of the park's maintenance vehicles.

Jack opened the truck door, and she slid outside.

"I think we should check out the park, see if we can get in the hotel," Jack suggested. He reached inside for the sack of food. "We travel light tonight."

She understood what he left unsaid. They could escape more quickly if they weren't carrying a hefty load.

Once inside, Summer could see that this was an older, small-scale park. The Ferris wheel and roller coaster appeared to be the zenith of the ride attractions. No two-hundred-foot free falls, no sky coasters, no Hollywood-scale high-tech illusions, no rides that promised to separate mind from matter. Fun Time was a kinder, gentler amusement park. Sadly Summer guessed that was the actual reason for its demise. "I guess it just couldn't survive today's world," she murmured.

Jack studied her face, then draped an arm around her shoulders. She sensed the comfort in his touch and allowed him to pull her close. "Everything has its time, Summer."

"I know. It's silly. I don't have an emotional investment in this place. I didn't even know it existed before today."

"That's why your heart's pure," he chided gently.

She smiled in the growing dusk. Then she spotted a pay telephone. "I wish I could call my mother. I know I can't, but I always feel so much better when I connect with her."

He nodded in understanding, but a flicker of pain crossed his face. "Nothing can take the place of family."

Summer felt the breach between them, regretted its cause, ached for the result.

Jack tried again to reach Tom Matthews without success. Quietly they walked together toward the Fun Time Hotel. But when they reached the inn, it was discouragingly dark.

"They've probably cut back to alternative electricity." Jack pointed to the few small overhead lights. "Just enough output for a few security spots."

Summer glanced at the deserted building. "The place looks as though it's still waiting for guests."

"Let's see if we can get inside."

The doors were firmly double locked, dead bolts in place. It seemed the owners had taken greater care in securing the hotel. They prowled the perimeter, searching for a breach in security.

"It doesn't look like we're going to get inside," Summer commented, absently patting Danny, who was kicking his feet, clearly ready to be let down to roam.

"Maybe..." Jack continued searching. "Here it is."

Summer looked, but all she could see was some metal tubing next to the basement window. "It looks like some kind of vent."

"Laundry vent," Jack agreed.

"I don't mean to be pessimistic, but we can't fit down that tube."

"No, but if I can loosen the vent, I can pry open the window."

Summer watched, amazed as Jack did exactly that. "Was one of your jobs burglarizing?"

"I try to stay on the right side of the law since that's why I'm on the run."

She smiled ruefully. "Good point."

"If you'll take Danny, I'll go in through the window and then open the door."

Summer took Danny from the backpack. "Let's go around the front, okay, big guy?"

He waved his arms and wriggled his legs, clearly wanting to get down.

"Not yet," she told him as they walked toward the front of the hotel. "We have to wait while Daddy checks to see if we have a reservation."

She heard a few thumps and clanks and winced, suspecting that Jack was connecting with more than he'd bargained for in the dark basement.

"Summer!"

She heard the call and increased her pace. "How are the accommodations?"

"Dark for the moment. I'm going to find the generator."

"Do you think that's wise?"

"Don't worry. I don't plan on a light-works display."

Summer climbed the steps to the porch of the hotel. She peered inside, but utter darkness greeted her. An involuntary shiver gripped her, and she cuddled Danny closer. "Let's wait for Daddy out here, okay?"

When she heard Jack's footsteps, she sighed in relief. Then a sudden, unwanted thought struck. What if it wasn't him? "Jack?" she called tentatively.

A beam of light flicked on, momentarily blinding her. It was lowered immediately. "I found a flashlight in the shed along with some candles."

Some of the fright lodged in her throat decreased slightly. "And the generator?"

He shook his head. "Not worth the time it took to find it. They only left connections to a few rides."

Summer trailed him inside, noting that with candlelight the interior didn't seem nearly as frightening. "It's kind of sad, isn't it? This place just being left to decay."

Jack walked around the room, pulling drapes so the light couldn't be spotted from the road. "I didn't realize you were so sentimental."

She was glad the near darkness hid the flush of her cheeks. "Permanence seems like something of yesterday, something no one values anymore."

"Sometimes life doesn't let you have permanence," Jack replied tightly.

No, and it wouldn't let this make-believe relationship become real, she realized with a pang. Because as he'd just reminded her, Jack couldn't have anything permanent in his life. She had to remember that their fictitious relationship was just that, despite her desire for it to be more.

Jack continued lighting more candles, then discovered a

full candelabra on the sideboard. Once lit, the room seemed warmer, less deserted looking.

"It looks better now." Summer glanced around. Shrouded furniture begged to be uncovered. "If we can find the dining room, we could eat. I imagine Danny's hungry."

"Good idea. You okay in here while I grab the food? I left it on the porch."

"Sure." So Jack had noticed her fright. Apparently she wasn't very good at concealing her feelings. She would have to watch that. She didn't want him to know of the longing that seized her for things that couldn't be....

Packing Danny on her hip, Summer located the dining room, uncovering a small table that would fit the three of them perfectly. Following Jack's example, she drew the drapes. Giving in to a whim, she used the flashlight to locate china plates. Holding her breath, she turned on the faucet in the kitchen, and to her relief water poured out. Admittedly it was brackish looking to begin with, but then it cleared.

Jack appeared behind her. "What're you doing?"

"Washing plates."

Jack placed his candles on the counter, then reached out and took Danny. "Is this an occasion?"

"Not really. It's just that this hotel and park seem like something out of the past, and maybe for the evening we could pretend that we've stepped back, as well."

"Pretend that the real world isn't out there?" he asked quietly.

"Something like that."

"That rarely lasts for long," he reminded her. Then his tone gentled. "But I don't suppose there's any harm in it for an evening."

That sly stroke of warmth crept in again. "I think I can find some glasses, too."

"We can use them. Cyndi slipped some wine into our food supply."

Summer's hands stilled for a moment. "I really liked her."

"Good." He shifted Danny. "She couldn't say enough nice things about you. Thought we made the perfect family."

Summer's gaze flew to meet his. But the dim light made it nearly impossible to read what lurked there. "It seems we've become masters of illusion."

Silence thundered between them.

Another beat passed before Jack spoke. "So it does." He picked up the freshly washed plates and carried them into the dining room.

Summer kicked the base of the cabinets beneath her, wishing she could retract the words. Stalling, she found silverware and glasses. Hunting a little farther afield, she located a linen tablecloth and napkins that were neatly pressed and folded. It was almost as though they'd been left there in anticipation of just such an event.

Taking a deep breath, she reentered the dining room. To her surprise, Jack had filled the room with candles. It seemed he'd lit all the candles he had found. Delighted, Summer smoothed the linen cloth over the table, then carefully arranged the place settings. She noticed that Jack had placed the food on the sideboard. It wasn't a terribly elegant selection, still he had fashioned it into a buffet of sorts.

She was wondering where Jack had gone when he appeared in the doorway. Holding Danny, he approached. Raising one hand, he offered her a small bouquet of flowers. "For you."

"Where in the world...?" Touched, she accepted the flowers, bending to sniff their sweet fragrance.

"Just wildflowers," he explained. "Growing in the uncut grass."

"They're better than hothouse roses," she murmured. "I think I can find something to put them in." She couldn't find a vase, but an old-fashioned glass pitcher worked almost as well.

While Summer looked for the container, Jack had located a high chair. Danny seemed content to sit in it, banging his cup against the wooden tray.

She smiled. "Looks like we're all set."

Jack watched her as she put the flowers on the table. With the increased light from all the candles, Summer could see more clearly. It seemed that his eyes darkened to nearly black. She wondered if it was a trick of the candlelight or her revved-up imagination. Suddenly nervous, she fiddled with the silverware as they filled their plates.

"This isn't exactly what I promised you, is it?" Jack asked quietly as they took their seats. "I didn't expect to keep you away from your home for so long, certainly not for a week."

Summer shrugged. "I doubt either of us could have anticipated what would happen."

"And now that Fisher and Wilcox know about you, I've put you in just as much danger."

Glancing up, she met his eyes, saw the regret etched there. "You didn't plan it. And you couldn't prevent it. Besides, it was my choice."

Jack reached over to gently disengage Danny's fingers as they curled around Summer's hair. He allowed his hand to linger for a moment before withdrawing it. "I'm not even certain it's safe for you to return home until this is resolved."

A spurt of fear erupted. "My mother—?"

"Shouldn't be in any danger. I'm not really certain they know your identity. But, if they do and they're close enough to trail us and you head for Edisto, they might split up and follow you."

So they were in this for the long haul, Summer realized. But as quickly she remembered that once they found sanctuary, their charade would end. Despite the feelings that she had developed for Jack, he would walk away. And once again, she would be left alone.

Silently chastising herself, Summer wondered how she

could have learned so little from her relationship with Tyson. Hadn't her disastrous ending with him been enough proof that trust no longer existed? That such fantasies were the stuff of fairy tales...that genuine happily-ever-afters didn't happen?

Jack leaned over, his hand gently bracketing her jaw as he tipped her face upward. "I'm sorry, Summer. You didn't ask to be part of this, and now I've fouled up your life. But I'll do whatever I can to make it up to you." A strange emotion darted through his expression, then vanished. "If that means setting things right with anyone who might be in your life, I'll do it."

What little appetite Summer had suddenly disappeared. "Let's just get you guys to safety, okay? Let me worry about my relationships."

His lips tightened, then relaxed briefly. "Of course."

A plate clanged as it hit the floor. Danny looked down at the damage he'd just caused, then banged his spoon on the tray.

The emotionally charged moment dissipated as they bent to clean up the mess.

"Okay, mister," Jack told him. "No more of that." He retrieved the sticky spoon. "I'll grab a towel."

Summer nodded slowly, her gaze focusing on Danny. Seeing he had her attention, the baby smiled winningly, his few teeth winking in the candlelight. "There's that jack-o'-lantern grin," she told him, her voice hitching. How was she going to walk away from him, as well?

"I guess he's bored," Jack apologized, returning to wipe up the baby food.

"Maybe we could take a walk around the park later," Summer managed, hoping she sounded normal. "If you think it's safe."

"It should be all right. Fisher and Wilcox have no reason to believe we took this side road." He paused. "You know, it's a good thing Cyndi packed all this food. It looked like the cupboards were bare in the storeroom."

"Probably to keep bugs and rodents away," she agreed, not particularly caring if the hotel had any food.

"Right."

The conversation between them remained strained as they finished dinner. Summer offered to clean up Danny as an excuse to escape the tension. But then, too soon, she ran out of excuses.

Jack held a flashlight as they picked their way across the grounds. "No telling just what's out here. Looks like this place has been empty for quite a while."

"It's old," Summer agreed.

Jack pointed upward. "You're right. That's a wooden roller coaster. Aren't too many of those left."

They strolled beside the closed concession stands, then through the alley of games that faded signs proclaimed once contained ring toss, darts and other games of chance.

"You can almost smell the cotton candy," Jack said, shifting Danny in his arms.

"Now who's the sentimentalist?" Summer teased. But she took a deep breath of the clean night air. "You forgot to mention the popcorn."

"I'm more of a caramel-corn kind of guy," he said with a grin.

"Ah. That explains it."

Danny chortled as Jack put him up on his shoulders as he swaggered down the sidewalk.

A matching set, Summer thought. They so belonged together. She couldn't imagine anything happening to either one of them. She guessed that Fisher and Wilcox wouldn't have any reason to harm Danny, but they could use him to flush out Jack if they ever got their hands on him, which put the toddler in equal peril.

Glancing upward, Summer spotted a moon that dominated the sky much like a Vegas headliner with lesser stars forming a background. The thought made her smile.

They walked past the flying-swings ride. Elaborate carvings graced the scalloped top encircling the ride. Old-style pictures of elaborately coiffed women of the nineteenth century decorated each cotton-candy-colored panel.

A little farther on, they came to the rides for toddlers. Miniature boats still floated in a circular tank. She and Danny both laughed in delight when Jack put him in one of the boats and pushed it by hand.

"The tiniest captain!" she exclaimed when Jack lifted him out of the boat.

Together they strolled along until they reached the carousel. "Look at it!" Summer exclaimed.

The carousel was an anachronism straight out of the Victorian era. Hand-carved horses galloped alongside a delightful assortment of other creatures. A sea dragon, giraffe, lion, zebra, tiger and frog marched in place alongside the horses.

Jack paused to run a hand appreciatively over a unicorn figurine. "These are probably at least a hundred years old. Collectors would pay top price for each one."

"Really?"

"They're considered American folk art. That's why there aren't too many of these carousels left. People break them up and sell the figurines separately."

"That's terrible!"

Jack shrugged. "From an architectural viewpoint, I agree. But they can easily sell for eighty-five thousand dollars each. With over one hundred figurines on a carousel, that's a considerable chunk of change."

"Even so, can you put a price on history? On something that can never be recaptured?"

Jack reached out to tuck a strand of wayward hair behind her ear. "I thought you were so practical. You keep surprising me, Summer."

She wished suddenly that she could always go on surprising him, that it wasn't completely bizarre to consider a future. "How's this for a surprise? I wish we could ride on it."

He grinned. "That's easily arranged."

"But—?"

"The generator's hooked up to some of the rides. If you'll keep Danny reined in, I'll turn it on."

"Is it safe?" Summer questioned, wanting to ride, but worried about attracting attention.

"For now. I don't know how long we'll stay here. I wouldn't risk it again after tonight. Fisher and Wilcox might backtrack when they don't catch up to us. But we should be okay now."

She reached for Danny, and Jack disappeared into the darkness. As she watched, lights on the elaborately carved roof flickered on. Bulbs of all different colors glowed against the many shades of turquoise and yellow. Each panel was decorated in a nineteenth-century motif. As the carousel groaned to life, music wheezed from the bellows-like pipes.

Jack appeared, holding out his hand in invitation. Barely hesitating, she accepted it, allowing him to capture her fingers in his strong grasp. With her other hand, she clung to Danny as they climbed aboard the carousel.

"Should we be doing this?" she whispered, her voice a mix of dread and excitement as she considered the consequences. She didn't need to form any more memories that would haunt her in the lonely days ahead.

"This once—yes."

Excitement won out as she picked an exotic-looking giraffe to ride on. Jack reached out and easily took Danny in his hands. Then he flicked on the start button before choosing a white stallion across and just slightly behind her. Unexpectedly dazzled, she was immediately reminded of a white knight as Jack sat astride the wooden horse. The carousel gained speed as the figurines moved up and down in accompaniment to the music.

Glancing over at Jack and Danny, she was again struck by the sight of the two of them. Jack, so tall and strong. Danny, so tiny and trusting. Fleetingly she thought of Tyson, his rigid principles, his determination to succeed at any cost. Somehow she couldn't picture him with a child in his arms.

But how could she trust her own judgment and instincts? Experience told her that she'd chosen poorly before. Was this just another illusion? Despite knowing what they shared couldn't be real, that no future was in store for them, Summer opened her heart. Even the mere possibility made her emotions soar.

Jack stood suddenly, putting Danny in the small Mother Goose side car, strapping him in firmly. Then he walked toward her.

"What are you doing?" she asked with a laugh, watching him maintain his balance despite the motion of the merry-go-round.

"I don't remember you buying a ticket for this ride." The corners of his lips edged upward, and his eyes glinted dangerously.

Summer only laughed harder. "The ticket taker was on a break."

Reaching her, Jack shook his head. "That's too bad. No ticket, no ride."

Still giggling, she saw that his eyes were changing, darkening with intent. Summer's laughter trickled away as a different emotion gripped her. And as she spoke, she discovered she was breathless, as well. "What did you have in mind?"

He swung closer with the motion of the carousel, his body now mere inches from hers. "I think we could come up with an acceptable forfeit."

"Sort of a token payment?" she questioned, her breath coming even shorter.

His hands closed over hers as she clung to the pole at the top of the giraffe. "More than a token."

"More?" Summer echoed. Then she watched in fascination as his hands lifted, one to rest at the hollow of her back, the other bracketing her chin.

"More," he affirmed. Then with painstaking slowness,

Jack tilted his head toward hers, his mouth seeking and finding hers.

Light and dark flashed as the sensations kindled. Summer fleetingly wondered if she was seeing the lights of the carousel or the stars...or simply feeling the flare of the fire he ignited.

His kiss was a gentle explosion, one that she willingly accepted. One of Jack's hands moved to cup the back of her neck. Like a willow bending to a persuasive wind, she leaned into his hold. As the exploration continued, deepened, incited, Summer loosened her hold on the carved figurine, instead weaving her fingers through the longish hair that rested on Jack's collar.

Like travelers finding exciting new destinations, they reveled in each discovery. And each visit was better than the last.

When Jack finally pulled away, Summer lifted one hand to gently touch his face, to trace the lines of his strong jaw, the more tender flesh of his lips.

"Da!" Danny called. "Da!"

Summer and Jack glanced back at the toddler, who looked as though his small face was about to crumple into tears at being left alone.

Reluctantly Jack released his hold on Summer and returned to his son. Unbelting him, Jack lifted Danny into his arms, then sat with him again on the white horse.

Her knight, Summer thought, watching them. Jack was making Danny smile again, and in moments both were laughing. Jack lifted Danny's arm, waving toward Summer. Valiantly she waved back, incredibly touched by both of them.

"We're gaining on you," Jack told her with a grin.

Secure in his father's arms, Danny flashed that sweet baby smile.

Over the lump in her throat, she managed to laugh, knowing her eyes were bright with unshed tears. "Want to make a wager on that?"

"You doubting us?" he questioned with a mock frown.

The carousel continued circling, the music danced across the night air and the stars lit the sky. "Never," she murmured. "Never."

Chapter 11

"I hate to leave," Summer said quietly as the amusement park disappeared from sight. "I felt safe there."

"Also hungry," Jack pointed out. "Food was the one accommodation the owner didn't leave us, and Danny's down to his last jars of baby food."

"You're right," she agreed.

Jack studied the rearview mirror, wondering just what route Fisher and Wilcox had taken. Dusk was overtaking the day, and soon all he'd be able to see would be the flash of anonymous headlights. He, too, hated to leave the relative safety of the amusement park, but they had stayed an extra day there, hoping to let their trail grow cold. Not knowing if there was a regular security patrol, they had been taking a huge risk by delaying. And although Summer had never complained about the minimized rations, he refused to have her going hungry.

Summer's calm temperament was a wonder. But that made him feel even guiltier. Jack glanced over at her, and wondered how he'd ever dismissed her. "Summer?"

"Yes?"

"I've been thinking."

"Good. One of us should be," she joked mildly.

"This would be a good time for you to get out. I know I told you it's not safe to return home, but you could go somewhere else, somewhere safe."

"What?" Shock colored her voice and darkened her eyes.

"I can't justify endangering you anymore." Jack thought of the kiss they'd shared, the tenderness he felt for her. He couldn't bear to think of bringing her to harm.

"We've already had this discussion," Summer retorted, a flush coloring her cheeks.

Why did she have to be so stubborn? It was difficult enough to let her go. "I don't want to blackmail you anymore. Danny and I will be fine."

"You haven't *blackmailed* me! I've helped because I want to." Summer twisted her hands anxiously. "Do you honestly think I could have a moment's peace not knowing if you two got to Washington okay?"

"I could call," he tried.

"Great! The only place I have to go is home and you said that might not be safe. So you're going to phone me…where? And since I wouldn't know how to locate you, I guess I could call you…..let's see…where? Gee, that sounds like a great plan."

Jack concealed the flinch he felt, knowing she was right. "If you insist on staying, then we have to find a spot that's really safe."

She slanted an ironic glance at him. "I thought that's what we've been trying to do."

"This time, we try harder."

Sunlight had long since struggled to replace the fading night as they rolled into a midsize, tucked-away town, nestled in the Virginia countryside. Even though she was exhausted, Summer noticed that the place fairly screamed bucolic.

"Where are we?" she asked, unsuccessfully stifling a yawn.

"Caleb Corners. It's remote enough to be a good hiding spot for a few days, but large enough that strangers go unnoticed."

Summer stared out the window. "I guess in a really small town everybody knows everybody and we'd be pretty obvious."

"Like flies on whipped cream. That's why people usually head to big cities to hide out, but we don't exactly have a glut of big cities to choose from on the route to D.C."

She glanced around at the gently rolling hills, the neat, carpeted fields punctuated by white farmhouses, sturdy barns and silos. It was a town that could have been conjured up from the pages of a Laura Ingalls Wilder book.

After driving past the surrounding countryside, they entered a prosperous-looking town. Old rock buildings attested to Caleb Corners's historical base while newer buildings spoke of continuing growth.

"It's a gingerbread town," she blurted out impulsively, immediately liking what she saw.

"Gingerbread?"

Summer squirmed, then sheepishly met his glance. "It's what I call places like…Caleb Corners. Places that seem warm, welcoming."

A few seconds passed.

"That's how it was," Jack admitted. "It's probably why I thought it could be again…why I thought this place might be *really* safe. And if Fisher and Wilcox checked out all the places I've lived, they should have come and gone from here already."

She nodded. Although Summer knew her instincts weren't as finely tuned as Jack's, she did know that this place simply felt better than the others had. Most of the mistakes she had made in her life had come from not following her instincts, not listening to the small voice of warning.

As they passed through the town, Summer wondered at the life Jack had been forced to lead since he had turned state's evidence. She guessed at times his small voice of warning must have sounded like a wailing banshee.

Then Jack slowed down. Braking, he parked and Summer looked at him in surprise. They had stopped in front of a Victorian-era church. Complete with a soaring steeple, the graceful old building could have been drawn from an old-time postcard.

"I was a handyman here after I joined the program," Jack explained.

Summer's eyes softened. "That must have been so difficult, working on buildings instead of designing them."

"I didn't have a lot of choices. But this was a good place to be."

"With good people?" she questioned, guessing the answer.

"Let me put it this way. This contact is trustworthy, certainly more trustworthy than Bart was."

"Why is that so easy for me to believe?"

Despite his fatigue, Jack managed a grin. "Good instincts."

"You reading my mind?" she asked, thinking that only moments had passed since she had been considering her instincts.

He cocked his head.

Summer waved away his question. "Never mind. Should we see if we're welcome?"

"I doubt that Pastor Steiger and his wife have changed. With them, what you see is what you get. No hidden agendas."

Despite her fatigue, Summer smiled. The Steigers sounded like just the prescription they needed after the harrowing journey they'd been on. Especially when the older couple whipped open the door, pulling them inside and gushing over Danny.

"This is my wife, Summer," Jack completed the introductions, seeing the Steigers exchange a pleased glance.

Summer managed not to widen her eyes at the introduction, smiling as she was drawn into their warm welcome.

"We're pleased to meet you," Don Steiger told her warmly, extending his hand.

"It's so wonderful," Mary Steiger exclaimed, her lively brown eyes dancing. "You've married and now a baby, too!"

Startled, Summer's gaze skipped to Jack's, but he glanced away. So, the Steigers hadn't known about Danny. Had Jack lived here before Danny had been born? Before he'd known what would happen to his late wife?

"And we've redecorated the guest room," Mary continued, oblivious to Summer's confusion. "We've changed things around a bit. Actually it used to be the gardener's cottage, and we've turned it into a guest house." She turned to Summer. "A *tiny* guest house, I'm afraid! But it should be just right for newlyweds."

"I'm sure we'll be very comfortable," Summer managed to respond, thinking again of spending time in an intimate room with Jack. Somehow *comfortable* didn't come to mind.

But Mary was clapping petite hands together. "And we have a wonderful nursery now, too."

"For our first grandchild," Don Steiger inserted. "She's a beauty. But the nursery's coed since we're hoping for more in time."

"And little Danny will love it," Mary enthused, reaching out for the baby.

Reluctantly Jack released him. "I'm...we're used to keeping him close."

"Ah, but you're practically honeymooners," Mary dismissed. "And little ones love having honorary grandparents around to spoil them rotten."

Helplessly Summer gazed at Jack. It seemed once again Danny had charmed his way into someone's heart.

"Jack, you must have heard our prayers because we can sure use you again," Don told him as Mary clucked over the baby. "The belfry roof is leaking." He shook his head. "And the list of repairs at the chapel might send you running."

"I don't think so, Pastor. It's good to be back here."

"Let's get you settled," Mary told them, still holding the baby. "Are you hungry?" Not giving them a chance to answer, she continued. "Of course, you must be. And I bet this little guy would like some of my homemade applesauce."

"Pastor, do you mind if I pull the truck into the old carriage house?" Jack asked, thinking he would feel better when the vehicle was out of sight.

"Certainly. There's room out there for half a dozen cars. You don't have to ask, son. Treat this like your home. We're happy to have you back with us."

Summer felt a prickle of grateful tears and bit down on her lip. Clearly the Steigers thought highly of Jack. And remarkably she already felt safe.

It didn't take long to unload their luggage and to install themselves in the guest house. As soon as the door closed behind Mary and Don, Summer whirled around. "Okay, spill it. How can the Steigers not know about Danny? I'm guessing we're not going to these safe houses in the same order you did originally."

Jack sighed, rubbing a weary hand over the day's stubble. He needed a shave, a hot shower and a hot meal. But clearly he was going to have to do some talking first. And that bothered him more than putting off the other three.

Reluctantly he began. "I told you my wife got caught in the cross fire that put her in a coma. Danny wasn't born yet. Eventually he was delivered by C-section." He paused, remembering. Pain and guilt still accompanied the memories. Clearing his throat, Jack continued. "I wanted to stay with Linda day and night. She was in protective custody within the hospital. I was afraid to leave her alone, afraid that someone would slip by the guards and get to her. But only one attempt was made—and it wasn't on Linda. It was on me.''

Jack walked toward the window, pushing the drapes aside and opening the pane so that fresh air rushed in. ''Tom Matthews convinced me that staying by Linda's side was putting her in danger. She wasn't the bait—I was. If...I left, she'd be safer.''

''So you left?'' Summer questioned.

He nodded. ''That's when I entered the program, and this is where I came first. Since Danny hadn't been born yet, the Steigers never saw him.''

''So we're both a surprise,'' Summer concluded softly.

''Yes.''

''Did they know you were married?''

Jack laughed bitterly. ''I told them I was a widower. I didn't know at the time it would be prophetic.''

She flinched, feeling his pain. ''Saying it didn't make it come true.''

He shrugged, but Summer could see the tension in his posture, the stiffness in his set expression. ''Maybe not. But I caused the situation that got her shot, then I wasn't there for her when she died.''

''You didn't cause it!'' Summer denied hotly. ''You did the right thing. Surely you don't believe Linda would have wanted you to stand by and do nothing?''

Since they were chillingly close to the reassurances Linda herself had offered, Jack didn't reply.

''From what I can sense about her, Linda wasn't the kind of person who would have wanted you to take the easy way out.'' Her voice softened. ''And I think she would approve of how you're raising Danny...how he's going to turn out because of you.''

A look of gratitude flickered in Jack's eyes.

Summer realized they were dealing with his innermost

feelings and decided she should back off in the face of his pain. "You're right. The Steigers seem like lovely people. Are you okay about having Danny in the nursery instead of with you?"

Belatedly Jack stared around the tiny cottage. Mary had decorated it in English country style, filling it with cabbage roses, plaid slipcovers and mellow pictures of hunting dogs, all meant to soothe and relax. But his eyes fell on the lone bed. The brass four-poster was a narrow double, a bed meant for one person, or two people on very good terms.

"Jack?"

Distracted, he glanced back at her. "Yes?"

"Are you okay about having Danny in the nursery?" she repeated.

"For now. We can put his playpen up and then snag him later. Right now, I could use about forty-eight hours of sleep."

In unison, their gazes fell on the solitary bed.

"Or a shower," Summer blurted, then wanted to kick herself. In a flash, she remembered barging in on a very naked Jack as he had showered. Every detail of the moment jumped out in her memory, sending warm blood to her cheeks.

Jack's gaze settled on her, and the warmth spread. A dangerous tension simmered in the air.

A quiet knock on the door startled them both.

Jack turned first, quickly moving to open the door.

"Sorry to interrupt," Pastor Steiger began. "Mary's got some hot soup and roast-beef sandwiches almost ready. She thought one of you might want to take a shower in the main house, rather than wait on this one."

Seizing that excuse to escape, Summer spoke up quickly. "How very kind of her." She grabbed her still packed bag. "I'll take her up on the offer."

As she scuttled out the door, she dared a look at Jack and knew she hadn't left the conflict behind.

* * *

Summer hadn't expected to resolve that conflict by singing. But that was what she was doing after she had stumbled onto choir practice at the church.

Enthusiastically she had been welcomed by the choirmaster, Chandler Morris. When Summer had admitted to being able to carry a few notes, she had been drafted.

And now, as Jack planed a sticking chapel door, Summer harmonized to the first song. A surreptitious glance around told her most of the other members were older women.

After the first song, the director looked at Summer keenly.

Nervously she smiled back.

"Looks like we could have a soloist in our midst," Chandler told her, not bothering to disguise the glee in his voice.

"Oh, no..." Summer tried to protest.

"We won't make you sing a solo the first time." Chandler paused for effect. "But after your second Sunday, nothing's sacred," he punned.

Summer could only stare. That would be keeping low-key, being the center of attention as the church soloist.

Ethel, a woman she had just been introduced to and who stood next to her, patted her arm in comfort. "Don't worry about Chandler. He always acts like a shark going after a fresh kill."

"So I should think of myself more as bait than a soloist?"

"Not much of a comfort, is it?" she responded sympathetically. "We'll try and draw him off the scent, if you like. But with a voice like yours, he's not going to give up permanently."

Summer cataloged this information, hoping they'd be in D.C. before she had to outwit the choirmaster.

"Where's Mary?" Frances, the woman next to Ethel, asked as the director turned again toward Summer.

Distracted, Chandler responded, "She'll be along."

Summer's brows rose. Mary was watching Danny…or at least that was what she understood.

Ethel turned to Summer. "Mary's our pastor's wife."

Summer nodded, but just then Mary rushed down the aisle, her arms filled with Danny and his carrier.

A collective aah sounded from the women in the choir.

"That's not your granddaughter!" one exclaimed, stepping down to greet Mary.

"Of course not," Mary agreed. "This is Danny." She glanced up toward the choir loft. "He's Jack and Summer Anderson's little boy."

Now the chorus of oohs and aahs was redirected toward Summer.

"You didn't tell us about the little charmer!" Ethel exclaimed. "How old is he?"

"Eleven months. He's—"

"Adorable!" Frances chimed in. "Simply adorable!"

"No wonder you're late to choir practice," another woman told Mary. "You couldn't pry me away from a baby that sweet!"

"Which is why he's coming to choir practice," Mary told them. "I've absolutely monopolized the little guy since the Andersons arrived and I started feeling guilty—thought his mother might like to see him."

When almost the entire choir turned in a simultaneous motion to look at her, Summer managed to smile weakly. "That was very kind of you."

"I brought this." Mary held up the carrier. "I thought we could put Danny right up front by you."

When Mary brought Danny closer, he chortled as he recognized Summer. "Hey, there," Summer greeted him softly, her smile tender.

"He'll help Mom sing," Mary explained. She leaned closer so only Summer could hear. "And keep her from getting too bored."

Surprised, Summer smiled at the twinkle in Mary's eye. But actually she was enjoying herself. While she wasn't a musical wonder, she had always enjoyed singing. And somehow with Danny at her feet so she could gently rock his carrier and hear his happy laugh, it seemed even more enjoyable.

Summer's mind wandered, and she imagined how it would be to sing little Danny to sleep each night, to know that every morning she would be greeted by that precious smile.

"Summer." Ethel tugged at her sleeve.

"Oh, I'm sorry. My mind was wandering," Summer apologized, wondering how long she'd been daydreaming.

"No problem," Ethel said with a laugh. "When my children were little, I took every possible opportunity for a mental vacation. We're taking a break, and I'm going to set up the coffee and doughnuts in the recreation hall. You want to come along?"

Mary and a few other women were crowding around, as well. Summer reached down and picked up Danny, giving him a cuddle.

"Don't monopolize her," Frances chided. "She'll want to get to know everyone."

Guiltily Summer looked at the circle of friendly, welcoming faces. She didn't know if they would be in Caleb Corners for a day or a week, but she did know she wouldn't be joining their community. And a bit of regret washed over her. To these women, she and Jack and Danny were the ideal young family. If they only knew.

"I'd be happy to help with the refreshments. Then Danny and I are going to beg off. It's been a really long day." The sleepless night was catching up to her in a big way.

"No need for you to help," Mary intervened. "I don't know what I was thinking. Of course you've had a long day. You and Danny go settle in for the night and I'll bring over a pot of tea—unless you'd rather I take Danny," she added hopefully.

Summer's grip on Danny tightened, realizing she didn't

want to give him up again so soon. "Actually I'd like to have him close."

Mary's smile was understanding, if regretful. "Of course."

"But you don't have to bring us tea," Summer added, not wanting to inconvenience her gracious host. "In fact, I can help with—"

"Shoo! Now, out with you," Mary replied. "I'll grab that tea and be over in a shot and then we'll all leave you alone."

"I'll see you on Sunday," Ethel told her. "We'll give you the third degree then." Summer's eyes flew open in shock, but the older woman was giving Danny's arm a friendly maternal pat. "I might complain about the days when my children were little, but I'd give anything to have that time back again." Her voice tightened, and a trace of tears glinted suspiciously at the corners of her eyes. "But once it's gone, it's gone. So you enjoy."

Her mind reeling with advice and welcoming words, Summer retreated to the tiny cottage. With Danny securely wedged at her hip, Summer glanced around, seeing the touches that spoke of Jack's presence. With a start, she realized she had become accustomed to the masculine accessories—from the blue jean jacket tossed casually over the back of a chair to the razor and manly-smelling soap in the bathroom.

"Looks like Daddy's been here."

"Da," Danny responded.

"He'll probably be back soon." Summer wondered if the butterflies in her stomach signaled anticipation or dread.

Danny's plump fingers curled around her thumb. Once again, his utter trust sent a rush of warmth through her.

"But after your bath, we have plenty of time for a story...." She paused. "And a song, if you like."

Within a short time, she had him bathed, powdered and dressed in his sleeper. Sweet-smelling, sweet-tempered, he was truly a joy.

Glancing around, Summer realized she hadn't thought to prepare a nighttime bottle for him. Just then, the intercom buzzed.

It took her a moment to locate the panel on the wall. Hesitantly she pushed the button. "Yes?"

"Summer? I have your tea and a bottle for Danny. Are you ready for me to bring it over?" Mary asked.

"You're too good to be true," Summer exclaimed. "I was just thinking I'd forgotten about Danny's bottle."

"Jack brought over some formula this afternoon. I had him collect bottles so they could get a good wash through the dishwasher. But there is a tiny fridge and microwave in the cottage to use later. Is this a good time to come over?"

"Certainly," Summer agreed, not really wanting to take Danny out in the night air right after his bath.

"I'll be right there," Mary replied.

"Your fairy godmother will be over momentarily with a bottle," Summer told Danny. "We're awfully lucky, you know." The irony of those words struck her. The child and his father were running for their lives, hardly an ideal situation, yet the Steigers had given her a renewed sense of hope. Surely something good would come of this.

Within a few short minutes, Mary brought over the tea and Danny's bottle. "I won't stay," she began. "You're probably both beat. I know Jack must be, too, but men always act so stoic, don't they?" Mary laughed as she headed toward the door. "But if you change your mind about needing some help with Danny, just buzz me on the intercom. I'll be over in a flash."

"You've been wonderful. Thank you so much."

Mary hesitated, then turned back. "We think a lot of Jack. I don't know as I ever met anyone in such pain. Not that he ever talked about it," she hastened to add. "But you could tell. One look and you could see loneliness, despair—he was a walking raw wound." Mary's expression brightened. "But he's completely different now. And I suspect you're the cause."

Startled, Summer gaped, unable to reply.

Mary only smiled. "You're good for him, and we're grateful to you for that. We've thought about Jack since he left. We've prayed for him...and hoped for him. It's good to know our prayers have been answered." With a smile, she left, closing the door quietly behind her.

Summer stared at the closed door. Only when Danny flailed his arms and struggled to get down did she move. Could the Steigers be imagining what they wanted to see? Or could there possibly be some truth to Mary's observations?

"What do you think, little one?" she asked Danny, twining her fingers so that he wrapped his hands over them.

Spotting a rocking chair by the window that she didn't remember seeing before, Summer shook her head in wonder. Mary Steiger was truly a kind and thoughtful woman. No doubt she'd had her husband bring the chair over while they had been otherwise occupied during choir practice. "Look, Danny. A special chair, one for just you and me."

His huge eyes fastened on her, obviously enjoying the sound of her voice. Encouraged, Summer settled with him in the rocking chair, watching as the light breeze gently ruffled the curtains. "Well, punkin, what story shall it be? *The Three Little Bears? Cinderella?* The 'Rugrats' meet the kids from 'South Park' and set them straight?" She laughed softly. "Or how 'bout how silly Summer met Prince Charming and found out he was really Prince Nowhere?"

Danny gurgled as his hands curled around the bottle, clutching it firmly. He was strong for a little guy. She held his warm body close as she thought of her broken engagement, the man to whom she had devoted four years of her life. Tyson had stolen more than her heart; he'd pilfered her trust, as well, and it was one theft that couldn't be replaced.

"I guess I wasn't very smart," Summer confided. "I thought all two people needed was love. I didn't know that social contacts and networking were just as important."

Danny cradled his head on her chest, and Summer stroked his silky hair. "But I guess they are...to some people." She thought again of the pain she had felt when without warning, Tyson broke off their engagement to marry another woman who possessed more social contacts—alliances that would further his career.

"For four years, he delayed the wedding and I built my life around him. When he decided to marry someone else, it knocked the props out from under me."

Danny's eyelids drooped.

Summer laughed humorlessly. "I know. It's not the most exciting story. I guess I should have stuck to *The Three Little Pigs.*"

The bottle began to slide from Danny's slack lips, and Summer gently retrieved it. "So, little one, how 'bout a song instead?" His head slumped to one side. Tenderly she stroked his soft skin as she adjusted him in her arms. In a soft, clear voice, she sang him a lullaby. Summer was surprised at how easily the words she remembered from her own childhood came back to her.

Reluctant to put him in the portable crib, she continued rocking, singing the songs of her childhood, allowing the soft moonbeams to illuminate the dimly lit room.

How was she going to walk away from this tiny person once Jack found Tom Matthews? Could she put her heart on hold again, pretend that the pain didn't matter?

She thought of Jack, working into the night despite the harrowing events of the past forty-eight hours. So much strength and determination. Another, sharper doubt assailed her. How would she be able to walk away from him? Would these wounds be the ones she couldn't put behind her? The ones that would change her forever?

Chapter 12

Jack stared across the church lawn, watching as Summer played with Danny. The Steigers had a baby seat on their ancient swing set, and Danny was loving being pushed in it.

A gentle breeze ruffled the elegant arms of the weeping willow as it shaded the verdant green lawn. Trees even older than the historic church building lent a permanence to the area. It was one of the things that had attracted him to the church. That and a need to be near something that might help him understand why his life had gone so crazily askew.

While the officials in the witness-protection program had chosen Caleb Corners because of its remoteness and population profile, Jack had found the job on his own. Initially Sedgewick, Jack's contact in the program, hadn't thought it would be a good idea for Jack to get a job. He felt that Jack's concentration would be so poor that he would attract attention.

After three days of idleness, Jack had ignored his mentor's advice and found this job on his own. And for some reason, he had never told Sedgewick about it. Part of it was a desire to have something in his life that was his own, something that hadn't been examined beneath a microscope and then hung out for everyone to see. Later, when Jack had moved from his apartment to the Steigers' guest room, he hadn't informed Sedgewick. His mail had continued to be delivered to the post-office box. And Jack had always contacted Sedgewick since it hadn't been considered safe for anyone in the program to call hidden witnesses.

Now Jack was immensely glad that he hadn't shared that knowledge. Fisher and Wilcox could learn about Caleb Corners, along with all the other towns he had lived in, but they wouldn't know just where to look. If he and Summer could keep a low profile, this could be a safe hideout.

He reached down for another handful of nails and frowned, remembering his discussion with Summer the previous day. Jack still wasn't certain how long he could keep her with them. He hadn't forgotten his promise to return her home safely. Despite her protests that she was with them because she wanted to be, his promise was losing credibility.

Jack thought, too, of what he had overheard the previous night. Trudging to the door of the cottage, tired to the bone, he had paused as he'd heard Summer's voice floating through the open window. Surprised by her painful confessions, he wondered what else he didn't know about her. He also wondered about the man she had been engaged to. Did she still love him? Was that why she had tried so fervently to hide her femininity?

Jack glanced at her again. To look at her now, it was hard to believe that he had once nearly mistaken her for a man.

"It's shaping up just fine, son."

Whirling around, Jack tried not to show that his heart had jumped into his throat from surprise. Relaxing his guard could prove lethal, and clearly he had done just that.

"Thanks, Pastor. But it's going to take more than a few nails to keep this together for long. We'll need to replace this section of the fascia board."

"If you say so. Wouldn't want it to fall on our parishioners, not that some of the hardheads would feel it."

Jack grinned. He had always loved Don Steiger's slightly irreverent approach to life. "I'll make a run to the lumberyard and get supplies."

The pastor nodded his head. "Just put it on the account like you used to. You might have noticed that nothing much around here has changed."

"That can be a good thing," Jack replied, hammering in a nail.

"And change can be equally good. Look at you and your new family."

Jack paused, his gaze following the pastor's. Summer had Danny in her arms and was twirling him around and making him laugh. Sunlight danced over her blond hair, illuminating it into a golden sheen while the breeze stirred the full skirt of her casual sundress. Something in his gut knotted, then warmed.

"I'd say you hit the jackpot, son. Lovely wife, fine son. A man can't ask for much more than that."

"I guess not, Pastor."

"She's a fine woman," the pastor continued. "Concerned more about the people around her than herself. I'll tell you from experience that counts for an awful lot. As the years pass, a lot of things fade, but compassion only grows."

Jack continued to stare at Summer and Danny. It seemed the pastor had seen—really seen—Summer. Had his own vision been impossibly clouded?

"I'm not telling you anything you don't know, Jack. After all, you're the one who picked her." He reached up and plucked a wayward piece of flaking paint. "Good thing you got here when you did. The place might have fallen to pieces."

Jack tore his gaze from Summer. "I doubt that. You take good care of your own, Pastor."

The older man nodded, his gaze again resting on Summer and Danny. "Apparently you do, too, son. I suspect you always have."

Startled, Jack met the other man's eyes but saw only compassion there. For an insane moment, he thought the pastor had somehow found out what had happened to Linda. As Don Steiger walked away, Jack turned his attention back to Summer, his gut knotted with conflicting emotions. Would he be able to take care of them this time? Or would history repeat itself?

Summer stood on the bottom step of the porch and listened to the night sounds: the bass quartet of bullfrogs from the nearby pond, the cicadas joining their harmony and the distant call of a roving owl. Undisturbed, a gentle breeze fluttered through the leaves of the towering oak trees. Summer smiled as she looked down the peaceful street, past rows of picket fences. Caleb Corners reminded her of home. Darkness blanketed the sky, and as people settled in for the evening it was as though all was right with the world.

Hearing footsteps creak on the wooden porch, Summer recognized them immediately. There was a cadence to a person's footfalls, as individual as fingerprints, and she had no doubt these belonged to Jack.

Turning, she smiled.

To her relief, he smiled back.

"Things must be okay," she guessed.

He nodded. "The Steigers are spoiling Danny rotten, but he's loving it."

"They're good people," Summer commented, watching Jack's face as the night shadows played over his features. Once again, she was reminded of a pirate, ferociously courageous, powerfully virile. But she knew this pirate didn't possess a black heart.

"I haven't asked, Summer, but what did your mother say when you called her after we docked the first night?" He paused. "Or that second call a few days later?"

"I told her we'd run into a few complications," she admitted.

"Nicely phrased. But isn't she worried about you?"

Summer shrugged. "I'd be lying if I said no. But she knows I'm a big girl, that I can take care of myself."

He stepped closer so that only the light of a moonbeam separated them. "Not such a big girl." His hand glided over to touch the hair that was tossed over her shoulder. "Standing down there, you look like a wee slight thing."

"Your Irish is showing."

Jack's teeth flashed in the dark night. "I'm just cracking open the cover."

"There's more to come?" she questioned, enjoying this side of him, wishing they had more time like this, wishing they hadn't met in such a bizarre fashion. But staring up at him, she realized they wouldn't have met any other way. They were so very different. Nothing less than the danger they were facing could have brought them together.

"There's always more to an Irishman than he lets on." Lazily Jack leaned one lean hip against the porch railing and stretched his long legs, pulling the denim tight against muscled thighs.

Summer was struck by the sheer maleness of him. Swallowing, she silently admitted the wealth of her attraction. Even the tranquillity of the evening faded as a rumbling tension ignited the warm night air. As distinctive as thunder that rolled in with a storm, Jack had changed the currents, electrified them.

Knowing this, Summer knew she should make an excuse and escape, flee from the feelings. Yet she couldn't move. Especially when he shifted slightly, moving a fraction closer, heating the air between them. Frantically she searched her mind for an excuse, but nothing surfaced.

"Nice evening, isn't it?" Pastor Steiger's voice broke

the exquisite silence and Summer whirled around, stepping back from Jack.

"Yes," Summer mumbled, not certain whether to be relieved or frustrated at the interruption.

The pastor chuckled. "Nothing like a warm summer night for young love." He scratched his graying head. "Seems I remember what that was like."

"I suspect it's not all memory." Jack's voice was even, mildly joking as he replied, and Summer wondered if he had at all been affected as she had.

Pastor Steiger smiled. "I suspect you're right." He tapped his pipe against the railing. "I won't disturb you two, just had to get away from the danged computer before I pitched it out the window."

"Problem?" Jack asked.

"Yes, but I don't know if it's me or the computer. Had a specialist out here the other day and he did some programming, said it was all fixed up, but I swear it's worse than before."

"I'd be happy to look at it for you," Summer offered.

"You know about computers?" the pastor asked, a note of hope rising in his voice.

"They're my speciality," she replied, watching Jack's brow rise in surprise.

"It..." Jack's voice trailed off to a sputter, which he covered by coughing.

She enjoyed the satisfaction of surprising Jack, knowing he didn't dare question her in front of the pastor. After all, one would expect that he would know what his wife did for a living. "I'd be happy to take a look, Pastor."

"Now, I don't want to interrupt...but I have to say I'd be awfully grateful if you could make some sense out of the thing. I've got to run a budget report and right now I don't think I can get it to even tell me our bank balance."

"No problem." Summer edged past Jack, unable to resist shooting him an enigmatic look. "Let's go see what's hanging it up. Could just be a coding problem, something in the software, but we'll run a diagnostic check.''

"You're a miracle straight from heaven!" the pastor declared. "I was telling Jack he was heaven-sent, but I didn't know the both of you were. So you're a computer whiz?"

She grinned. "Let's just say I get along with computers like you do with your parishioners."

"I hope not. Hate to say it, but some of them are pure knot heads."

A few hours later, Summer stretched as she made her way to the cottage, easing the ache in her lower back. She wasn't certain what sort of "specialist" had worked on the church's computer, but the man had made a mess of things.

Low lamplight illuminated the interior of the cottage as she slipped inside. Careful not to wake Jack or Danny, she tiptoed toward the closet to grab her gown.

"Got the computer back in business?" Jack's low voice rose from the near darkness.

Startled, she clutched the wall, relieved it was Jack and not one of their pursuers. "You scared the life out of me!"

"You didn't think I was Fisher or Wilcox?" Jack's tone was a cross between disbelief and amusement.

"Is that such a leap?" Summer's hands fluttered toward her chest where her heart still pounded. "In case you've forgotten, they're an unsavory pair, and we *are* running from them."

Jack rose from the low, overstuffed chair. "Sorry, I didn't mean to startle you."

Summer took a deep, cleansing breath to even out her racing pulse. "It's okay. No more surprises, though."

"Like yours?"

Puzzled, she stared at him through the filtered light. "What do you mean?"

"Computer whiz? That doesn't exactly tally with being a boat mechanic."

"Why not? Do you think most mechanics are illiterate?"

He snorted impatiently. "Of course not."

"Auto mechanics are required to have a lot of training." Deliberately she made her voice noncommittal. "Surely you know that cars are computer controlled."

"You're not an auto mechanic," Jack pointed out.

"Nor a boat mechanic."

He stared at her. "What do you mean?"

"I help at my mother's shop, but that's not my chosen career."

Jack plowed one hand through his hair. "Then what is your job?"

"A computer-security programmer," she replied, enjoying the edge of surprise she'd held over Jack.

But he didn't seem amused. "Why are you just now telling me?"

"You didn't ask."

Impatiently Jack made a gesture of frustration with his hands. "You were working on the boat—"

"And you assumed that was the epitome of my ability— that I didn't have to be able to excel in intellectual pursuits."

Jack had the grace to look chagrined. "I didn't mean—"

"Yes, at the time you did."

He moved a bit closer, and she could see the regret in his eyes. "I'm sorry for that. But you'll have to admit that most women can't repair a boat engine."

Summer smiled. "Most women didn't grow up in their father's shadow. I learned the ins and outs of a boat engine the way most girls learned about makeup. I guess I'm still a slow learner in that category."

He reached over to tip up her chin. "Not from what I see. You look...just fine, Summer." His voice deepened a shade. "Just fine."

It wasn't a raving declaration, but somehow it suited her needs and Summer smiled again. "So, you're surprised that I use my brains instead of my brawn?"

A slow smile eased over his face. "Not so surprised."

Jack's glance strayed over her feminine form. "Just wondering what you're doing on Edisto Island if you're a hot-dog computer specialist."

"I'm lucky. I telecommute, so it doesn't matter where I live."

"But couldn't you advance your career faster if you were in the city?"

Summer shrugged. "Probably. And someday I hope to have my own consulting firm, after I find another capable mechanic to help at my mother's shop. But it's not worth the trade-offs."

"Such as?"

"My family's on Edisto—which amounts to my mother and the people she's collected over the years, like Lloyd, who doesn't have any family of his own. My mother would never admit it, but she needs me. Not just with the shop, but because she's getting older. I can't imagine living far away, leaving her alone, not being able to see her, to check on her."

A shadow passed over Jack's face.

Horrified, Summer realized what she'd just said. "Jack, I'm so sorry! I didn't mean to make you feel bad about your family."

He shrugged.

Impulsively Summer laid a hand on his arm and she felt the automatic flinch. But she was offering comfort and refused to be deterred. "Jack, everyone has different challenges, different solutions. I didn't mean to sound glib about my mother. Actually…" She drew her courage together. "I gave up a lot to stay on Edisto—not so much with my career, but in other…ways."

"Did that other way involve a man?"

Startled, she looked at him for a moment before lowering her eyes. "I'm afraid so. When I wouldn't leave Edisto, he thought I was far too backward to fit in the sophisticated network he was establishing."

"And was it worth it?" Jack asked quietly. "Giving him up?"

For a moment, she could scarcely remember the pain Tyson had caused. Somehow it had dulled more than she had expected. Yet she probed the quiet questions in his eyes, wondering what had placed them there. "As I said, there's give and take. But…I think I made the right decision."

Her answer vibrated between them.

Gazing into her eyes, Jack realized that if in some part of his mind he had wondered if they could have a future together, she'd just killed that hope. Family was too important for her to ever become part of his life. Always running, never being able to contact those she loved, she would be miserable. True, it wasn't a choice he would have voluntarily made, either.

"I thought I'd made the right decision, too," Jack answered finally, unwilling to let her know just how far his thoughts had strayed. When had she managed to sneak into those thoughts? he wondered. And how had he not seen it coming?

"Of course you made the right decision." Summer gestured toward Danny, sleeping peacefully in the portable crib. "He's worth everything."

"That's never been in question." Jack paused, considering again how she had infiltrated his thoughts. "I see how important family is to you."

"But family's equally important to you, as well!" She gazed at him earnestly, her eyes darkening to nearly jade. "Just as your duty to yourself and your beliefs is. Otherwise, you wouldn't have been willing to sacrifice as you did to stand up for those beliefs." Again her glance strayed toward Danny. "It's evident how much you treasure your son, how you want to raise him with the same strong sense of right. Could you have lived with yourself if you'd turned a blind eye, refused to become involved?"

"No," Jack admitted, feeling a wave of pain that had

never completely faded. "But by involving Linda, I stole his mother, something I can never replace."

"You did not!" Summer denied hotly. "Those criminals stole Danny's mother. And Linda wouldn't have married you if she valued a man of lesser principles. She wouldn't have wanted Danny raised to be a coward and weakling. She believed in you, Jack. Can you do any less?"

Slowly he shook his head.

Summer gentled her voice. "What kind of future do you see for yourself, Jack?"

A charged silence hung between them for a few moments, then he met her eyes steadily. "A future for Danny that doesn't involve running and moving constantly. I want my son to grow up free, strong and courageous. And I'm afraid it won't be possible." He refrained from telling her that he longed to fill the empty place in his heart…that he didn't dare open himself to that kind of hurt again.

"I don't know exactly how, but I know you'll manage it," she replied.

Surprised, Jack realized there was true solace in her words, advice that rang true. For the first time, he felt some measure of peace about the decisions he made. "You sound very sure."

Summer's voice softened, as gentle as the breeze that fluttered at the windows. "You made the supreme sacrifice. And that sacrifice must count for something."

Jack turned toward Danny. "I intend to make sure it does. And nothing's going to stand in my way." He felt the chill his words carried. "Nothing."

Chapter 13

"**Y**ou and Summer have to attend!" Mary Steiger had insisted, refusing to accept any of the excuses he had offered. In fact, the pastor's wife insisted on baby-sitting Danny.

Her words rang in Jack's head as he glanced around the church hall. For the night, it was decorated to resemble an 1850s church dance. The next day, following historical tradition, they would have a box supper on the church lawn.

Jack had hammered up calico festoons, hauled in bales of hay and assembled long tables to hold the cider and an assortment of pies, cakes and homemade taffy. He had to admit it looked both festive and fairly genuine. He also had to admit he didn't want to be here.

The key to their safety was in maintaining a low profile. Uneasily he glanced around the relaxed group of parishioners clearly enjoying the event. None of the townspeople presented a threat, yet he didn't want to do anything that would make Summer and himself stand out in their memories.

"You keep scowling like that and everyone's going to wonder what's wrong with us," Summer chided from behind a glass of bright red punch.

Jack turned to her, his uneasiness momentarily distracted. Summer wore a dress that Mary Steiger had insisted on loaning her. While it was a perfectly proper historical costume, the well-fitting silk hugged Summer's curves in a way Jack had never seen her dressed before. The thrust of her breasts, the curve of her waist, the flare of her hips—hers was a silhouette that made his throat dry in appreciation.

Keeping with the 1850s theme, Summer had drawn her hair back from her face, letting it glide over her shoulders in soft curls. She had fastened it with an emerald ribbon that matched her dress and emphasized the color of her eyes. A gold locket nestled between her breasts, winking out an invitation Jack found difficult to ignore. Her lips were full, and as he painfully remembered, luscious to the touch.

"Jack," Summer repeated, reaching out to touch his arm.

Jerking his attention back to her face, he cleared his throat. "Yes?"

"The props are so authentic and well put together. The pastor said he couldn't have done this without your planning and imagination."

At the moment, Jack cursed that imagination. Since they had been on the run, it had been torture each time he and Summer had slept in the same bed. Now with Summer's tantalizing image making the situation more complicated, he wasn't sure he would be able to keep to his side of the bed. And the tiny cottage they'd been assigned had the smallest bed yet. Couldn't Mary have loaned her a shapeless calico dress that didn't fire the imagination?

"It's all decorated wonderfully!" Summer enthused, clearly enjoying the party.

"It doesn't look nearly as good as you do," Jack replied, daring to say aloud what he was thinking.

Flustered, Summer smoothed a hand over her hair. "I'm not sure if you're being sincere or merely kind, but thank you. Mary insisted on the hairstyle and dress. I was afraid I'd look ridiculous."

"You may look many things, Summer Harding, but ridiculous isn't one of them."

Further flustered, she glanced down at her cup of punch and then away. But her thoughts fled instantly to the kisses they had shared, the magic Jack had created with a simple touch.

Frances, one of the women Summer recognized from choir practice, materialized at her side. "Now, now! What are you two doing on the sidelines? Newlyweds should be dancing!"

As much to escape the woman as not to attract further attention, Jack held out his hand to Summer. "You heard the nice lady. Dance?"

Summer stopped short of curtsying, but accepted his outstretched hand. "Delighted."

It was a public dance, a church dance, the setting very proper, the mood certainly chaste. But when she stepped into his arms, Jack was hard-pressed to remember any of those things. Instead his body responded to the soft crush of her breasts against his chest, the impossibly small span of her waist beneath his encircling hand. While they moved to the slow beat of the music, Jack could feel their exchange of heat, the rhythm of their bodies as they moved like one.

Even the touch of Summer's hand in his marked the contrast of larger to smaller, stronger to weaker, male to female. Her skin was soft, her fingers long and nimble. The tips of them curled within his hand, and he found himself feeling irrationally protective.

Summer angled her head closer to his, and he inhaled her uniquely fresh aroma, the scent of roses and sunshine. Circling the floor, Jack suspected he would remember that fragrance long after they said goodbye.

Something swift and unexpected tightened in his gut at that thought. Despite how often he'd told her that she must leave for her own safety, he wasn't ready for goodbye.

Responding instinctively, he drew her closer and felt Summer's surprise as she stiffened.

She tilted her head back. "Jack?"

"We're supposed to be newlyweds, remember?" he responded gruffly, not allowing her to draw away.

Summer nodded her head next to his, the soft, shiny hair gliding across his cheek.

Jack wondered about the man she'd been involved with. Had she been in love with him? Was she still?

Her hand still curled trustingly within his, and he wondered, too, if she was still hurt over the broken engagement. The man was clearly a fool, Jack decided.

Summer tilted her head back a fraction. "Do you suppose they had worries like ours back in the 1850s?"

"You thinking of a little time travel?"

She laughed, a gentle, infectious sound. "No. Just thinking that times must have been simpler, so perhaps the worries were, too."

"No electricity—therefore no computers for you. A woman couldn't help with the family boat business. It would have been unacceptable female behavior. No social programs for the needy, no cure for most diseases, a civil war looming on the horizon. I don't know...all in all, I'd say they had their worries, too."

"I suppose they did—their own brand of Fisher and Wilcox. I was just thinking that it's too bad life isn't always like this dance tonight...simple, uncomplicated...but I guess that sounds silly."

"Not so much," he replied, his gaze drawn into her bottomless eyes. They reminded him of the sea, a multitude of shifting shades that came together in one glorious burst of color. "Maybe for tonight, we could pretend that this is how our life is." Jack paused, not daring to voice the rest of his thoughts: that in a different life he could be holding her in his arms, that she could be his wife in every sense, that there were no barriers keeping them apart. That there would be no goodbyes.

"I'd like to pretend—" Summer's eyes met his "—even if it is only for the night."

Time passed. It could have been minutes, it could have been hours... Jack couldn't say. Only when the band took a break did he reluctantly release Summer.

"Okay, folks, we're going to play a few parlor games," the pastor announced.

Moans and groans echoed through the hall.

"None of that! You all wanted a genuine 1850s party. Well, that's what you're getting. For those of you who didn't major in history, there weren't any VCRs or CD changers back then. They had *parlor games.*"

Laughter punctuated his words.

The pastor smiled. "It won't be as bad as it sounds. In fact, you young folks might decide it's better than a video arcade."

While most of the kids pulled faces and rolled their eyes, the ladies organizing the party began lining people up for the first game.

Pastor Steiger raised his voice to be heard over the babble and chatter. "The object of the first game is to pass an apple from person to person—without using your hands. I'd suggest that if you have your eye on someone special, get in line behind him or her."

Jack and Summer glanced at each other ironically as their hands were bound behind their backs with brightly colored scarves.

He leaned over to whisper in her ear. "Fisher and Wilcox catch up to us now and we're done for."

Seeing that he wasn't particularly worried, Summer relaxed a fraction and whispered back. "All trussed up like the sacrificial turkey at Thanksgiving."

Jack winced. "Somehow I have the feeling I won't ever

be able to look at Thanksgiving dinner in quite the same way again.''

"Looks like we're ready to begin," the pastor announced. "The team to pass the apple down the line first wins."

It wasn't easy to hang on to a slick-skinned apple with just your chin, Summer soon discovered. As their teammates cheered them on, she and Jack had to practically meld their bodies together in order to fit their chins into apple-passing position.

His hard chest jutted out, accepting her softer form. It was a supposedly innocent intimacy, which made it seem that much more titillating.

The apple bobbled, nearly slipping as they pushed their cheeks together. Since everyone else had contorted into equally ridiculous positions, Summer and Jack didn't hesitate to push even closer together.

Faces pressed cheek to cheek, she felt the strength in his close-shaved jaw. Despite their awkward posture, Summer began to smile as she pictured Jack with that jaw set, firmed to take on the world.

"What could you possibly be smiling about?" he managed to ask with a grunt as he tried to balance the apple.

Summer's grin widened. "Don't tell me we've discovered something that's beyond the scope of your expertise."

"Funny," Jack muttered, straining to hang on to the slippery apple.

Feeling an imp egging her on, Summer reached toward him and gently nipped the soft underside of his jaw.

Eyes widening, he allowed the apple to fall unchecked to the floor. But he didn't grunt in exasperation as she expected. His gaze never veered toward the forgotten fruit. Instead it centered on her lips.

Warmth sent new signals. And she wasn't having any difficulty reading them. But nothing in her consciousness activated to heed the warning.

His lips were warm, strong and overwhelming. But she

welcomed each feeling. The room and everyone in it paled next to the sensations. But that didn't surprise her. Each time she was this close to him, common sense disappeared as something else took its place. Something that bordered on desire. And it wasn't a feeling she wanted to examine.

When he finally pulled back enough that they parted, she was breathless. But the passion had to be postponed, she realized when she heard the people around them chuckling at their display.

"This must be your honeymoon," Frances teased with a huge wink and hearty laugh.

Summer collected herself with an effort. "Not exactly."

Frances waved a plump hand negligently. "I vaguely remember being young and in love. Enjoy, my dears." With that, she scooted away, leaving a trail of overpowering perfume in her wake.

"And to think I told the pastor the parlor games weren't such a great idea," Jack told her.

Summer cleared her throat, still feeling the imprint of his lips on hers. "You've changed your mind?"

Jack's gaze caught and held hers. "What do you think?"

Uncertainly Summer paused. She wanted to believe that Jack had felt the same measure of giddy attraction that she had. More, she wanted to admit her feelings, hoping he would reciprocate. But, afraid to take the plunge, instead she tiptoed into the water, testing Jack's reaction. "We made a convincing couple."

Jack's expression stilled for a moment at her cautious reply, before his smile flashed. "That we did. You're quite a player, Summer. If someone didn't know the difference, they'd believe we really were a couple."

She'd believed…but clearly he hadn't. Firming her chin, Summer tilted it upward. "Then I guess we did a good job."

"So we did, Summer. And we fooled just about everybody."

* * *

Summer tried to straighten the quilt over the grass, but it was rapidly becoming apparent that it was a futile gesture. No sooner did she straighten it than Danny would crawl forward, trying to escape. And recapturing him crumpled the quilt each time.

"You might as well give up," Jack advised lazily from his supine position. A hat perched over most of his face, he seemed far too content to lie in the shade. Of course he had good reason to be resting. The boiler in the recreation hall had burst the previous evening soon after the dance had ended, causing him to work all night.

After their kiss, Summer had wondered if they might have a different conclusion to the evening, but Jack hadn't arrived back at the cottage until the early-morning hours. And by then, Danny was wide-awake and ready for breakfast.

"You're going to become bug bait if you don't move," Summer teased, knowing he was genuinely tired.

"Is it my watch?" Jack questioned, referring to Danny.

"Not especially. You simply look too comfortable."

He grunted and rolled on one side. "Okay, I moved."

Summer spotted Danny revving up for another escape effort. "Oh, no, you don't." Scooping him up, she put his wriggling body on her lap. "What do you see over there that's so intriguing?" She glanced across the yard. "Oh, some kids. Punkin, I'm afraid they're a little too big for you to play with. They're playing dodgeball and they'd probably get you mixed up with the ball."

Jack chuckled. "Now, that's quite a picture."

Summer ignored him, turning to the baby instead. "Why don't we see what Daddy has that we could pilfer?"

"Daddy doesn't have anything worth jail time," he warned her.

"I don't know. How about that hat? I bet Danny would love to wear that."

"That's a 49ers hat from the Super Bowl," Jack protested. "Genuine article."

"Danny won't mind that it's old and a little worn," she replied sweetly. "Would you, punkin?"

"You're all heart." Yet he placed the hat backward on Danny's head when Summer plunked the baby down next to him. "You realize that will keep him entertained all of about thirty seconds."

"Probably," she agreed. "I thought we'd walk over to the pond and look at the ducks. They're bound to be good for at least ten minutes of entertainment."

Jack groaned. "Danny, my boy, how 'bout a nap instead of some ugly ducklings?"

In response, Danny tried to crawl off the blanket again.

"It's Sunday afternoon, Danny, have a heart," Jack tried again.

Danny crawled even faster, laughing when Summer scooped him up and tickled him.

"I thought an old-fashioned box supper meant R&R," Jack groaned.

"As in racing and running after Danny? Then you're right."

"I don't think I'm getting a lot of sympathy," Jack responded, propping himself up on one elbow.

"Right again." Glancing across the lawn, Summer spotted Danny crawling at top speed. Instantly she jumped up and headed after him.

Jack watched them and saw that she had the situation under control. But then he hadn't had to worry about Danny with Summer around. She had already sprouted that extra set of maternal eyes in the back of her head.

Summer captured Danny before the baby reached the older kids. "Okay, you, why don't we go find something safe for you to play?" Making him giggle by blowing kisses on his tummy, Summer took him over to the swing set designed for toddlers.

Jack sat up slowly, watching them together. It amazed him that even in the face of danger, Summer could make the baby laugh. It occurred to him suddenly that Danny had been happier since Summer had joined them. Although the baby was too young to understand either the situation or the dynamics, clearly he liked Summer. And Jack had always thought babies and animals possessed a keen intuitive sense about people.

She pushed the swing as Danny chortled with glee. After several minutes, Summer allowed the swing to slow down, finally plucking Danny from the seat and walking back to Jack. He enjoyed the view coming and going, even the view as she put Danny in his stroller.

"Okay, folks," the pastor announced from the top of the steps. "Time to bid for box lunches. You men better bid high if you want to share lunch with the lady of your choice."

Jack watched the good-natured auction with amusement until Summer's box supper came up for bid. Not expecting competition, he watched with lazy interest. But when two or three bids surfaced, Jack straightened up and searched the crowd for the men who had made them. He guessed the men didn't know Summer was with him. Most of the time since they'd arrived at the church, he had been occupied with repairing one thing or another.

Standing up, Jack made his considerable height evident. The last offer for Summer's lunch had been ten dollars. He decided it was time for a preemptive bid. "Twenty-five dollars."

The pastor's gavel banged down immediately. "Sounds like that man's either hungry or wants to make sure no one else eats lunch with his wife!"

Amused laughter broke out, and the other bidders smiled good-naturedly and retreated from the bidding.

"I didn't realize you were that hungry," Summer told him as she approached, her lips curved in a knowing grin as she put Danny in his portable playpen.

Jack started to joke, but the lighthearted emotion failed him. "More than you'll know."

Her grin faded. Suddenly Summer knew the hunger he

spoke of. Her own pangs were laid bare as their gazes locked.

Without comment, Jack pulled her close, his lips saying the words that remained unspoken. It was a fierce possession, a promise that demanded...then delivered.

The picnic, the parishioners, the world, in fact—all were forgotten as thwarted longing demanded satisfaction.

Summer felt the bunching of his muscles as her arms snaked over his shoulders. The strength and power excited her, lured her, compelled her to wish for an end to this frustration.

"Hey, you two!" Mary Steiger called out as she approached. "Three, I mean!"

Jack and Summer reluctantly parted.

Mary reached for Danny. "How 'bout coming with me so your parents can eat lunch?"

The toddler settled for a moment in her arms, then wriggled fretfully to get away.

"Looks like he wants Mama," Mary said regretfully.

"Mama," Danny repeated, holding his arms out to Summer.

Jack stared at Summer, but for an entirely different reason this time. Could the child be bonding with Summer so completely?

A staggering set of complications struck him—ones he wasn't yet ready to examine.

He felt a spurt of unfamiliar guilt. What would Linda think of her son calling another woman mama? And what would his late wife think of his increasing feelings for that same woman?

Overly full lips twitched nervously, since the man knew the questions to come. He wasn't disappointed.

A hand slammed viciously against the metal desk. "You said the profiler would find them!"

The graying man swallowed. "Radison is the best, but Anderson's not following his normal course of action."

"The *best* should have anticipated that," the pale-eyed man replied in a quiet voice that was more terrifying than if he had thundered the words.

"Radison is trying another tack. He'll look outside the scope. My guess is Anderson anticipated what we'd do and countermoved."

"Brilliant deduction." The man moved to the window, presenting his back. "You've just used up another one of your chances."

Sweat broke out beneath graying hair. "I'm doing my best."

"You'd better hope not. I wouldn't waste any more of your chances." Pale eyes skewered the other man to the wall as he turned around. "Remember, the kind and the cruel kill in equal quantities."

He ran his tongue over fleshy lips. "And which are we?"

The nearly maniacal laugh shot terror through his heart. "If you don't know, your chances just ran out."

Chapter 14

How could one day take so long to pass? Summer wondered as she watched the church choir assemble. It seemed that aeons rather than hours had passed since that moment with Jack on the lawn. Her lips still tingled with his imprint. Without volition, her fingers strayed to trace their outline, remembering the feel of his kiss. Just a kiss, she reminded herself. But that was scant comfort when her body burned with a fire that refused to be quenched.

Singing, Summer told herself. She could lose herself in the singing. Determinedly she joined the other choir members. It was an extra practice since the group was scheduled to perform at an all-city concert the following week.

At first Summer had feared the exposure. But she'd learned they would dress in matching choir robes, providing some anonymity, and making the excursion relatively safe.

Though she had been certain the rehearsal would distract her building tension, one hour and four songs later, she was only more anxious.

Resolution. That was what was needed, she decided,

striking off her first solution. She and Jack couldn't go on as they had.

When the rehearsal ended, Summer looked for Jack, but discovered that he was working on the ancient boiler again. Stymied, she sought to ease her restlessness.

She played with Danny until the exhausted child fell asleep on her lap. Guiltily Summer realized she had delayed his nap time so that she could play with him, rather than face her own thoughts.

Reluctantly she returned him to the crib in the Steigers' nursery. Unable to push the whirling thoughts from her head, she volunteered to clean up the church lawn. Although most of the church members had conscientiously cleaned up their picnic things, there was still some litter—an errant cup, paper plates and napkins.

People lingered to catch up on news and to simply pass the time, but Summer didn't let them deter her. She cleaned around the people, causing more than one quizzical stare. Unfazed, she ignored both the adults deep in conversation and their children, who used the gathering as an excuse to run and holler. She inspected every foot of the lawn, but that chore didn't take nearly long enough and still the time dragged.

Deciding there was a strong possibility that she might go crazy, Summer cleaned the tiny guest cottage with a vengeance at odds with the pleasant surroundings. When she was finished, the soft glow of the well-polished furniture competed with the fresh aroma of lemon wax.

Impulsively she clipped some roses, hydrangeas and peonies, knowing that Mary Steiger encouraged the practice. Once arranged, they became a soft focal point. Following the same impulse that led her to cut the flowers, she tossed some petals on the bed. If Jack asked her about them, Summer decided she would tell him that it was an act of whimsy.

"Whimsy," she said aloud. The innocent petals on the

bedspread seemed to mock her. "It's one way to put it," she muttered in quiet defense.

Since the cottage was so clean it practically squeaked, Summer reluctantly put away her cleaning materials. After ten minutes with a magazine, she found herself tossing it down to pace the small confines of the room.

"Enough!" she told the cottage as she left. Patience had never been her strong point. Her mother had always said that when the good Lord was handing out patience, Summer had been too impatient to wait in line. Stomping across the lawn, Summer decided that her mother just might have been right.

Jack searched through the toolbox as he looked in disgust at the old boiler.

"Damn thing should have been put out to pasture a hundred years ago," he muttered. Uncharacteristically he punctuated the words with a well-aimed kick at the solid base of the boiler.

When the clang subsided, Jack sighed. Then he ran an apologetic hand over the surface. "We'll get you through this crisis, too."

Jack knew the source of his frustration and although the old boiler could try his patience, it wasn't the cause. He knew exactly why he was frustrated.

And her name was Summer.

Summer of the contradictions, mesmerizing eyes and huge heart. And partner to a sexual tension that heated the air, stunned the senses and nearly made him forget the past.

But could he forget that past?

The picture of his late wife was something he carried in his heart, but it had faded a bit of late. How could that be? Had he sacrificed Linda only to forget her?

Unexpectedly he remembered Summer's fervent defense. She didn't believe he was responsible for Linda's death. Summer had pointed the finger at Fisher and Wilcox. Could she be right?

He had never intended to become involved with anyone again. But he had never expected to let anyone intrude on his emotions, either. How had Summer managed that? And what in the world was he going to do about it?

The interminably long day had been filled with noise and people. By comparison, the night was starkly quiet. But nothing about the verdant green of the canopied trees or the rich swath of velvet sky was stark. Summer dawdled as she crossed the lawn toward the cottage.

Her earlier impatience hadn't disappeared, but now resembled a fire that had burned down to softly glowing embers. While they no longer danced in crazy abandon, the sparks were still alive, simply waiting to be flamed back to life. But Summer had accepted that she had to wait until Jack was free to think about extinguishing that fire.

And Summer also knew she had to decide whether she was willing to take that step, knowing that Jack had pledged his love to someone she couldn't compete with. Summer wondered if she dared allow herself to become any more deeply involved with him, knowing they had no future together. Would crossing this last barrier wound her heart for all time?

It was a lazy, late-summer night. Crickets chirped while the perfume of trailing honeysuckle scented the air. The Steigers' perfectly groomed rose garden with its freshly turned, loamy soil and the huge magnolia tree added their own rich aromas.

Far away from the big city, where a multitude of lights didn't compete with the stars, each constellation seemed nearer and brighter. Summer remembered a favorite childhood tale about capturing stars just within her reach. Somehow that seemed probable on this night ripe with possibility.

Reaching the cottage, Summer saw that the door was ajar and she hesitated. Jack had still been finishing his work on the boiler when she saw him last. With danger dogging their every move, she was wary. He could have finished early or—

"Summer?" Jack's voice carried through the open door.

Relief made her sag for a moment, before she braced her voice to hide it. "It's me."

"Good."

The solitary word warmed something deep inside. Summer's pace quickened and she stepped into the cottage, closing the door behind her. Dimness and the glow of candlelight struck her first. The lamps had been turned off, and only the flicker of the candles illuminated the room. Somehow it seemed smaller than it did in the daylight...more intimate.

"Where's Danny?" Jack questioned.

"Staying with Mary and Don."

"For the night?"

She swallowed. "Yes." As she uttered the word, Summer knew that when she'd told the Steigers they could keep Danny overnight, she had made a conscious decision. One she now faced.

Jack took a few steps forward, then planted his feet apart. At once she was reminded of the first time she had seen him on the deck of his boat. Again he resembled a pirate from bygone days, his presence filling the entire space of the shrinking room. He seemed at once overpowering, overwhelmingly male and unmistakably virile.

Suddenly all the tension and desire that had thrummed between them leaped to the surface, demanding to be heard. No more interruptions, no more artificial barriers—the reckoning was now.

"You bought my box lunch," Summer blurted out, forgetting to be coy, disregarding pretense.

"I didn't want to share you with anyone else," Jack returned, taking another step closer.

"You didn't?" she whispered, feeling her heart crumble, remembering every fantasy she had entertained about them. Fantasies in which he wanted her as much as she longed for him, fantasies that culminated in them being together forever. Perhaps they wouldn't have forever, but they could have the night.

Jack's eyes blazed, the blue deepening beyond black. "No. I don't ever want to share you."

Hope, ridiculous or not, pierced her.

His eyes simmered with a promise she dared not try to discern. "If you want me to stop, tell me now, Summer."

Yearning at once both sweet and sharp swamped her. The sweetness filled her heart. The sharpness propelled her across the room, each step taking her closer to a destination of promise. "I'm telling you...."

His face began to close.

She reached out tentatively to trace the strong, implacable lines of his jaw. "Don't ever stop."

Jack felt his paralyzed pulse race again as he reached for her. Awash in emotions he didn't dare analyze, he pulled her close, fitting her body next to his. Her breasts crushed against his chest, hip bones abraded hip bones. Their bodies aligned, sighed together, soared together.

Mouths fused, and their tongues danced in anticipation.

Gentleness battled with impatience for prominence. Jack forced gentleness to win for the moment. He smoothed back her wheat-colored hair, a sweep of silk against his arms, then reached for the buttons that ran down the front of her dress.

As he freed each one, he saw the telltale flutter of her pulse, the betraying beat that signaled her desire. Then he met the unguarded emotion in her eyes, the trust that brought the green and gold of her unusual eyes to one glorious burst of color.

Savoring each anticipated moment, he pushed the dress from her shoulders, letting it pool at her feet. The dress, though simple, was conservative, almost prudish—which made the lacy bra and silky panties she wore beneath that much more exciting.

Sucking in his breath, Jack allowed his gaze to take in

each curve and inch of flesh he had imagined. His hands rested on her shoulders, straying near the slender straps that represented one of the last barriers.

But impatience was testing them both.

Tentatively Summer reached toward the buttons of his shirt, tugging them loose. He pulled the shirt free and shrugged it away. Her fingers explored his chest, then drew a line down his abdomen. He inhaled sharply as pleasure struck so intensely it resembled pain.

Impatience raced toward abandon.

Lifting Summer in his arms, Jack carried her to the narrow bed. The mattress seemed to rise to meet them as they pressed eagerly against it, all hands, mouths and feeling.

He couldn't seem to touch her enough, to journey across her supple body. The skin beneath his fingers was as soft as the dew-kissed rose petals crushed beneath them, her response even more exquisite.

Summer arched toward his seeking touch, shamelessly wanting and needing each nuance he created. His mouth traveled a path from her throat downward. His lips fastened over one nipple, deliciously abrading her sensitized skin through the delicate fabric. The sparse barrier was somehow more exciting than nudity since it intensified the anticipation, heightened the awareness.

He nibbled a trail that dipped and swerved, somehow concentrating on each tender, highly charged spot as though guided by an internal map. She couldn't still a moan when his lips pressed against her inner thighs, then nipped the crease behind her knees.

She reached for his belt buckle, but he restrained her hands, lifting and putting them behind her head as he captured her lips again.

Anticipation and satisfaction warred, but Jack favored the fire of anticipation. Releasing Summer's hands, he slipped the straps of her bra over her shoulders with aching slowness, taking what seemed infinite time with each.

Hearing her withdrawn breath, he drew a slow, slender

line between her breasts before unfastening the bra hook centered between them.

Staring at the spill of her breasts, Jack drew a ragged breath of his own. Reverently his gaze lingered before he reached to fill his hands with their lush weight.

Suddenly he wanted to feel skin to skin, all restraints removed. As though reading his mind, Summer slid her hands over his hips to his belt buckle. This time, he helped her rip it free. His jeans followed quickly.

When he reached for the last remaining wisp of fabric that separated them, Summer sucked in a deep breath. Then the satin, too, was gone and nothing stood between them except the hunger that had been growing for far too long. No longer could it go unappeased. No longer did either of them offer any resistance.

Jack buried his face in the sweet flesh of her throat. Wrapping himself in the sound of her whispered sighs and throaty groans of pleasure, he lingered over each bit of skin, each new discovery.

His hands traveled over the valley of her waist, the slope of her hips, the incredible length of her legs. She opened up to him without hesitation, trembling beneath his touch. And those quivers heightened his anticipation, fueled his already runaway desire.

Summer clenched his shoulders, her fingers biting into the muscled flesh. Beyond imagination, beyond experience, beyond intensity, each touch signaled a promise to reach destinations never before imagined.

Feeling his initial entry, she hesitated for only a moment. Then trust took over.

Her body rose to meet each thrust, then coiled in a whipcord of release as she cried against his lips…sighed against his heart.

He brought her again and again to that edge. Jack treasured each trembling response, each shudder that gripped her body. Taking exquisite care to ensure her pleasure fueled his own. His thrusts deepened as he sought to seal his brand. Magic erupted.

In the explosion that followed, he carried them both to places previously unknown...and took his heart along for the ride.

Chapter 15

Jack worked silently as he ripped the rotted boards from the overhang. Part of him wanted to whistle in satisfaction. The other part of him was eaten up with guilt.

Having told himself his exchange with Summer would only be physical, that his emotions weren't involved, he had tangled those precious lines beyond recognition.

Wearily he laid the hammer down, then wiped his brow. He had vowed to remain faithful to Linda. And that vow had been shattered.

Along with every preconception he'd had about Summer.

For a moment, Jack leaned against the weathered brick wall. He needed every bit of concentration to focus on out-witting Fisher and Wilcox. And he hadn't given the pair a thought since Summer had consumed his heart.

"Jack?" Don Steiger's quiet voice broke into his thoughts.

"Pastor?" Jack abandoned his relaxed pose. "Just thinking about what needs to be done next."

"I suspect you don't mean the overhang."

"I'll get it done—"

The pastor waved his hands in dismissal. "No one's checking up on you. I think this is one of the few breaks you've ever taken while working here. You've gotten more done since you've been here than the last two handymen have in months." His kindly gaze was deceptively benign. "Something worrying you?"

Jack longed to spill his mixed feelings, the confusion, the guilt…but knew he couldn't. "Nothing worth bothering you about."

"That's my job, son. You don't want to put me on unemployment, do you?"

Jack managed a smile. "Pastor, I suspect you have a long line of people just waiting for your help."

"But none of them are wallowing in guilt because they love their wives."

Jack's head snapped up. "What?"

Don Steiger smiled gently. "You might as well be wearing a hair shirt."

"It shows that much?"

"Sackcloth and ashes would be more subtle," the pastor replied. "From the pain you were in when we met you the first time, I'm guessing you loved your late wife a great deal."

Jack swallowed, remembering. "Yes."

"And you think you're dishonoring her memory by caring for Summer?"

Jack nodded his head slowly.

"Don't you think your late wife would have wanted you to be happy?" He paused. "Do you think she would have wanted you to be alone the rest of your life? To spend an empty existence—no children, no life's partner? I suspect she would have wanted you to create a new family. I don't think you'd hold her memory so dear if she had been selfish or uncaring."

"Of course she wasn't like that!" Jack denied hotly.

Pastor Steiger smiled. "I never thought she was, son.

That's why I'm sure she would have wanted you to be happy. Now, you have to allow yourself to be happy.... You have to let go.''

Jack clenched his hands. ''And forget her just like that?''

''Of course not. You'll always remember and love her. And that's good, too. You're richer for all that you shared. But now it's time to share with someone else...and not to feel guilty when that person makes you happy.''

Troubled, Jack stared at the older man. He'd always known Pastor Steiger to give wise counsel, but this was a true leap of trust. And Jack wasn't sure he possessed that much trust.

Summer couldn't quite define Jack's mood. Quiet through dinner, he then played with Danny, bathed him and put him to bed. She wondered if Jack was regretting the previous evening—or, worse, trying to decide how to tell her it had been a mistake.

Danny had kept her busy all day. Cutting a new tooth, he was cranky and out of sorts. But seeing how swollen his gums had been, she couldn't get annoyed with him. And as soon as Jack had finished work, he had taken Danny off her hands.

But now with the baby nodding off to sleep, they were virtually alone.

Jack dimmed the lamplight, then stepped into the tiny kitchen. Summer fidgeted nervously on the settee.

''Wine?'' Jack asked, returning with a bottle of merlot and two glasses.

''Sure.'' She smiled uncertainly.

He poured the wine, left his glass on the side table, then flicked on the radio, tuning in Kenny G. If she didn't suspect that his mind was on something else, she would have considered this the perfect setup for seduction.

Jack parted the curtains, opening a vista to the full moon that danced across the dark horizon. Nervously Summer sipped her wine, raising her eyes above the rim of the glass to search Jack's face. But his expression didn't reveal any more than the casting moon.

He moved to stand in front of her, and Summer held her breath. Would he tell her now? Admit that he'd made a huge mistake? Perhaps suggest they remain friends?

Jack held out his hand. "Can I have this dance?"

Summer felt the wide, silly grin overtaking her face before she could prevent it. "Dance?" she echoed.

He lifted the wine stem from her hand and placed it next to his. "You aren't going to let me stand here with egg on my face, are you?"

She shook her head as she rose. Lifting her hand, Summer traced the lines of his jaw. "That wouldn't do at all."

The evocative music swirled around them as they matched their steps to its sensual rhythm...and to each other.

Circling the room, they tested the fit of their bodies, the response of each movement. And each turn seemed better than the last.

Warm, strong, powerful—Jack's embrace was all that. Sinking in his arms, Summer luxuriated in the safety she found there...and more.

His mouth slanted over hers, and she tasted the tenderness, the restraint. Both whetted her hunger, stirred her yearning.

The reckless abandon of the previous evening gave way to the luxury of prolonged anticipation. And each slow moment was one to savor.

Jack's hand rested just below her waist, guiding their movements to the music...and a beat uniquely their own. His knees nudged hers. Their hips met, teasing...then undulating in unison. Each movement was an unplanned duet of perfectly matched steps.

Although the music continued playing, they finally drew to a standstill near the bed. But tonight there was no frantic tumble to its surface, no frenzied race to disrobe. Instead each moment stretched out with aching intensity.

Lips sent a promise of their own as they discovered,
tantalized, teased. But Summer knew the fulfillment that
awaited her. Quivering at the remembered responses and
the new ones he was creating, she wondered that the room
didn't quake, mirroring her anticipation.

Summer remembered her anxiety, knew they'd only
postponed the inevitable. As Jack's gentle but sure touch
started that journey, she knew she would travel to that destination despite the future they would never share. She
knew they stood on the edge of goodbye…but what made
the blood slow? Or stilled the yearning?

Because for now, she would pretend there were no tomorrows, no danger…no goodbyes. Because she was learning that there was no greater power than that of goodbye.

The weatherman had promised rain, but not a cloud scuttled in the pure blue sky. The onlookers burst into applause
as the last strains of the song faded. The members of the
Cherry Avenue choir tried to look humble in light of the
praise, but they weren't succeeding too well.

Jack stood on the sidelines, watching Summer bask in
the glow. The all-city concert brought together the churches
in the community. Jack suspected the spirit of cooperation
was one of the reasons Caleb Corners remained a kindly
place.

He and Summer had needed the breather—a place to lie
low and regroup for a few days. Caleb Corners and the
Steigers had provided that. It was going to be difficult to
leave. Under the protective umbrella, he had almost been
able to forget the danger they were running from. He hadn't
dared to call Tom Matthews since they had arrived, not
wanting to take the chance that the call would be immediately traced.

He saw Don Steiger edging through the crowd toward
him.

Jack leaned against the bowed trunk of a live oak tree.
''You're looking pleased with yourself, Pastor.''

The older man grinned. ''I didn't have one thing to do with that performance, yet everyone's crediting me with the choir's success. It's a nice change. I have to take the flak when things go wrong—whether I'm involved or not. Can't help enjoying it when it works the other way.''

Jack nodded, his eyes straying to rest on Summer. Sunshine danced over her tumble of wheat-colored hair, and as he watched she tipped her head back in laughter. For the moment, he could almost forget that their days were numbered.

''You staying for lunch?'' Don asked. ''Burgers and hot dogs on the north side of the park.''

''I probably couldn't pry Summer away with—'' Jack glanced up, the words forgotten. A cold pit formed in his stomach.

Across the square, he spotted Fisher and Wilcox heading into the hardware store. Mind racing, he tried to formulate the best way to round up Summer and Danny. His son was home with Mary Steiger. She had insisted on keeping the teething toddler with her so that Summer could enjoy being part of the concert. And now those he cared about were split in two directions.

''Jack?''

Forcing himself not to bolt across the park and grab Summer, Jack managed to sound fairly normal. ''No, Pastor, I don't believe we will.''

Don Steiger searched his face, then clasped one hand on Jack's shoulder. ''Whatever it is, son, you have friends here.''

Startled, Jack ripped his gaze away from Summer. ''You don't—''

''I don't need details, Jack. But if you need help, I want to know about it.''

Jack gambled, then decided he had to take the first step toward trust. ''We'll be leaving Caleb Corners.''

The pastor didn't look surprised, but he did show his concern. ''Is that the only solution?''

"I can't say any more, Pastor. It's better…for all of us. Right now, I have to get Summer and—"

"Meet me by the car, Jack."

"But—"

"It'll be faster. From the look on your face, I suspect that's important right now."

Jack's throat worked. "You don't even know what we're running from."

"No, but I know *you*, and that's all I need to know."

Jack thought of everything he wanted to say—everything he couldn't say—and settled for a firm nod. He kept his pace just beneath a run as he rapidly covered the ground between the audience and the choir. Luckily Summer stood on the second tier of the risers.

Her face brightened when she spotted him. Jack didn't pause, striding up to the group. The women on the front row parted, allowing Jack to reach for Summer's hand.

"Jack!" she began with a laugh. When he didn't respond, her smile faded, along with her voice. "Jack?"

"We have to leave now."

Fear bloomed in her eyes even as she tried to school her expression. "Of course. I nearly forgot," she improvised for the benefit of the curious onlookers. Quickly she stepped off the risers, ignoring the surprised glances from the choir members.

Jack gripped her hand in his as they walked quickly away from the group. "Fisher and Wilcox just headed into the hardware store."

Fleetingly Summer followed his gaze. "Then Danny's all right?"

"For the moment, but we don't have any time to waste."

"I wish I'd driven here," she fumed.

"The pastor's driving us home," Jack told her, forcing himself not to run across the park and draw attention.

Shock widened her eyes. "He knows?"

"No. He just knows that something's wrong and we have to leave. Knowing any more would endanger all of us."

The pastor was waiting in his car with the engine running. As soon as they were inside, he pulled away from the park and headed toward the church.

"Won't they miss you back there?" Jack asked, craning his head backward to see if anyone had followed them.

"It'll give Chandler a chance to shine. He loves the spotlight." The pastor's glance widened to include Summer. "Besides, I have the feeling I won't need to be gone all that long."

Pastor Steiger was right. They bundled their belongings in record time.

Jack tossed a duffel bag in the bed of the truck.

"Hold it, son."

Surprised, Jack paused. "Pastor, I appreciate your help, but we have to hurry."

"And my guess is that truck doesn't move very fast."

Jack's eyes narrowed. "Your point?"

Pastor Steiger tossed him a set of keys. "Take the car."

Flabbergasted, Jack could only stare.

"We have two," the pastor continued. "And we want you to take it."

Mary stood beside him, nodding in agreement.

"I can't—"

"Yes, you can, son. I'm not sure exactly what's going on, but you don't want to put Summer and Danny in greater danger because of your pride."

Jack swallowed a lump of gratitude. "It's only a loan, Pastor."

"I'm counting on that. Now, you'd better hurry and get going."

They quickly loaded their belongings in the car, and Summer bent to strap Danny in his car seat before sliding inside.

Jack closed her door, then skirted the hood. He paused before opening his own door, then shook the pastor's hand. "I'm not sure why you're doing this, but thank you."

"Just remember what I said, son. Your late wife would have wanted you to be happy. Once everything's straightened out, don't forget that."

The words tantalized, then were stashed away as Jack concentrated on leaving Caleb Corners without attracting any attention. Still, stray thoughts kept assailing him. Would Linda have been happy to have someone nurturing Danny? Or would she feel betrayed as he'd always believed?

Despite the daylight, Jack decided he couldn't afford any more detours. He had to get to D.C. and find Tom Matthews. Perhaps he could find out where the agent had gone. A terrible thought occurred to him. What if Fisher and Wilcox had targeted Matthews out of revenge, just as they had once targeted him? He didn't want to chase a miracle—or a ghost, if that were the case—but someone had to believe him; somehow the truth had to be revealed.

Summer's gaze met his. "I hate leaving here. I hate that they found us."

Jack nodded in agreement. He'd been certain Fisher and Wilcox would have dismissed Caleb Corners as their hideaway, but the dirty agents must have revisited the safe places listed in Jack's file.

And Caleb Corners had been the perfect sanctuary. Grimly Jack was realizing that *temporary* seemed to be the operative word for them.

Summer could see the disgust on Jack's face as he slammed the pay phone back in place. She saw his lips move and guessed she was better off being out of hearing range.

He pulled the car door open and shut it with a tad more force than necessary.

"No luck, I'm guessing," Summer stated rather than questioned.

Jack's fist punctuated her words as it landed on the steering wheel. "There has to be a way to reach Tom Matthews."

"Isn't there *someone* at the agency who could help us?"

Grimly Jack shook his head. "Not unless we know who double-crossed me."

"You mean who wiped out your file?"

"Exactly."

"Would that really help?" she asked. "I didn't think you were interested in getting into your file. I thought you considered it a lost cause."

"Until I know who's helping them, I can't trust anyone at the agency."

"I wish I'd realized that," she muttered.

"What?"

"I said, let's go find out who's behind this," she replied calmly.

"Just like that?" Jack snapped his fingers. "Now, why didn't I think of a solution that simple?"

"Do you want to find out or not?"

"Of course, but—"

"Then we have to find a computer."

"And then...?" Jack asked cautiously.

"I crack the code and find out who the turncoat is."

"Look, I know you're a computer programmer—"

"A computer-security programmer," she corrected him. "My speciality is designing programs to protect computers from hackers."

His gaze narrowed as a flicker of understanding dawned. "And to do that...?"

"I have to know all the hacker secrets and tricks so I can set up security screens."

"You're a *hacker?*" he asked incredulously.

"Not exactly." Summer grinned. "But you're getting the idea. All I need is a computer." Her hands fairly itched to reach a keyboard.

Jack still looked skeptical. "I can't believe it's that easy."

"I'm not saying it will be. First we have to find a computer that's hooked up to a modem. And we can't do that on the run in a car."

He frowned, then slanted a glance at her. "I'm guessing you have an idea."

"We need to find a local newspaper, something that shows the entire region," she replied, thinking furiously. "And a good-size bookstore that carries the latest computer magazines."

His expression was wry. "I suspect it's best I don't second-guess you at this point."

Jack's subtle acknowledgment pleased her—almost as much as his original assumption that she was intellectually challenged had annoyed her. "I'm not making any promises, but it's our best chance."

He reached for the map. "At this point, it may be our *only* chance."

Chapter 16

The computer trade show in Weston, Maryland, only an hour from D.C., was a stroke of luck. And they were far overdue for some good fortune.

Summer and Jack strolled through the crowded aisles, pretending interest in the displays as she searched for the setup she needed. A working modem connection was essential, but she also needed a fast processor and sufficient memory.

"There!" She grabbed Jack's arm, careful not to wake Danny who rode in a carrier on his back. She pointed out the phone connection and a sign indicating the lightning-speed processor and extensive memory. It was located prominently in a row of computers in a nearby booth. "That looks perfect."

Jack nodded in agreement. "I'll distract him," he said, referring to the vendor who looked ready to pounce on the next customer.

"Right. I need enough time to make a connection, then

find the back door to the agency without setting off any alarm systems.''

"The extent of my computer expertise is a few designing programs and basic Web surfing. Just do what you have to do.''

She started to walk toward the computer, when Jack reached out suddenly, grabbing her arm. ''Alarm systems? Don't do this if it's going to put you in more danger.''

Summer crossed two fingers behind her back to cover her fib. ''I don't think we could be in any more danger. Besides, I know what I'm doing.''

After logging on to the computer, she quickly ran through the numerous links it took to reach the agency. Glancing up, she saw that Jack was still keeping the vendor busy with his concocted tale about his architectural firm's need for a complete new computer system.

Concentrating on her task, Summer wanted to cheer out loud when the last link brought her to the agency. At just that moment, Jack wisely diverted the salesman's attention to a computer at the far end of the display.

After a few more moments, Summer couldn't control a sudden grin. Her firm had created a proposal for the government, which had been ultimately rejected, that had included a test program identical to this agency's system. It was a proposal designed to keep hackers out of the records.

Her grin widened. Seeing the vendor glance quizzically in her direction, she tried to control her expression. But it was difficult because she remembered the back door into the program.

Within moments, Summer accessed the command operating system. Then she was into command interface. Remembering all the key information she had discussed with Jack, in a short time she was able to resurrect his file. Trying to hurry before she activated any alarm systems, she copied the file.

Knowing she was walking a thin line, Summer quickly

printed out Jack's report and then deleted the file so that it wouldn't tip off anyone who might be searching for it.

Catching Jack's attention, she signaled him with a thumbs-up sign. The now suspicious clerk glanced between them.

Jack shook the man's hand. "Thanks for all your help. As I said, I'll have to discuss the system with my partner. It's a fairly large capital expenditure."

As Jack spoke, Summer triumphantly held up the newly printed report, then edged out of the booth toward the exit.

The salesman was clearly perplexed. "You didn't leave me a card."

Jack smiled. "Not necessary. I have yours." Leaving the clearly aggrieved vendor, he joined Summer at the end of the aisle that led outside.

"We did it!" she whispered as they exited.

"A clean getaway?" Jack asked, shifting the straps of Danny's backpack.

She swallowed, glad that his gaze was diverted. "Probably."

His head jerked back around. "Probably?"

"I didn't dare stay online any longer—that might have really tripped an alarm. But it didn't shut me out, and that's a good sign."

"What did you find out?"

She held out the considerable stack of paper. "You up for a little light reading?"

Pale eyes scanned an urgent, confidential report. "The system has been breached."

"I can't believe he knew how to crack the code!" Fleshy lips twitched in agitation.

Controlled fingers tapped the metal surface of the desk. "He didn't. But that woman he's with did. Why didn't you know about her?"

The other man shrugged. "Anderson even threw the profiler off track. He's good. How was I supposed to guess he'd hook up with some hacker?''

Cold eyes paled further. ''Not that it will do them any good. At least he's leaving tracks now.''

''Ones we can follow.''

The laugh chilled more than the cold eyes. ''This time, the leak is lethal. And Jack Delancey is flat out of places to run.''

Frowning, Tom Matthews reread the wire services' alert. What was a picture of Jack Anderson, aka Delancey, doing on the report? A man like Jack didn't sacrifice the woman he loved, a successful career, and virtually his entire life to adopt instead a life of crime. It looked as though a lot had happened while he had been away on an undercover assignment.

He reached for the phone, jabbing in the number of the witness-protection program. Told that Sedgewick was unavailable, Tom reached a clerk instead.

''No, sir. No Jack Anderson or Jack Delancey. I'm afraid you're mistaken, sir. He's never been in the witness-protection program.''

Tom remained calm. ''Have you worked very long in this department?''

Indignation flowed through the telephone wires. ''Although I'm a recent transferee, I can assure you that I'm fully briefed on all operations. Your Mr. Anderson has *definitely* never been part of our program.''

Tom paused. ''Could there be a computer error?''

''Our system is state-of-the-art, sir,'' the clerk replied pompously. ''And it's in perfect condition. Perhaps you should recheck the name and identity you're requesting.''

Perhaps. Tom replaced the receiver. And perhaps he'd better find out what the hell was going on. But he didn't plan to tip anyone's hand doing so.

Sunlight streamed over the roadside picnic area they stopped at a few hours later. Set back far enough from the highway to be undetected by passersby, the area provided a perfect place for Summer and Jack to study his file. Danny napped in the portable crib while they nibbled at hamburgers and French fries and waded through the information, trying to isolate something that would help them.

Surreptitiously, Summer concealed the pages detailing Jack's wife's murder, which included a picture of the soft, gentle-looking, pretty woman. A woman whom Summer knew Jack had loved. Right now, she knew he didn't need to be reminded of his loss.

Jack tapped one page of the report. "Look, it says here that Donald Sedgewick—my original contact in the agency—has been promoted. If that's the case, I wonder why he was never available to take my calls."

She followed the line of text he pointed out. "It doesn't indicate that anyone else has been assigned to your case. Do you suppose someone's been blocking your calls to him?"

Jack shrugged. "That would be my guess."

Her gaze skipped farther down the report. "Jack, look at this. You've been listed on the wire services as an escaped criminal. It wasn't an isolated poster I saw." When he didn't say anything, she clasped his hand. "You were right all along. The police never would have helped us."

"It wouldn't give me a grain of satisfaction to say I told you so. I wish we had been able to turn to them."

Briefly Summer rested her cheek against his solid shoulder, drawing comfort from his implacable strength. With the ugly truth spread out before them, how could either of them believe in good conquering evil? Or in any sort of tomorrow they could share?

"Summer!" The note of excitement in his voice reached her. "Look at this!"

She blinked away the sheen of tears that had prickled and followed his gaze. But the words disappeared when he turned her toward him to plant an exuberant kiss on her mouth. His lips lingered, then he pulled away. "Summer, you did it! Here's an alternate number for Tom Matthews."

She hated to dash his enthusiasm, but Summer knew one of them had to consider reality. "How do you know it's not the same dead end as the one we already have?"

"Because not only is this an alternate number we didn't have, but his primary number is different, as well. We've been chasing shadows, but this is real." Jack paused, his face suddenly darkening. "Unless you think they set up a dummy file, thinking we'd find it."

Summer smiled confidently. "I don't want to sound like an egomaniac, but there are few people with enough expertise to crack the agency's safeguards. Think of it like a Navy SEAL operation. The quarry is surrounded by minefields, automatic nuclear warheads and a hail of gunfire. Few people can even reach the minefields, much less tiptoe through them."

Jack looped an arm around her shoulders. "My own little G.I. Jane." His grin widened. "And just when I thought you were enjoying the *girlish* thing."

Summer stiffened momentarily, then relaxed a trifle when she saw the admiration…and seeds of something else lurking in his eyes. "The girlish thing?"

"I know I'm enjoying it."

She swallowed, uncomfortable with the compliment, but inordinately pleased by it. "Maybe we should find a telephone."

As she started to rise, Jack reached out to cup her chin in his hands. "Thank you, Summer." His eyes searched hers. "I don't know what I—we—would have done without you. You've given us another chance."

The sudden lump of emotion that lodged in her throat was nearly her undoing. Resolutely she swallowed, knowing the closer she brought him to what he was seeking, the closer she was to saying goodbye. "We all deserve another chance," she finally managed to say, not wanting him to see the agony she was feeling.

Reluctantly Jack released his hold. "Time to find a telephone. And hopefully, some answers."

Jack clutched the receiver as he punched in the last digit of the telephone number. If this didn't work, he wasn't certain where he would turn. Half-expecting another recording, or a canned operator's voice telling him the number was disconnected, Jack nearly jumped when he heard a live voice.

"Tom?" Jack cleared his voice. "Tom Matthews?"

"Yes." The voice on the other end was equally cautious. "Who's this?"

"Jack Anderson."

A long silence echoed over the phone wires.

Jack clenched his fist, trying to remain calm. "Are you there, Tom?"

"Can you prove who you say you are?"

"Can you?" Jack parried, suddenly wondering if the phone number in the file had been a trap.

"This sounds like a standoff neither of us can win," Tom replied. "I suspect we're going to have to meet face-to-face to prove ourselves."

Jack hesitated. If this was an impostor, he would be walking into an ambush.

"I can't hear what you're thinking, but I suspect I know. You pick the spot—neutral territory. But I'm not too fond of dark wharves or warehouses in the middle of the night."

Something clicked in Jack's memory, but he couldn't remember exactly what. Uncertain whether that was a good thing, his mind raced as he tried to think of a safe meeting place. All the government places were out of the question. Security guards could have him locked up in seconds. He considered other public places like schools, but he wasn't going to endanger any more innocent bystanders. "How about the Ford Theatre?"

There was a pause at the other end of the line. Appar-

ently the irony of the location where Lincoln had been as-
sassinated wasn't lost on the other man. "Fine. Inside?"

"No. Outside—in front of the entrance." Jack glanced
at his watch. "In two hours."

"If this *is* Jack Anderson, it's time to come in."

"Just be there," Jack replied. Replacing the receiver, he
hoped he hadn't just set up his own assassination.

Chapter 17

"Son, the only people who meet in dark wharves and warehouses in the middle of the night exist strictly in the movies. And, frankly, I'm no movie star."

Jack whirled at the words, his heart thudding as he stared at the man who had managed to walk up behind him, despite the vigilant watch he'd been keeping.

The other man stood his ground. "So, you really are Jack Anderson."

Jack swallowed everything he wanted to shout, settling instead for a quiet voice rich with emotion. "And you're really Tom Matthews. No wonder I thought your words today sounded familiar." They were the ones Tom had spoken the first time they'd met when Jack had naively suggested just such a meeting place.

Their hands clasped in a sturdy, heartfelt handshake.

"I have you covered," a voice warbled from behind them.

Both men froze.

Summer crept from the lengthening shadows. "Don't turn around."

Jack swallowed a second rush of adrenaline. "It's really Tom Matthews, Summer." He glanced at the other man. "Tom, this is Summer Harding."

"Are you absolutely sure, Jack?" she asked, her voice still trembling.

"Yes. And if I'm not mistaken, Tom's armed, so you'd better lose the weapon."

Tom turned slowly to confront Summer.

Sheepishly she withdrew the Pez dispenser from her jacket pocket as she glanced at Jack. "I was worried about you."

"Pleasure to meet you, Ms. Harding." Tom offered his hand.

"Summer, please." She started to extend her hand, remembered the Pez dispenser and switched the toy into her other hand, accepting his handshake.

"Summer," he agreed, his perceptive gaze sweeping over her. "Now that we know all the players, I suggest we switch locales. This is a little too public for my taste."

Danny yelped just then, clearly startling the older man.

Summer reluctantly turned around, revealing Danny securely strapped in the backpack carrier. "Actually, *now* you know all the players."

Tom shook his head as Jack's story drew to a close. "I'm sorry you had my old telephone number. Of course, after it was changed, the new number was sent to all the relevant files." He winced. "Which didn't help you much. I'd like to tell you that you've got the wrong idea, that your file just got misplaced and that now it's restored." He glanced first at Jack and then Summer, who sat in matching club chairs in the small hotel room. "But I can't. I've been doing some checking of my own since I saw your picture on the wire services. Nothing's added up since."

"What do you think has happened?" Jack questioned.

"Same thing you no doubt do. Internal corruption. I've been running a low-profile check of my own. There's no other explanation."

"But now that you know, you can help Jack, can't you?" Summer asked anxiously.

But Tom didn't offer any immediate reassurance. Instead he studied Jack. "We can set up a new ID, new hiding spot, but Jack won't be safe until we find out who's behind this."

"But you can do that, can't you?" she asked again, her anxiety visibly increasing.

"Not without help," Tom replied.

"Then get help!" Summer leaped to her feet to pace. "You have the entire government at your disposal. Surely you can find enough help."

"There's only one person who can help," Jack answered for him, meeting Tom's eyes.

"What do you mean?" Summer asked.

"A sting operation," Tom replied. "To flush out the turncoat."

"That sounds good," she admitted.

"With Jack as the decoy," Tom continued.

"No!" Summer all but shouted.

"It's the only way," Tom replied quietly. "We have to expose the insider who betrayed Jack, or he'll be running the rest of his life." Tom paused. "Talk it over between yourselves and let me know. We can iron out the details later." Not waiting for an answer, he let himself out of the hotel room.

"He's right," Jack responded slowly as the door closed behind Tom. "I can't run forever. It's best for Danny to end the hiding and constant relocating. This isn't the kind of life I want for him."

"But there must be another way! I don't want you and Danny to be running forever...." Summer's voice wavered as she fought the emotion choking her. "But there has to be another way!"

Jack took her hands. "There is no other way."

"But you could get killed!"

"There are worse things than dying," he replied quietly, searching her expression, pained by the tears he saw pooling in her eyes. "I have to do the right thing. I don't want to orphan Danny, but I can't raise my son to be a coward, to walk away from a moral obligation."

"Surely there's a less dangerous way to do that!"

"You told me you thought I'd done the right thing by getting involved in the first place, then testifying despite the risks. You even told me that you thought Linda would think so, too." Jack gently squeezed her hands. "I believe you said that the reason I can live with myself is because I made the honorable choice. It isn't time to end that sacrifice, to take the easy route."

The tears now spilled down her cheeks. "You talk as though you know what's going to happen…that you're willingly going to walk straight to your death."

Jack continued to hold her hands. "You asked if Linda would have been happy knowing Danny could grow up choosing the easy, less honorable path if I'd set that example. I think you were right. I couldn't live in that shadow of uncertainty."

Chagrined, Summer listened as he parroted her words, knowing that what they'd shared had clearly meant a great deal to him. He had measured what she'd said and valued it. Desperately she clutched at straws. "How can you think of depriving Danny of his father?"

"Have a little more faith in me, Summer. I intend to come out of this alive. If not, Danny will still be better off being raised by someone other than a cowardly father who doesn't live by his principles." Jack increased the pressure on her hands. "Which brings me to another point. If something happens to me, would you want to raise Danny?" He paused. "I've seen how good you two are together…I can't imagine him being happier with anyone else."

Summer thought of the child she'd grown to love as much as his father. "Of course I want Danny!"

"We'll rough out some papers…make it legal."

Summer brushed at the tears on her cheeks. "Sure. And if everything goes all right…"

"You won't have to worry about the papers, because I'll be around to take care of Danny."

Her heart wrenched. She'd given him the opportunity, but he hadn't said anything about her remaining part of their lives if he succeeded and came back safely. Obviously he didn't envision her being part of his future. Instantly she was reminded of the trust she'd lost with Tyson, the trust she'd thought she was rebuilding. Bitterly she realized she hadn't rebuilt anything. Rather, she hadn't built anything lasting with Jack.

Seeing that he awaited her reply, she shored up her courage, steadied her voice. "Of course."

His gaze fastened on hers, probing. Then something akin to resignation registered. He gently touched her cheek. "I'm counting on you, Summer."

Jack worked out the details with Tom Matthews, who had put out the bait at the Drug Enforcement Agency. Matthews told everyone at the DEA that his old contact, Jack Anderson, had resurfaced and that they were planning a meet. Then he gently let slip the details of where and when Jack could be found. He also made very sure that the same information made its way to the agency in charge of the witness-protection program.

Now, wired with a transmitter, Jack drove to the appointed meeting spot, rechecking his map to make sure he was in the right place. Ironically he glanced around at the location Tom had chosen. Despite the other man's distaste for "dark wharves," he'd chosen a place surrounded by water, with a bridge the sole connection to land. The only other way to access the spot was by boat.

Jack wondered briefly if Tom had reconsidered his desire

to be part of a drama. The place fairly reeked of atmosphere. A row of metal buildings, admittedly not a warehouse, dominated the pitted asphalt lot. Potholes the size of small craters threatened to swallow unsuspecting vehicles. The buildings themselves were badly in need of paint, possibly even bulldozing. Assorted weathered railroad ties and old tires were piled around the buildings. A few covered trucks sat haphazardly in the lot. It was difficult to tell whether they were parked or abandoned. Jack rolled down his window. The smell of ripe barnacles and brackish water tainted the air.

He couldn't see Tom or any of his men; they were hidden cleverly. Resisting a shudder of premonition, Jack admitted that Tom had chosen well. Anyone would have an ominous feeling, he decided, knowing he was purposely walking into a trap.

The car rolled to a stop. Jack ignored his own misgivings as he left the car. He checked the doors on three of the buildings before he found one that was unlocked. Taking a deep breath, he entered.

Immediately he was hit by the gloom. The pervasive darkness threw him for a moment as he tried to regain his bearings. From the layers of dirt and dust, it didn't look as though anyone had set foot in the place for years. Another shiver skittered up his spine. Resolutely Jack threw off the feeling. If the place looked like a welcoming living room, it wouldn't be a convincing backdrop for the meet. Besides, Matthews knew what he was doing. The DEA commander was one of the best.

The door creaked open. Jack took a deep breath. It had all come down to this moment.

Summer pounded on the back of the driver's seat. "Can't you go faster?"

"Yeah. But it ain't worth it for me to get a ticket."

"I'll pay the ticket," she pleaded.

"You gonna pay my insurance premiums for the next

five years? They'll hike 'em up past my boot tops.'' The driver ignored her, shaking his head. "You'll get there, lady. Won't take more'n five minutes."

"You don't understand! It's a matter of life or death!"

The cabbie rolled his eyes. "In this town, it always is."

Despite her continued pleas, he wouldn't move any faster. Gripping the door handle with chilled fingers, she counted off the minutes until the place came into view. Leaning forward, she strained to see. Trying to remember the map she'd glanced at so briefly, Summer wasn't sure it looked like the right address. Her heart still jumped as she remembered Tom Matthews's surprise.

"What do you mean the map sent over by courier?" Tom had asked. "I didn't send anything by courier." Then he had sworn, briefly but eloquently.

"What's wrong?" Summer asked.

"Hell, I promised him—"

"Won't his transmitter lead you to him?" Summer demanded.

Tom shook his head. "We haven't activated it yet—there won't be a signal." He paused. "Did you see the map?"

"Just for a minute."

"Do you remember it?"

"Some of it…I think." Briefly she told him what she remembered, hesitating at a few of the street names, not certain exactly what some of them were.

"You stay put, Summer. I'll take care of it."

But she couldn't stay behind. Immediately she had dialed the front desk and asked about a sitter. While she explained that it was an emergency, the manager on duty responded immediately, taking Danny into his care.

Now Jack was alone with two men intent on killing him. And increasingly, as the cab driver helped her to negotiate them to their destination, she realized she'd given Tom Matthews the wrong directions.

As he'd feared all along, Jack had walked right into a trap.

* * *

The slash of daylight from the opening door penetrated the thick darkness.

Swallowing that flash of premonition, Jack stepped forward. "Tom?" he asked as he had been instructed to do.

A mocking laugh answered him. "Hate to disappoint you, Jacky boy. But it's not Tom." Fisher flashed a humorless grin. He gestured with his thumb toward another man, but Jack was surprised to see that it wasn't Wilcox, but some younger, unimportant thug. "Gee, Jack doesn't look all that happy to see us."

The second man laughed as though Fisher had said something humorous.

"How'd you find out I was here?" Jack challenged, remembering his role.

"You didn't think you could run forever, did you, Jack? Hell, we liked giving you lots of line, just so we could enjoy reeling you in that much more."

Jack felt the warm rush of anger and restrained it. Now was not the time to show his true feelings. He had a deeper purpose.

"So you've found me. What now?"

Fisher's laughter, like the man, held a mean quality. "Oh, now we're going to have a good time, Jacky boy." He advanced.

Jack forced himself not to plant his legs in a fighting stance.

The second man, who had yet to speak, took a step forward, as well.

"What happened to your partner in crime?" Jack asked. "Or is he still in prison?"

"Wilcox? Don't you worry about him. He'll be along. He wouldn't miss this for the world."

Jack sensed there had been a shift in power. He'd always thought Wilcox and Fisher were pretty much equals. But he guessed that had changed. It looked as though Fisher had been put on the front line while someone else was giving orders. "You his flunkie now?"

Fists slashed out, blindsiding him.

"Watch your mouth, Jack, or you won't last till Wilcox gets here. And I'd hate to see him miss out on the big moment. He's been…anxious to see you again."

Jack shrugged away the pain. "And I guess you snap to his commands."

"You always were a slow learner, Jacky boy."

Jack prepared himself for the blow, but didn't expect the flash of the switchblade from Fisher's sidekick. The quick slash opened his arm, spilled the first blood. He clapped a hand across the wound, ignoring the burst of needlelike pain, refusing to acknowledge it to Fisher. "So, I take it Wilcox's coming to the party?"

Fisher's ugly laugh echoed through the empty building. "Now you're getting it, Jacko." His mouth curled downward into a surly scowl. "But don't press your luck. If you don't last till Wilcox arrives, I won't get too choked up."

"Maybe Wilcox won't agree with your plan," Jack countered, knowing he needed to draw Fisher into revealing the turncoat within the agency.

Fisher's laugh was another ugly bark. "It's his plan, you idiot."

"But you two didn't work alone, did you? You must have had some help getting all my information, then wiping out my file."

"Too bad you weren't so smart before, Jacko."

"Was it Matthews?" Jack guessed, hoping the absurdity would lead Fisher into talking.

"Maybe."

Jack's senses reeled. Had he been so wrong? Was his every instinct off base?

Fisher laughed again. "You're too easy, Jack. Too bad we don't have time for a few hands of poker. I'd make a fortune."

Jack remembered to breathe again. "Then who?"

"Sedgewick."

It took Jack a moment. Was Fisher toying with him again? "Donald Sedgewick?"

"If you're waiting for the gotcha, you'll grow old before you hear it." Fisher's nasty laugh rang out again. "Oh, I forgot. You aren't sticking around long enough to grow old."

"You're telling me the head of the agency sold me out?"

"Don't take it too personal, Jacko. Sedgewick would sell out his own mother if the price was right."

Jack's mind raced furiously. "So you paid him enough to copy my file and then delete it?"

Fisher's smile was pure evil. "He's doing the paying this time. We paid him enough for his tips when he was part of the DEA. Now it's payback time."

"So you're blackmailing him? That's why he wiped out my file?"

"Very clever, Jack." Another voice carried from the doorway. "Money soothes most consciences." Pale eyes cut through the gloom as Wilcox joined the group, accompanied by another man who remained in the shadows. "Too bad you couldn't have learned that for yourself. You might be facing financial independence instead of death." Then his chilly gaze rested on Sedgewick, who hesitantly emerged from the darkness. "Right?"

Donald Sedgewick's fleshy lips twitched. "Right."

Shocked, Jack stared at Sedgewick, willing himself to remain calm until Tom and his men had enough evidence on tape. He hadn't believed Sedgewick was involved until he saw him step into the light. It was still hard to believe.

"Not so talkative now, Jack?" Fisher laughed, but he ended it quickly when Wilcox sent him a quelling glance.

"Talking too much has always been a problem for Jack," Wilcox inserted. "You could have walked away with a fortune. Instead you cost us almost everything." Nearly colorless eyes radiated with venom. "And for that, you'll pay."

Jack could scarcely keep the triumphant grin from his face. Any moment Tom Matthews and his men would be rushing the room, and Wilcox's and Fisher's smiles would be wiped out.

"You deaf, Jack?" Fisher asked. "Most men don't smile when they hear a death sentence."

"I'm not like most men," Jack replied, wondering what Tom Matthews was waiting for. Surely they had enough evidence by now.

"No, most men are smart enough to know a good thing when they stumble onto it. Now the only thing you'll stumble into is a grave."

What was Matthews waiting for? For him to become a corpse?

In the ominous stillness, Jack realized that something had gone desperately wrong.

Summer stared from the doorway, wondering what she could do to create a diversion. And what if she did something and made things worse? She'd given the cabbie a huge tip and asked him to call Tom Matthews on his cell phone. Now she was torn. Should she find a phone herself? Or should she go for the diversion and hope for the best, hope that Jack understood and would make a successful bid at escape?

Before she could decide, the choice was snatched out of her hands. A stray cat brushed by her leg. Startled, she screamed. Horrified, she scrambled to escape before she made things worse.

"Run, Summer!" Jack shouted.

Suddenly a shot rang out.

Paralyzed with terror, she froze. What had she done? Hearing footsteps thudding toward her, she made her legs move. But she wasn't fast enough.

Long arms reached out to grab her. "Hang on there, little lady." Fisher raised his voice so he could be heard inside the building. "Looks like we have some company."

Summer fought his hold, then realized it was useless. Pushed inside the building, all she could see at first was a murky darkness. As her eyes began adjusting, she could pick out the forms of the men.

When her gaze focused, she spotted Jack. And for a moment, her heart seemed to still.

Blood trickled down his arm, and a wider, darker splotch stained his side. Although she'd only heard one shot, apparently he'd been wounded at least twice. "Jack!" she whispered.

"This must be the woman traveling with our boy," Fisher deduced.

Wilcox glanced between Jack and Summer. "So you found a replacement for the wife?"

Although Jack's face remained stoic, Summer winced for them both. The motion didn't go unnoticed.

"We've put a lot of thought into your…ending, Jack, but we wouldn't want to exclude your new lady. As you know, we like to…include everyone." Wilcox's pale gaze remained on Jack.

But Jack didn't give them the response Wilcox had obviously been hoping for. "Things aren't always what they appear to be."

Wilcox wasn't easily fooled. "You think that by not claiming the lady, we'll leave her alone? Don't delude yourself, Jack. You also thought the program would protect you."

Despite his wounds, Jack laughed. "You don't really think I came into this by myself, do you?"

Wilcox glanced around the deserted building. "You expecting the cavalry?" His laugh was as chilling as his eyes. "Matthews doesn't have any idea where we are."

Remembering the map, Summer gasped.

Wilcox whirled around, his eyes narrowing. "Do you know something you'd like to share with us?"

Gulping, Summer shook her head.

"Your fight's with me," Jack told him, advancing toward Wilcox despite his wounds.

Wilcox laughed, the maniacal sound bouncing off the metal walls.

Fisher flipped up his gun. "We're shaking, Jacko." Then he turned the gun toward Summer. "Shaking."

Jack didn't know what had happened to Matthews, but he realized he was on his own. He also realized he couldn't let anything happen to Summer. He loved her and he wasn't going to let her come to harm. "You can shoot her. You can shoot me. But you won't know where we stashed the evidence."

"Evidence?" Fisher barked. "You think we're as stupid as you are?"

Jack kept his gaze on Wilcox. "How 'bout you, Wilcox? You think it's smart to wipe us out without knowing?"

Wilcox didn't reply, instead shifting his gaze between Jack and Summer. "You already turned state's evidence."

Jack thumped the side of his head. "Done deal, huh? That's why it was so easy for Sedgewick to arrange for your early release? On what, a technicality? Sure. And that's why the DEA is working with me—'cause it's a done deal."

Wilcox's nostrils flared as he clearly tried to maintain his control. His gaze shifted to include Sedgewick.

The nervous man began visibly sweating, and he pushed at the gray hair matted at his forehead. "You aren't going to believe him, are you?"

Jack edged closer to Summer. "Ask Sedgewick how we always kept one step ahead of you," he directed, seeing the immediate flare of suspicion in Wilcox's eyes.

Sedgewick's chunky lips twitched. "He's going to say whatever will save his hide. He was just lucky, that's all."

"Lucky all that time?" Jack mocked, surreptitiously moving closer to Summer. He saw her eyes widen and silently urged her to remain quiet and still.

Fisher turned toward Sedgewick, too, his brow pulled into a quizzical line. "You said the profiler was wrong."

Sedgewick backed away from Wilcox. "He was! They have a high accuracy rate, but they're not perfect!"

"Dead wrong was more like it," Jack inserted, inching close enough that he could nearly reach Summer.

"That's the pivotal word for you!" Sedgewick shouted at Jack. "You're the one who should be dead!"

Fisher's gun wavered between Summer and Sedgewick.

Seeing the opportunity, Jack shoved Summer toward the door. "Get out," he managed to order between gritted teeth.

Summer hesitated.

Jack saw Fisher's indecision. Anticipating the shot before he saw the flash and heard the thunder, he flung himself in front of Summer, ignoring the tearing pain in his side. Her scream punctuated Fisher's shot.

The force of the bullet's entry knocked him back, yet he didn't fall. His spirit refused to accept that he would lose Summer. He had to stay strong until she was safe.

But Summer refused to stay out of Fisher's gun sight, instead reaching toward his newest wound. "Jack, oh God."

With the last of his strength, he pulled himself upright, blocking Summer from Fisher. But the man's gun didn't waver. As though in slow motion, Jack watched Fisher pull the trigger back and knew he faced death. Jack thought of his son and the woman he loved.

The door crashed open, the rusty hinge screeching in protest as metal clanged against metal.

"Hold it, Fisher!" Tom Matthews shouted. "You pull that trigger and you're dead before the shell hits the ground."

Again Fisher wavered. Wilcox didn't. The man opened fire and in seconds Fisher joined him. But a barrage of gun fire from Matthews's men dropped both men.

Summer knelt beside Jack, who'd slumped to the ground,

running her hands over him, tears dampening her cheeks. "Jack, please don't die," she pleaded, voice trembling.

Tom Matthews patted her shoulder awkwardly. "I radioed for an ambulance when we got here. It should be here any second. Thank God your cabbie got through to us."

Summer gripped Jack's hand. "We need you.... Danny and I need you so much." Her voice broke. "I love you, Jack Anderson. I don't want to live without you. Don't you dare die on me!"

The shrill wail of a siren pierced the air. "Thank God it's here," Tom Matthews muttered, rushing away. In seconds he returned with the paramedics.

Summer reluctantly released Jack's hand only at the paramedic's instructions. "Ma'am, it's better for him. We'll be able to help him."

They loaded him quickly on a stretcher, hustling him to the ambulance.

Vaguely Jack felt them working on him, the prick of the IV insertion, the low murmurs of their voices. Wavering between consciousness, Jack forced his eyes open. If he wasn't going to make it, he couldn't leave things unfinished. He reached for Summer's hand. The paramedic covered his face with an oxygen mask. He felt another prick, and consciousness faded. An overwhelming sense of loss filled him. It couldn't end this way. It just couldn't.

Chapter 18

"The federal prosecutor plans to ask for life without parole for Sedgewick," Tom Matthews told them. "Fisher and Wilcox were dead on the scene."

"Do you think the charges will stick?" Jack asked from his supine position in the hospital bed.

"The prosecutor does, and that's what I'm banking on. His sort tend to be conservative in their estimates, and he doesn't think Sedgewick will ever see daylight outside of a federal prison again. He's charged him with several counts of murder and two counts of attempted murder. With that many counts, Sedgewick won't even come up for a parole hearing in less than eighty years."

Summer battled with the words she knew she must say, the words that put them that much closer to goodbye. "So Jack and Danny are safe now? They can resume their old lives?"

Tom Matthews smiled. "This is the good part of my job. I'm able to say yes. Sedgewick is the weak link. He wouldn't have the stomach or nerve to try anything—in or out of prison. You're a free man again, Jack *Delancey*. No more running and hiding.''

Jack's eyes flickered shut briefly. ''Then Danny's future is secure.''

''As is yours, Jack. You've sacrificed more than any man should be asked to. But the rest of your life is your own.''

The nurse entered the room. ''Mr. Anderson, it's time for lights out.'' She glanced pointedly at Tom Matthews.

Tom picked up his hat. ''I'm on my way, Nurse.'' First he glanced at Jack. ''By the way, I got the car returned to the Steigers.''

''Thanks. I didn't want them to think we were running a con.''

''Somehow I doubt it ever entered their minds.'' Settling the hat on his head, he left.

The nurse, accustomed to Summer's nearly around-the-clock presence, didn't shoo her from the room. Even though he was still pale and weak, Jack looked remarkably well to her, considering the shape he had been in when the ambulance had rushed him to the hospital.

He had nearly died from his wounds. The surgery had been touch and go, and the doctors hadn't been optimistic. Jack had lost so much blood, and the trauma had been extensive. But he was a fighter and a survivor.

Summer's eyes pooled again with tears never far from the surface. Terrified to leave his side, lest he slip from life, she had called her mother while Jack was still in surgery. Louise Harding had been on the first plane to D.C. Since then, she had competently cared for Danny while Summer was at the hospital with Jack. It was just another bond that Summer knew would be painful when severed.

The nurse checked Jack's IV and vital signs. ''Looking good, Mr. Anderson. Pretty soon, you'll be tap dancing.''

He smiled at the young woman. ''If you saw my two left feet, you wouldn't say that.''

The nurse winked at Summer. ''I'm sure you're just being modest." She clicked off the overhead lights, leaving only the dim glow of a night-light. "Try to get some rest."

"That's all I do," he muttered as the nurse left.

Summer studied Jack's face, memorizing each feature, painful as it was. "You want to get better so you can go home to Danny."

"I sure miss that little guy."

Summer willed away the anguish, knowing how much she would miss the baby, too. "He misses you. My mother says he keeps asking for you."

Jack managed a grin. "I don't think I've been in here long enough for him to be speaking in complete sentences."

Somehow she smiled over her own pain. "Da-da." Her voice hitched. "He asks for Da-da."

Jack reached for her hand. "What is it?"

"I was just thinking how much your family will enjoy seeing Danny again." Summer swallowed, raised her face, then ducked it again, unable to meet his eyes. "From what Tom Matthews just said, it's safe to call them. I imagine your mother would love to take over for mine."

"Does Louise need to get back to the business? I didn't mean to take advantage of her."

The hitch in Summer's heart matched the one in her voice. "We both should be getting back. You're out of danger now, and your family will get here as soon as possible, I'm sure." She managed to lift her head again, willing the tears to stay at bay. "You'll want to get on with your life."

The silence between them vibrated with all the unspoken emotions of two wounded souls.

Jack increased the pressure on her hand. "A life without you, Summer?"

She tried to smile, but failed. The agony was too intense. "You'll have Danny as you planned...and now your family."

"I could fill my life with a hundred people, but if you're not in it, it would still be empty."

Tentative hope bloomed. She raised her gaze to meet his. "It would?"

"Don't you know you are my life, Summer?"

She shook her head, the emotion clogging her throat, stinging her eyes.

"Do you know what my biggest regret was when I thought I was dying? That I wouldn't have a chance to love you...to share my life with you."

"It was?"

"I realized that if you love someone, it's worth taking the chance that someday you'll lose them." He reached out, tipping up her chin. "The joy you give me is worth whatever the future holds...because you are my future. I love you, Summer."

She shut her eyes briefly, then lifted their clasped hands and gently touched them to her heart. "I believe this is yours."

Moonbeams pushed past the utilitarian drapes hung at each side of the window. Gentle fingers of shrouded light touched faces already glowing with promise. Their lips met—tenderness, banked passion and emotion colliding in a pledge of commitment, a vow that would carry them far beyond the night...far beyond what either had dreamed...into the promise of tomorrow.

Inland from the gentle coast that didn't boast of cliff and boulder seascapes or storm-whipped surf, was a place of low islands and saltwater marshes. And beyond the marshes, narrow country roads meandered through tunnels of massive old gnarled live oak trees, their tops growing together at the center of the roads to provide a living canopy. Tendrils of gray moss dripped from their branches, trailing in easy abandon against the shell-topped roads.

Sunlight dappled through the leaves, and beyond the turn in the road, a restored plantation seemed to rise up from meadows of fallow green. Surrounded by cotton fields long since abandoned and palmetto trees that bent with the ocean breeze, the house shone with a new coat of paint. An even newer sign at the mailbox declared it was the home of Delancey and Delancey Enterprises.

One of the double entry doors burst open suddenly, and a fair-haired woman nearly danced across the veranda. Her laughter spilled through the magnolia-scented air as she rushed forward, a dog at her heels.

Jack looked up, seeing Summer framed between the two huge white pillars, the dusky pink of the house a soft background. He raised a hand in greeting, his lips already turning upward in a smile that seldom left his face.

"Jack! Your folks called! They're coming for a visit!" she sang out as she neared him.

Automatically his arms reached out to catch her. "Whoa! Unless I miss my guess, we have a day or two to prepare."

"Possibly," she said with a smile.

"Mama!" Danny demanded, toddling on chubby legs to reach out and grab her skirt.

She lifted him in her arms, gently tickling him and making him giggle in delight. "How are my two wonderful men?"

Jack swooped closer to steal a kiss, his eyes brightening. "Better now."

"Rascal." But she reached out to trace his jaw, warmth evident in the touch.

"Besides, how do you know it's not *three* wonderful men?" he questioned.

"It may be old-fashioned, but I told you I don't want to know," she retorted, her hand automatically reaching toward her gently swelling abdomen.

"I suspect it will be a girl," Jack replied ruefully. Then he leaned a bit closer. "As beautiful as her mother."

Summer swallowed the emotion that was never far from the surface. She used to fear that if she blinked, she would wake up from this incredible dream. But each day, as steadily as the last, Jack proved he was around to stay.

He had purchased a dilapidated plantation, one of many that remained on Edisto, and had renovated it into a home of such stellar design that it had been featured in style magazines across the country. And architectural clients had poured in.

Luckily Jack had planned for two business areas in the house since her own computer firm was flourishing. She had more time to develop her business now that she no longer needed to work at Harding Boat Rental and Repair Shop. Jack's younger brother had relocated to Edisto, bringing with him his love of boats and a desire to work in Louise's shop. They were so very lucky...to have each other and their families.

Summer blinked away tears.

Jack reached out to gently brush her cheek. "Summer, what is it?"

"I'm just so happy."

He smiled in understanding. "I hope it's a permanent condition."

Her reply was as soft as the breeze that stirred the air. "Always."

Danny struggled to get down. Knowing it was safe for him to run and play, Summer released him. As Danny toddled along with the Australian sheepdog that seldom left his side, Jack pulled Summer close. "And even that won't be long enough for me."

The dog barked, the sound mingling with Danny's happy shrieks. Sea gulls swooped in from the coast, and the memories of past ghosts shimmered, then disappeared. Happiness surrounded them, a renewal that had just begun...and would continue as sure as the seasons that changed...as sure as the love that connected them for all time.

* * * * * *

SILHOUETTE
SENSATION®

AVAILABLE FROM 19TH MAY 2000

INVOLUNTARY DADDY Rachel Lee

Under Blue Wyoming Skies

Undercover cop Rafe Ortiz suddenly had a newborn son to protect from his very dubious relatives. So he came to Conard County to see his half-brother, and met Angela Jaynes—the kind of woman a man married...

EMILY AND THE STRANGER Beverly Barton

Mitch Hayden had come into Emily's life to try to right the past, but the pretty widow had tumbled hopelessly in love with the ruggedly handsome man she barely knew. A man too dangerous to love...

THE HORSEMAN'S BRIDE Marilyn Pappano

Shay Stephens had run away with Easy Rafferty because he was her one true love, but guilt had followed them and wrenched them apart. Now Easy was back and Shay was determined to prove to him that home was right here in her arms.

ANNIE AND THE OUTLAW Sharon Sala

Gabriel Donner had sinned enough for two lifetimes, and now he had to earn his way to heaven. Sweet Annie O'Brien desperately needed a guardian angel and Gabriel eagerly rode to the rescue. Loving Annie was heaven, losing her would be hell. But his time was running out...

HEARTBREAK RANCH Kylie Brant

Jed Sullivan was ruthless about getting what he wanted—and he'd set his sights on Julianne Buchanan. He'd always controlled the sparks between them, but she was coming home and he was hungry...

AN OFFICER AND A GENTLE WOMAN Doreen Owens Malek

Michael Lafferty had arrested Alicia Walker for murder. He was supposed to be helping to convict her, but instead all he could think of was seducing her and proving her innocent!

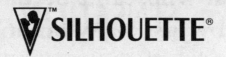

Men who can't be tamed by just *any* woman!

We know you'll love our selection of the most passionate and adventurous Sensation™ hero every month as the Heartbreaker.

HEARTBREAKERS

FREE!

2 Books
and a surprise gift!

We would like to take this opportunity to thank you for reading this Silhouette® book by offering you the chance to take TWO more specially selected titles from the Sensation™ series absolutely FREE! We're also making this offer to introduce you to the benefits of the Reader Service™—

> ★ FREE home delivery
> ★ FREE gifts and competitions
> ★ FREE monthly Newsletter
> ★ Books available before they're in the shops
> ★ Exclusive Reader Service discounts

Accepting these FREE books and gift places you under no obligation to buy; you may cancel at any time, even after receiving your free shipment. Simply complete your details below and return the entire page to the address below. *You don't even need a stamp!*

YES! Please send me 2 free Sensation books and a surprise gift. I understand that unless you hear from me, I will receive 4 superb new titles every month for just £2.70 each, postage and packing free. I am under no obligation to purchase any books and may cancel my subscription at any time. The free books and gift will be mine to keep in any case.

SOEB

Ms/Mrs/Miss/Mr ....Initials...........................
BLOCK CAPITALS PLEASE

Surname...

Address...

....

....Postcode ....

Send this whole page to:
UK: The Reader Service, FREEPOST CN81, Croydon, CR9 3WZ
EIRE: The Reader Service, PO Box 4546, Kilcock, County Kildare (stamp required)

Sometimes bringing up baby
can bring surprises —and
showers of love! For the cutest
and cuddliest heroes and
heroines, choose the Special
Edition™ book marked

That's my

baby!